MONICA LA PORTA

GAIA

WORLDS APART SERIES

To keep up to date with Monica's new releases and promotions scan the QR code with your smartphone or mobile device.

To Mom.

TABLE OF CONTENTS

1

I first saw him in a crowded street, in a crowded city, on a sunny summer day. I was on vacation with my family, visiting Greece for the first time. I was eighteen, with long, ash-blond hair and hazel eyes always on the verge of changing to a dark green.

Athens was warm that day, the sun kissing my skin, the radiance of the daylight caressing my eyes like a lover's hand. My father had just parked the car, and I was happily basking in the Mediterranean light while the constant humming of the engines passing nearby made me feel drowsy. The only sound out of register was my sister Clara's crystalline voice laughing at something silly I had just said, which kept me from falling asleep right there on the sidewalk.

A playful wind tangled my hair and brought to my sensitive nose the smell of freshly baked honey-dipped pastries. I smiled, turning my head to see where the bakery was, when a single sunbeam touched only my lips, warming them. Then, something happened. The air stood still, the sweet aroma disappeared, and the wind stopped moving my unruly hair—even the luminosity waned, coloring the ancient city in an ethereal light. I became suddenly aware of something—someone.

A sudden sparkle of electricity in the air gave me goose bumps. My whole body reacted as if magnetized, and I turned my head slowly toward a precise point in the middle of the street, where I singled out one car slowing to a halt. I don't remember the make or the color of the car at all, but I will always remember *his* eyes staring back at me—light blue, with a hint of green and lots of gold, full of wonder and relief and sadness all at the same time.

I had only a few seconds to contemplate his face, but it felt like a lifetime to me. He was tanned, with regular features. His nose was beautiful and straight, his mouth a faded pink, cracked by exposure to the sun and the sea wind, his curly, untamed blond mane equally sun bleached. He had a Mona Lisa smile, his lips curved upward even though he wasn't smiling at all.

I existed out of time, content to be pulled by the invisible force emanating from his eyes. I had never in my life experienced such an overwhelming attraction to another person, but I wasn't scared. On the contrary, I felt serene. Whole.

And then, all of a sudden, I was brutally thrown back into reality. The spell was broken. His car moved, and everything seemed to come to life once more; the traffic was humming again; people were walking by like nothing had just happened; my sister was still chuckling at my silly joke.

The moment I lost contact with his eyes, sadness possessed my soul. The world seemed less cheerful, the aroma from the bakery less tantalizing, the sky not so blue anymore. I felt I had just said goodbye to a loved one. That sensation of being alone burned my heart and stayed with me the rest of the day. That night, I lulled myself to sleep with warm thoughts of calming, light-blue eyes and smiling lips.

His memory didn't fade, and it kept me company during the rest of the trip. My parents noticed my mood swings and asked several times if I was okay. I honestly didn't know how to answer, and after a while they let me be. My sister was more insistent, but for all her prying, she didn't make me confess. I just couldn't talk about it.

What was I going to say, after all? That I'd had a vision? That I couldn't forget some stranger's eyes? It wasn't romantic; I sounded delusional. Clara would surely laugh at me, but only after diagnosing me with a clear case of heatstroke and dehydration caused by the Athenian sun. So I kept my thoughts and my memories to myself, and I tried my best to enjoy the rest of the trip.

Not that I had to force myself to like Athens. That summer, I had graduated from an Italian classical high school, and all my studies about the great civilizations of the past were still fresh and ingrained in my brain. The trip to Greece had been a special graduation gift. I was grateful my parents were giving me the opportunity to see with my own eyes all the places I had only studied in pictures.

But I couldn't fully enjoy the experience even though I really wanted to. It was unsettling how I longed for someone who was slightly more real than a figment of my imagination.

The whole trip, I kept looking around to see if he was there, even while swimming in the Aegean Sea. Only when my parents and sister started exchanging meaningful glances when they thought I wasn't looking did I realize I had gone too far. When I needed a break from their scrutiny, I made a show of reading from a battered old Greek mythology book that had belonged to my mother, from whom I had inherited the passion for archeology. I kept reading from it while my father drove from one excavation site to the other, from one monument to the next. I paused from my reading only to admire the luscious landscape of the Attica region, and whenever possible, I asked my father to stop so I could draw the scenery in the sketchbook I took with me everywhere.

Our trip was already packed with a busy itinerary, but my father indulged me on several occasions. He managed to carve out some time to let me stroll through olive orchards full of green leaves and darker, succulent olives. He gave me time to wait for the right shadow to reach a whitewashed rock wall covered in crimson and orange bougainvillea, so I could shoot my perfect picture, immortalizing the contrast of pure, blazing white against the fiery explosion of flowers framed by the cerulean sky. Once, I made him stop the car because I wanted to take a break under a beautiful pomegranate tree. Another time, the view of the sea from a small copse of pine trees was just too irresistible to pass up, and I sat on the warm, dry soil and sketched the scene while breathing in the resin mixed with the salty breeze.

The memory of his eyes was with me the whole time. I collected images of Greece because I felt a compulsion, but taking pictures wasn't enough. A few times, I felt something nudging at my mind like a light, feathered knock on a closed door, and my mind was filled with images of swirling blue-and-green waters and warm golden sands. The experience was pleasant and relaxing, and in the midst of conflicting emotions I couldn't understand, I took the time to enjoy it. And I was happy while it lasted.

We saved Cape Sounion and the Parthenon for our last day in Greece. Watching the sun disappearing behind the temple of Poseidon should have been the crown jewel of my graduation gift. Bathed in a glory of vivid red and orange, with a warm, salty breeze caressing my wet cheeks, I closed my eyes, and in the reverent silence of this natural display, I tried to imagine Byron carving his name while kissed by the same sun. But the only thing I could think of was that maybe *he* had enjoyed this soothing breeze from the sea, sitting under the same fig tree I was standing by.

Still shaken by the storm of emotions Cape Sounion had evoked in me, I left and followed my family to the car—next stop, the Parthenon. The ruins of the most celebrated temple in Greek history moved me deeply. I lingered dreamily, at peace with the rest of the world, wanting to prolong that moment forever as I listened to the ancient stones whispering their story through the wind. I experienced a strong communion with the long-lived nature of the local flora; maybe the solitary and contorted olive tree where selfish lovers had carved their names had been giving fruit when the Parthenon was still painted.

We stayed there until the starry night reminded us it was once again dinnertime. I felt sad the vacation was coming to an end. I knew I wasn't coming back soon, and I was worried I didn't have enough time to memorize all the little details that would remind me of *him*. I reluctantly entered the car, hoping my skin had been marked on a cellular level with the astonishing beauty of the panorama. I finally let my father drive away, after having extorted the promise that I would be allowed to come back another summer. I told them I needed more time to draw sketches of the Acropolis.

Since it was our last night in Athens, we decided to do something touristy and parked a few blocks away from the busy district overlooking the day-lit Acropolis. We strolled between the vendors selling cheap replicas of monuments and statues and breathed the wonderful smell of Greek food exploding in colorful, assorted trays lying on wheeled stands.

Finally, we decided it had been a busy day and we had to sit down and eat. We found a little restaurant overlooking the Acropolis and sat outside under a hundred-year-old olive tree. We ordered a feast of Greek culinary triumph, but I wasn't hungry. I let my mind wander, taking in the view, and for the second time that day I felt I was exactly where I was meant to be. The sweetness of the food in the air and the warm darkness of the night were helping me relax when I felt the familiar sparkle of electricity, as if a thunderstorm were approaching.

In the busy, well-lit street, I immediately found the source of my sudden interest. I was drawn by his eyes staring at me.

Time stopped. Once again.

Life paused, the festive lights dimmed, and the smell and the color of the plates full of delicacies retreated from the reach of my senses. Reality blurred until it became a faint memory of things that had been once but were no more. The world faded into a dull sepia picture, still and uninteresting. My awareness could only encompass two distinct lights, brilliant pools of crystalline Aegean Sea water. It was *him*, inside his car. Nothing else mattered; nothing else made any sense at all.

The first coherent thought I had was how improbable, in a city as big as Athens, meeting the same stranger twice was.

The second was a mere question. "Who are you?"

His lips arched, shaping that smile I remembered so well, even though I had only seen it once. He seemed to say something that, even in the complete stillness of the night, I couldn't hear. His eyes were happy and liquid at first, more intense than the first time I saw them, and then all of a sudden they were sad, radiating a sorrow that reached my soul and made me shiver. The corners of his lips were still up, but he wasn't smiling anymore.

I wanted to cry. I hugged myself in the attempt to keep at bay the cold seeping through the light fabric of my summer clothes. I felt the irresistible urge to run to his car and talk to him, and I stood up without thinking, a mechanical reaction from my body, when a question my mother was asking took me back to the reality of the restaurant, and I looked away for a moment.

Without answering her, I looked around, but he was gone.

2

Rome in May is spectacular. Life is easy, and you know that summer is there, around the corner, waiting for your legs and shoulders to come out again. I love Rome, even with the constant traffic; it is a city that makes you feel part of history. I have always been proud to have been born in Rome, "la Città Eterna," the eternal city.

I was wearing a jeans skirt, very short but not a mini, and a white Lacoste that perfectly matched my brand-new white Superga tennis shoes. While I was waiting for the bus to arrive, I had time to reflect on some thoughts bothering me. A eucalyptus tree was protecting my freckles from the morning sun, and a very pleasant breeze was keeping me relaxed and perspiration free.

I had been dating a guy on and off for the last six months, but I couldn't decide if I wanted something more from him or not. Marco was good-looking and funny, an outdoor kind of guy, always dressed perfectly for the occasion, whatever it might have been.

We had met at the university, during a protest against who knows what. At La Sapienza, there was always something to protest against. Marco was there at the right moment; he protected me from the angry crowd, removing me at the last moment from someone's trajectory. Thanking him and having coffee with him had been easy, as if we had known each other forever.

And that was why I was pondering under the eucalyptus tree. All my friends had asked me what was wrong with me and why exactly I wasn't considering Marco for something more serious. The worst part was that even Marco was starting to wonder. During the bus ride to the university, I tried very hard to make a list of pros and cons. By the end of the ride, I still wasn't sure there was anything wrong with him.

Marco had plans for us that night, so I was running all my errands at the university before my second-year classes started, to have some time to change before our date. Marco was a romantic guy, and he had said he wanted to surprise me because it was a special occasion. Therefore, I needed time to make myself pretty, and I was already thinking about what to wear for the night; maybe that nice top that showed a little bit of lingerie and that silky skirt that blew over my legs like air.

Once I reached the campus, I had enough time to buy the books I needed for sociology class, to put money on my lunch card, and finally to reach my friend Sara at the small coffee place known as the Bar. It probably had been "Bar dell'Università" at some point, but the neon sign was burned out, and only the word "Bar" was readable.

"Ciao, Gaia!" Sara was the ever-happy friend, the one who knew everything and anything about me, and because of that she was a big fan of Marco. Sara knew how lonely I had been and knew about my problems with intimacy.

"Love your hair today. New highlights? The blond is shinier." She had good taste in everything and, as I liked to say, especially in friends.

"Instead of wasting time in complimenting me, you should be preparing for tonight. What are you doing here?" She raised an eyebrow, and her lovely blue eyes sparkled in annoyance.

"Oh, don't worry. I've plenty of time, and as you can see, I already shaved my legs." I playfully turned my leg right and left to show her my smooth skin.

"Are you taking this date seriously?" She raised an eyebrow.

"Marco called you, didn't he?"

One corner of her lips turned up, but she didn't confirm my suspicion. Instead, she ordered breakfast for us. After eating the cornetto—the Bar had the best croissant in the whole city—and drinking the cappuccino—which in turn was just passable, but everybody was there for the cornetto anyway—she said, "If I were you, I'd wear something sexy tonight."

I wanted to pounce on her to extract the truth from her lips, but we didn't have much time left before our class started. "Sociology is starting in five. We should hurry."

She looked at the sky. "Too sunny to sit in class."

I made a face. "You're the worst friend ever."

She blew me a kiss in response but then followed me to class.

Sprinting up and down hallways and stairs, we finally reached the classroom. Professor La Mora was already at his desk, answering questions. An unusual chattering echoed through the high-ceilinged room. I tuned in on the closest conversation. "What's this all about?" I asked one of my classmates.

The girl looked surprised by my ignorance. "Haven't you heard of the scholarship?"

I shook my head. I had missed two classes recently. I looked at Sara, sitting at my right, and she shrugged as well. No surprise there. She was the reason I had missed the classes in the first place. She had made me volunteer at a dog shelter where a "friend" of hers worked. The lesson started, and I didn't have time to ask anything else.

Today, Professor La Mora's lecture was about social structure in the Etruscan society. Projecting slides onto the whiteboard on the front wall, he explained the Etruscans' fascination with the afterlife and how their mausoleums were exact replicas of their houses. The curator of the Etruscan Museum in Tarquinia had provided pictures and even a few artifacts. The topic interested me, and I forgot everything else. I was fascinated by the exotic shapes and colors of the ancient objects carefully encased in clear boxes and now exhibited on the professor's desk. Some of them were nothing more than broken fragments, once elegant statements of the owners' wealth, now shards of pottery. Still, I could imagine them whole. At the end of the hour, a student passed me a stack of papers to sign if I was interested in applying for a scholarship.

"What's this?" I asked the guy.

"Professor La Mora and the departments of anthropology and archeology are organizing a two-year course with Professor Rayne at the University of Washington, in Seattle, USA," he answered.

"Why?"

"La Sapienza has been asked to collaborate in a worldwide project."

"Which is?"

"Classifying archeological findings and trying to better understand ancient societies," the guy recited. "So, do you want to apply for the scholarship or not?" He showed me the pen with an annoyed gesture.

"Why not," I said under my breath, and as soon as I signed, I passed it to Sara and was out, running to the next class.

After that, the day fast-forwarded without pause. In what seemed the blink of an eye, I was heading to the bus stop to go back home, where I still lived with my family—one of the perks of living in Rome. My mom knew about my plans, so she didn't try to feed me. Clara tried hard to play cosmetician with my face, but I didn't let her. After a shower, strategically placed perfume, combed hair, and several changes of heart, I decided to wear some sexy but elegant lingerie. Sara's words had been playing in my mind the whole day. I looked at the mirror and thought I was finally ready to go out. My sister, looking at my reflection, said yes with her eyes, meaning *Yes, do it,* without saying anything in front of my mother. I blushed and felt warmer at the idea. Marco called at the intercom as my father was arriving from work. I saluted everybody with a pirouette, trying to ignore the look on my father's face, and off I went into the night.

Marco was down at the door, waiting for me, looking nervous. He smiled, taking my hand in his. I felt electricity in the air, and my heart went crazy for a moment. I automatically turned to find what was causing the butterflies in my stomach, but Marco brought me back to earth with a soft kiss on my lips. I smiled back. The buzz stayed with me.

"You're so beautiful tonight, Gaia."

"You look nice, too." Truth be told, Marco looked more than nice. He looked handsome. "So, what are the plans, and why all the mystery?"

"Be patient, and you'll see, traffic permitting, in maybe half an hour."

Yeah, good luck with that in Rome, I thought. Being stuck in the crowded streets with him wasn't bad though, so I didn't complain.

Actually, if I wasn't the one driving or looking for a parking spot, I normally enjoyed cruising through the city. Especially if the tour was taken during spring or summer nights, when everything seemed bathed in magic and you could hear music everywhere. I loved seeing the light pouring out from the colored windows of Catholic churches, radiating calm and serenity through the darkness, promising scented incenses to the believers.

Marco drove unhurriedly, talking of nothing in particular, glancing at me often, and humming tunes from the radio when I didn't supply any further topic of conversation. I wasn't feeling very talkative although I was at peace with the whole world. I was even glad for the traffic. Rome was glorious at night, and the slow ride was exactly what I needed to contemplate details lost during the day. I noticed how brilliant were the lights reflecting on the Tiber River near the ancient hold of Castel Sant'Angelo and how beautiful was the structure of the bridge leading to the hospital on the Tiberina Isle. I liked to be reminded that I could always discover something new about the city, even after years of living in it.

After a while, I stopped seeing places, monuments, buildings, street names, and only focused on details: a faded inscription in Latin, warning not to trespass—a solitary, bygone memory in marble hanging on a brick wall; a holy water basin that, after centuries of indiscriminate remodeling and reuse of sacred spaces, now had found its final life as a swimming pool for birds; a beautiful carved door with a single blackened brass knocker decorated with a lion's head, which had a dark stamp on the wood frame; an iron guardrail constraining a first floor window and preventing who-knows-how-many nocturnal escapes, destroying love stories and dalliances alike.

I was happily lost in my dreams of all the stories behind those apparently insignificant Roman details when Marco slowed down and smiled one of his smiles.

"Here we are," he said expectantly, parking the car in a private garage.

I looked around and realized I didn't know where we were.

"I wanted to show you my apartment," Marco explained in response to my puzzled look.

He looked nervous, and I was starting to wonder why. It also passed through my mind that I had never asked him to take me to his place. I knew he lived by himself and had an apartment in Trastevere, one of the most sought-after neighborhoods in Rome. We had talked about it at the beginning of our dating, but I had never asked him to bring me there—at first because I didn't feel comfortable being alone with him so soon, later because we had settled on a routine I was very comfortable with instead. We normally saw each other at the campus during the day. The nights he wasn't working at The Well & the Moon, the bistro his family owned, we went out for dinner. He knew all the off-the-beaten-path places, and we tried a new cuisine every time. I had never felt the need to present him to my family. Since we had steered clear of the bistro, I had thought we were on the same page where formalization was concerned.

Like the perfect gentleman he was, he opened the passenger door for me and led me to the liberty-style elevator at the end of the garage, where he held that door for me as well. The brass-and-iron architectonic jewel hummed and halted every few seconds but finally reached the attic floor, and we stepped out to face an elegant foyer decorated with mirrors and freshly cut flowers.

Marco reached one of the only two doors on that floor, and after fumbling with the key for a second, he showed me the threshold with a theatrical gesture. "Welcome to my humble abode. Come this way. There's a view I've been dying to show you for a while."

Maybe I imagined it, but Marco seemed even more nervous. He took my hand, and we entered his apartment, which was beautiful, full of windows and elegant furniture, and lit with so many candles I felt dizzy. He pushed a series of buttons on a remote control, and music started pouring into the place, a melody sweet and peaceful. He ceremoniously walked me to the terrace outside and then paused before whispering in my ear, "It's all yours tonight."

I almost gasped at the view. Rome was there, shining in the night before my eyes, vibrant with sounds and colors, the most beautiful city in the world.

Marco, visibly satisfied by my reaction and regaining some control of his nerves, put his hand on my waist and started dancing slowly to the sound of the music. I let the magic of the moment embrace me, and I relaxed in his arms, my head on his chest while he gently kissed my hair. I closed my eyes and felt that maybe he could be the one after all. Marco, tall and elegant, with his dark-brown hair, his intense eyes, and his full red lips.

The melody changed, and he gently brought us to a halt. "I cooked for you. I hope you'll like it." He smiled, and I smiled back.

"Let's sit." Marco, or maybe someone else for him, had dressed the table with the finest linen, elegant crystal goblets, and silver cutlery.

We ate the whole dinner "al fresco." I was transported by his porcini mushroom risotto accompanied by lemon scaloppini and followed by an arugula salad. By the time Marco served the dessert, a millefoglie with wild berries and cream, I was in awe of his culinary skills. "So, you forgot to mention you're a chef?"

"Cooking is a passion of mine, but I'm never allowed to cook at the restaurant. My dad wants me to become a lawyer."

"Well, judging from your perfect grades, I can see why your dad thinks so. But you'd be an excellent chef." I lazily took another bite of the dessert. "This is heaven, I swear." I even moaned in satisfaction.

"Thank you. It means a lot to me, coming from you." He took my free hand in his and slowly started kissing every finger.

I closed my eyes. With only the stars and Rome witnessing our happiness, I felt cherished like never before.

The music pouring from the apartment was soft and relaxing, and the temperature outside was just what I needed to avoid melting down in his arms before the coffee. Something in the air that night was making me particularly aware of how handsome Marco was. Maybe it was the combination of stars and candles or the aromatic food accompanied by the most beautiful view in the whole world. Maybe it was just the intensity in his dark, shining eyes. Whatever it was, I was feeling dizzier by the second and could barely talk, worried about ruining the enchantment. I could read in his eyes the same struggle to keep the conversation flowing.

After a few minutes of uneasiness, he put his chair aside and helped me out of mine. "Let's go back inside." His eyes glanced at the white leather couch just inside the living room, a few meters from the terrace. I nodded, and he breathed and then led me gently to the couch, pulling my hand without looking away from my eyes for a moment. We sat, our bodies facing each other. He caressed my hair, touching the contour of my right ear. After a moment of hesitation, he moved his face closer to mine and whispered with berry-scented breath, "I love you, Gaia."

And all of a sudden, I realized the precise meaning of this night. Marco had prepared everything to the last detail because he wanted to say the "L" word out loud. The first pang of panic tore through me, and my breathing altered slightly, but he didn't seem to notice, too occupied with my lips, then my neck, and then my shoulders. His hand ran up and down my naked back, triggering two different reactions at once: the first, one of physical response to his fingers on my skin; the second, one of repulsion. Inexplicably, I recoiled from his touch. Cold shivers ran down my spine, and a bitter sensation gripped my stomach.

While I was still trying to understand what was happening to me, Marco was lost in the moment and didn't have a clue. He pushed me softly onto the couch, and my mind gave up when he gently covered me with his body and I lost control of mine and started shivering.

"My love." Marco's hand was still caressing my bare back, and at that precise moment I finally realized what was wrong with me.

My eyes were staring at the room, at us lying on the white couch. My senses were aware of the perfumes of the candles. My ears were listening to the music. I was there, but I wasn't. I wasn't lost in the happiness I should've felt at being with him. My heart wasn't skipping beats for him. I didn't feel lightheaded. I didn't feel at all.

Until that moment, I had really thought that tonight could have been *the* night. I had hoped that Marco would be *the one*. I had confided to Sara that I felt he could be my first. Tears poured out silently and without my consent rolled down my cheeks. I couldn't stop them because nothing felt right anymore: his hands on me, so gentle and soft; his lips on my neck, so warm; his hair caressing my chin, smelling so good.

I desperately wanted to go back to the moment before, when everything had been perfect. The candles and the music and the superb view and Marco so handsome and fragile, touching my body. Nothing was perfect anymore. I realized in horror that I didn't want his kisses, I didn't want his eyes on me, and I didn't want to feel his hands on my skin.

He stroked my face and found it wet. "My sweet little Gaia." Marco looked at me for a moment, his eyes becoming liquid, and then gently kissed mine closed. "Your first time will be beautiful. I promise."

I shook my head, unable to say the words out loud.

"I'll be gentle."

I looked at him. "It's not that."

He narrowed his eyes. "Don't be afraid. I would never—"

I finally found my voice. I owed him that much. "I can't."

He stood up, removing his hands from my body, creating as much distance as he could manage on the couch, and staring at me with sad understanding. "I thought you felt the same."

His voice was painful to hear. I wished with all my heart I could avoid confronting the pain in his eyes, but I knew Marco deserved better than that. "I'm sorry."

"You didn't say you love me back." He was astonished by the realization, as much as I was. "You didn't say it."

"No, I didn't." I had to run away. I couldn't stand looking at him anymore. I didn't belong there, and it was the only feeling left. I didn't fit in that room. I wasn't supposed to be there with him. The air wasn't breathable; my lungs were struggling to pump oxygen in and out. My eyes couldn't see anything, and I felt a weakness in my legs as if they were made of lead, but I knew I had to escape from all that. From Marco.

I fled the apartment without finding the courage to explain. Marco tried to stop me at the door. "Please don't leave."

By the time I reached the elevator, I had already dialed Sara's cell phone number.

"Gaia?" Sara sounded worried. "Shouldn't you be—?"

"Please…" I could barely talk. "Come and pick me up at Marco's."

"What happened? Are you crying? Did something happen?" Sara was getting anxious, so I tried to stop her before she started worrying too much.

"Sara, it's okay. Just come now." I gave her the address, and she agreed to come as soon as possible.

Marco was still there, outside his door, looking at me with his face now a pale mask. He leaned back on the doorframe, his lips closed in a thin line.

"Marco, I'm so sorry." I was crying in earnest; trying to be calm wasn't an option anymore. I entered the elevator cabin, unable to say anything else.

While the door was closing, I heard Marco whispering, "Why don't you love me back?"

I was wondering the same.

3

May, June, July, and almost all of August passed in a blur. After that fateful night where everything went wrong, I attended classes every day, took my exams for the quarter, went on vacation to Spain with my family, and came back to an uncomfortably warm Rome.

"Would you go check the mail?" Mom asked me first thing in the morning after a long night driving back from Barcelona.

The asphalt melting outside, my mood swinging toward the bluer tinges inside, I went downstairs to the lobby to collect postcards, bills, and unwanted advertisements.

"Sara's on the phone," Clara announced, fanning the phone before my eyes as soon as I entered our apartment, juggling the bulk of mail accumulated during our absence. "Isn't it early to chat?" she mouthed to me, covering the speaker.

"No, it isn't," I mouthed back and took the phone, thanked her, gave her the pile of scattered papers, took a swig from the iced tea she was drinking, and thanked her again. "Sara?"

"Do you remember the forms we signed several months ago? The socio-anthropological exchange program with the University of Washington?"

"Of course I remember. All people could talk about was how awesome it would be to get in." I walked to my room and sat at my desk. "What about it?"

"You won't believe it!"

"I won't believe what?" My head felt heavy, and I moved to my bed where I sank in, eyes on the ceiling. The glow-in-the-dark stars I'd stuck there when I was twelve were slowly but inexorably peeling away, bringing down with them chunks of white paint from the ceiling. "Wait—did you get in?"

"I just received mail from the university—"

"And?" I waited for her answer, but I could only hear giggling for several seconds. When I was about to yell at the phone, she finally blurted out, "Got full scholarship!"

Clara passed in front of my door, exclaimed, "Ah! There you are," and then came back, waving an envelope under my nose. "What is this?"

I swatted away what looked like a regular magazine subscription request. "Not now, don't you see I'm busy?"

Sara started tapping on the receiver with her nails. I recognized the horrible sound. "Are you listening to me? Are you there?"

I hated when she made that sound. "Yes, I'm here. Give me a sec to strangle my sister, and I'll be back." I switched to speakerphone.

The tapping stopped. "Take your time."

Clara yelled, "Hey! Thank you!"

Sara laughed. "Love you, too, Clara."

"Sara was telling me something important. Now, can you please wait a second? Please? My head's killing me—" I started closing the door to have some privacy.

My sister gave me an exasperated look and pointed with her finger at a corner of the envelope she was still waving at me. Meanwhile, Sara had kept talking. "Just a sec," I told her and then turned to Clara. "What?" But my eyes had already seen the purple logo on the stationery, and I grabbed the mail from Clara's hands.

"It says University of Washington." My sister followed me to the bed, where she sat on the duvet cross-legged while I stood at the edge of it.

It was Sara's turn to yell. "What is it? What's that Clara just said?"

"I got mail too." I looked at the white envelope, weighing it in my hands. It was light.

My friend emitted a sound that resembled a high squeal. "What does it say?" Another squeal. "Did you get in too?"

"I don't know." I was afraid I hadn't been accepted.

"What are you waiting for? Open it!" Clara bounced up and down on the bed, and I almost fell over.

"So?" Sara asked.

"Oh, come on—do it!" Clara's hand reached for mine, but I was faster and tore the seal open before she could snatch the envelope from me.

I scanned the mail once then twice. My heart galloping inside my ribcage, I silently nodded. Clara took the paper from me and then ran away screaming, "She got accepted to the UW program!"

Sara's happy squeals became rather loud. "Did you, really?"

"It seems so." I couldn't believe it. For the first time in a long while, I felt excited about something.

A long silence ensued from the other end of the line; maybe she had fallen from whatever she was sitting on, and then Sara laughed. "So, are we going?"

"Are you kidding me? Of course we're going. Let's go study about Native American tribes!" I had made the decision the same moment I opened the envelope and read the first line.

Sara started singing, "Go Huskies!"

"Uh?"

"You know, huskies…? Like the UW's mascot?" Sara sighed, but she did sing it again.

"I haven't slept the whole night. We just got back to Rome. I haven't turned on my brain yet. Anyway, huskies… I like it. It's good luck. Rome's soccer team's mascot is a wolf, so they're related. Good." I rambled some more before she stopped me.

"How was your vacation?"

"Great. Absolutely fantastic." I didn't want to talk about my vacation. Clara saved me from one of Sara's notorious and relentless drillings by coming back with the rest of my family in tow. Everybody started shooting questions at the same time, and I had to say goodbye to Sara.

As soon as I hung up, my father asked me, "Do you want to go?"

My family knew I was going through a sad phase. The vacation in Spain had been their way of trying to help me with the blues. Strangely enough, when they had asked if I wanted to go back to Greece, I said no. I was looking for something different. I hadn't found it in Barcelona.

"Yes, I do," I answered. "Nobody in their right mind would refuse a full scholarship to study abroad." Truth be told, I was running away from Marco, and I knew it.

"I wouldn't have." My mom smiled at me. "The change of air is going to do you some good." She patted my head in that way of hers that meant she had read my mind and wasn't going to ask questions. "We should start packing then."

"It will be so much fun." Clara was almost as excited as if she were the one going.

My father made a face I knew all too well. He had started wearing that terrified expression the first time I went out on a date. "Well, try not to have too much fun. You know what they say about American colleges and their parties—"

I laughed and winked at him. "I'll try my best."

* * *

Something I hadn't foreseen was how much I would miss my parents and sister. People normally complain about Seattle's rain, but what really made me sad all the time was the lack of interaction with my family. Mostly, I missed Clara.

Once I landed in Washington State, after a few days of sightseeing and hiking on Mount Rainier, I spent the first three months on the phone, talking to my sister about everything I was doing or—to be honest—what I wasn't doing. I didn't even try to mingle with the other students. Sara was at the end of her patience with me.

Variations of "This doesn't happen to everybody!" or "Do you know how many people would gladly take your place?" were normally followed by "Let's go out to do something." The one sentence she repeated almost every time was, "I don't understand you."

And I didn't understand myself. I agreed with Sara. I should have been partying every night and exploring new places every day. Seattle was a melting pot of cultures and languages, and there was something new to discover on every corner if I would only let myself enjoy the moment. Something was wrong with me. Or something was missing.

"You should be having the time of your life." Sara had even written it down on a pink Post-it and stuck it on the fridge in our rented apartment, as a reminder for me to ponder upon.

And ponder I did, every time I went to open the fridge. I had run away from Rome, and now I wanted to run away from Seattle. I should've had closure with Marco, but I chickened out at the last moment. Before leaving, one hot and humid September morning, I had called his cell phone. It went to the answering machine after a few rings. I didn't leave any message. I felt guilty.

"I love studying here," I repeated every time Sara complained about my moodiness. There I was telling the truth. The only thing I was really enjoying was participating in the research. We were studying artifacts from a Native American village found a year ago in Bremerton. The combined action of a small earthquake and the construction of a new parking lot had unearthed native remains. Local tribes had asked for the discovered items to be placed in the ground immediately, but representatives from the University of Washington had obtained special permission to study the unusual findings—normally, Native American cultures didn't leave a lot behind—before putting them to rest again. After making a detailed catalogue of everything the archeologists had dug up, we would eventually come up with a theory about the villagers' lifestyle. *Objects speak*. It was the statement in our papers.

It was a fascinating project, and it kept me busy. I could go for days buried in my notes, verifying theories with other students, and drinking lots of coffee. Thankfully, among all the places in the United States, I had ended up in Seattle. I still couldn't find a decent Italian espresso, but at least the entire city seemed crazy about caffeine. The concept of a "bar" like what we had in Italy hadn't arrived yet, but there was a coffee place at every corner. I liked spending time at the neighborhood's Starbucks with a fuming, double-sleeved paper mug in one hand, laptop opened on the table, eyes on the street behind the wall-to-wall windows. Maybe it was due to the constant shortage of sunlight, but architecture in Seattle tended to favor open spaces and a great deal of glass.

While I was spending time by myself, nurturing my ill moods, Sara, true to her words, was having the time of her life. And why not? She was free, smart, beautiful, and definitely the best dressed in town after having shipped all of her wardrobe from Italy. Despite my attempts at ruining our friendship, she kept me company, made me smile, and, most importantly, never pried for details of what had happened between Marco and me. I couldn't have asked for more, and that's why it bugged me so much that I hadn't confided in her.

One late afternoon, I finally mustered the courage to tell her what had made me run away from him. We were sitting on the couch of our tiny rented apartment in the University District, sipping American coffee in colorful ceramic mugs. I tapped my nail on the mug, in sync with the silent rain dripping outside the window. "Love these colors."

Outside the glass barrier, the autumnal wind created a rainbow vortex, thousands of leaves raining down in the streets. Shades of sun-bright yellow, candy orange, deep red, and chocolate brown, ever so shiny because of the water, soon covered everything. Dogs, big and small, barked at imaginary dangers. Kids walked by, kicking mounds of leaves. Seattle was beautiful in a nostalgic way, and maybe the reason was the music we were listening to, a local band, or maybe someone's dark eyes passing by, but I thought of Marco. "It wasn't his fault," I said without preamble.

Sara looked up at me and stopped playing with Pallino, our cat— actually her cat. As soon as we had landed, she had single-mindedly decided we needed a pet and dragged me to the animal shelter, asking for the cat who was going to be euthanized next. I couldn't have said no even if I'd wanted. Pallino stretched his paws and ran into the kitchen.

"Wasn't Marco's fault, you know?" I wanted to talk, to explain, but I was afraid she wouldn't understand. I wouldn't have.

Sara gently laid one hand on mine. "You don't have to say anything if you don't want to."

I tried to smile at her. She had respected my privacy and never asked anything, even though she had witnessed my ill-concealed unhappiness and tried to help. "No, I want to. It's just that I don't know how to explain what happened that night."

She squeezed my hand in support. "You know you can talk to me."

I took a moment to organize my thoughts, opened my mouth once, thought better of it, and then tried again.

"It's okay—"

Finally, I blurted out, "I felt someone."

"You felt... *someone*?" Sara's eyes widened.

After a few seconds of tapping my nails on the ceramic mug, which now contained cold and undrinkable coffee, I managed to continue, "Yes, I did. I felt that someone else was there with me... someone who wasn't Marco, and the only thing I really knew was that I didn't want to be with him. I could only think about the other guy." I rushed through it without breathing, almost horrified to have finally said it out loud to someone else.

Talking about that night brought me back there. I was there again, feeling both the pain for rejecting Marco and the ecstasy for feeling *him* close to me. "When I closed my eyes, while we were kissing, I saw someone else's eyes, and I felt his hands on my body and his lips on my skin." My own words triggered vivid memories playing in my mind like a 3-D movie. I was swept away by the intensity of the images. I remembered his blue-green eyes looking at me, his gentle, warm fingers caressing my skin where Marco was touching me, his lips kissing me softly where Marco was kissing me. It had felt like hell and heaven at the same time.

It was still painful remembering why I had pushed Marco away, an emotion so strong that just thinking about it made my stomach churn. That night, I had felt I was betraying *him* with Marco. Incredible as it sounds, that was the reason stopping me from responding to Marco's touch. I felt disgusted at the mere idea of enjoying Marco's attentions. Just being there with him felt wrong. "I knew I didn't belong with Marco. He wasn't the one I have been looking for all this time."

Sara blinked. "How can you be so sure?"

"I just am." For months, I had been daydreaming of *him*, longing for his brilliant eyes, for his sun-cracked lips. I went to drink a glass of water because my mouth felt dry, but now that I had started, I felt the urge to finish and tell the entire story even though it sounded absurd to my own ears.

"You aren't talking about that blond guy you saw in Athens, right?" Sara jokingly asked. Then she saw the serious expression on my face and shook her head. "But… it was two years ago—"

"I felt him. He was there with me, and I couldn't lie to Marco because I would've been making love to someone else. "

Sara winced, and I realized my choice of words wasn't exactly smooth. In my eagerness to say everything, I was cutting the story short without properly explaining what I meant. But I wanted her to understand how I had sensed *him* that night, how his presence had been tangible to me to the point that I'd had to leave Marco for him. I wanted Sara to know I was still aware of his presence. I knew his essence had followed me to Seattle. At the same time, I was aware I sounded obsessed.

Sara's eyes were starting to narrow a little bit while she kept fidgeting with one of Pallino's toys, a nervous habit she had recently developed. "Hmm, I'm not sure I understand what you're saying, and don't get me wrong, I'm really happy you decided to open up about what happened, but…"

For a moment, I wasn't so sure that talking was going to help me after all.

"I thought… everybody did… that you got terrified because it was your first time…" she paused, bit her lower lip, and finished the sentence, "and that Marco did something. Maybe he rushed you… and you didn't like it."

"No, he didn't do anything wrong. He was perfect—"

Sara stopped me mid-sentence. "He didn't? You had been waiting so much for that. What else could I think?" She was slightly exasperated and seemed at a loss for words. Sara was never at a loss for words. She wasn't the type.

Any other time, I would have laughed at the situation. I had finally managed to shock my friend. Not the way I wanted my confession to go, not at all, but deep inside I felt relieved. "I know what I'm saying sounds insane, but I assure you I didn't hallucinate. *He* was there with me in that room. Not his body, of course, but his thoughts were there with me… for me. I know it was him because I recognized him." I paused to let her take in the meaning of what I was trying to say. When she didn't stop me, I kept going, "I could never forget the intensity of his eyes when he looked at me that first time in Athens."

"It was more than two years ago. You probably idealized him. It's normal." Sara had stopped fidgeting with the toy.

"No, I didn't."

Sara raised one expertly trimmed eyebrow.

"Don't worry, I'm not crazy, and talking with you is helping me a great deal." Sara's eyebrow shot higher, but she didn't interrupt me. "I think he's getting closer to me. *That* night, I felt this electricity in the air, and it was the same feeling I had in Athens, and now I've been feeling it here as well."

She waved her hand in the air. "A coincidence."

I was clearly getting on her nerves. Sara was a no-nonsense kind of person, and that was her biggest virtue. It was the same virtue that added so much to our friendship. "How do you explain that after two years I can still see his face, as if he were in front of me, here in this same room, sitting by my side?"

Sara shifted her body slightly and then sighed and gave me another of her silent stares. A few seconds later, she said, "I'll tell you how I explain it. You left Marco because you're still fantasizing about someone you never actually met, a mythical figure of a perfect boyfriend that you can recall at pleasure. Bits and pieces of some romantic dream. Someone who's never going to disappoint you."

"No, it's not like that. You know me."

"How is it, then? Let me understand."

"I know I won't be happy until I'm with him."

She threw her hands in the air. "Oh, for crying out loud! You saw him two years ago in Greece. You're in Seattle now, two long years later. It's not that you exchanged numbers or anything. You only saw this guy twice and by chance both times. You never had a conversation or anything like it with him."

"Yes, but think about it. I *did* see him twice in a city as big as Athens, and in two different places."

She finally rolled her eyes. "A coincidence, nothing more, nothing less."

"I know it isn't a coincidence." I didn't say so, but I could have sworn his presence was stronger than usual at the moment. Another look at Sara convinced me she'd had enough of the conversation. "Thanks for being my friend." I took her hand and squeezed. "What would I do without you?"

"Sometimes, I do wonder." Sara finally smiled. "Go out, meet people, and by 'people' I mean real people, young and possibly very attractive guys." When she saw that for once I hadn't said no right away, her smile widened.

I let her think she had found a way to end the uncomfortable conversation while proposing once again her medicine to cure every malady: dating.

"We could have fun! *Can you imagine it?* Think about the possibilities of having a life in Seattle. Picture it, just for a moment. Isn't it appealing?"

"If you say so."

"Let me help you end your self-imposed monastic life. You know it isn't good for your health."

"Sure." I knew what she was going to say next. Earlier in the morning, I had heard her talking with a classmate about some outing.

"Guess what? We could go out tonight. Sam told me that at El Corazon there's a nice band from Mukilteo playing, Lions and Lambs, I think they're called, and I really want to go. But if you don't want to, I won't leave you alone."

It was my turn to give her the eye-roll. "I can't believe you just played my Catholic school sense of remorse and guilt for preventing you to have fun. That was low, even for you." I laughed at the innocent expression on her face. My best friend had the gift of making me feel better even when I was trying to sabotage myself. "You win, but don't even try to set me up with Sam's friend, what's his face…"

She frowned at my remark as if it was a personal insult. "What's wrong with you? He's really cute, with his Bruce Lee kind of charm."

"He's all yours." I was going to point my finger at her for not even remembering the boy's name, but she anticipated my move by speaking first.

"What if you like him after all?" Sara's satisfied smile illuminated the whole room.

"Listen to me. There's no *what if*, there's no *but*, and if you keep on callously playing matchmaker, I'll ruin your night." The smile dimmed considerably, and I felt a petty pleasure in it. "I swear," I added just to be sure she got it once and for all.

"Actually, I already told Sam you wanted to meet his friend—"

I was going to reply, but she raised one hand in peace.

"It's not a big deal, like a double date or anything. Liz and Samantha are coming too. By the way, did you know that Samantha went to the same high school as the guitarist? Isn't it crazy?" She said the last part in English.

"Totally," I mocked her equally in English, the saying sounding funny to me. "Okay."

"Okay?"

"Don't get too excited." Even though I would have never confessed as much, I knew I needed a night out. I liked the other two girls, and I needed to practice my English a bit. My knowledge of the language was more technical than colloquial; talking about something other than bones, chipped mirrors, and broken pieces of pottery was going to be beneficial to my experience in the States. I told her as much. I left out that I thought it would be beneficial to my sanity as well.

After rummaging through Sara's extensive closet, I went for something sexy but not revealing, dark skinny jeans and a cute black top that fit my petite torso well. I thought the little red bleeding heart design on the top was kind of appropriate for the place we were going. The idea made me smile; at least it could be a topic of conversation.

Before we left the apartment, I sprayed my favorite perfume, Anaïs Anaïs, all over the room so I could shower in it. The fruity scent sent my mind back two years. Anaïs Anaïs was the perfume I had been wearing when I saw *him* in Greece. I decided not to mention this detail to Sara. I had tested our friendship enough already. "So, how do I look? Good enough for the local band?"

Sara took a moment to assess my need for any accessories and then gave her verdict. "Yes, perfect for the local band." The odious smile made another appearance. "Sam's friend is going to be speechless."

And again, I crushed it remorselessly. "I already told you what I think about what's his face."

"Okay, okay, chill. Let's go out and have some fun, my little Joan d'Arc!"

Hearing voices and a virgin. I deserved it.

The only thing I had close by was the colored mug I liked so much. Unfortunately, it missed Sara's laughing face by a breath and crashed on the hardwood floor in a thousand pieces.

4

The night turned out to be pleasant. More so than I'd expected, in fact.

Sam and his friend Drew, what's his face's name, were nice. I started to like them even better when it became obvious they weren't interested in making fun of my accent... too much. It was still a sore spot for me. While Sara had a perfect cultivated British accent, mine was still very Italian and got me in trouble sometimes at the grocery store. The boys didn't seem to mind that I had to think twice before saying anything, and Liz and Samantha were delightful as usual. The concert was energetic and the band good. Even the conversation, when we managed some sort of word exchange, was light and fresh. Our research was mentioned once or twice. After all, everyone was from the same department.

At the end of the concert, we met with other people we knew from UW and decided to end the night at Sam's house. Sam, born and raised in Seattle, was one of the few aborigines—Sara had affectionately named him thus—which by itself was interesting in a city where everybody was from somewhere else. He lived in Queen Anne, a beautiful neighborhood with an unobstructed view of the Space Needle and the Experience Music Project Museum. He had inherited an apartment big enough to fit everyone inside. As Sara had promised, the conversation at Sam's was invigorating. Everybody talked freely about politics and religion, and nobody got offended. During my first days in Seattle, I had learned the hard way that some topics were taboo. More than once, I'd had to apologize for saying something I thought completely innocent.

I had fun talking without having to parse words but after a while got tired from thinking in a language that wasn't mine and went outside to admire the famous view. The night was cold but refreshing. Sam's apartment had become uncomfortably stuffy, and

I needed fresh air. A few tourists and some couples were taking pictures. I sat inside an abstract sculpture at the edge of the paved floor of the terrace, wondering briefly if I could do that, and went on with my thoughts. I turned on my Zune to listen to some quiet music. I was in the mood for some romantic sweet melody and opted for *The Piano*'s soundtrack.

I closed my eyes for a moment, lost in my thoughts, when I suddenly felt a shift in the air, wet wood and wildflowers playing with my nostrils. A warm, gentle breeze surrounded my body, shifting and changing. I opened my eyes and gasped.

He was there, with me, looking at me, sitting on the edge of the parapet. He was exactly like I remembered him, two years older.

Time stopped. Things in my peripheral vision didn't exist anymore. My music seemed amplified, and it sounded like an open-air concert playing live and not from my little device. I had eyes only for him, for his eyes, and I could see him smiling at me. I stood up and then froze.

Trying my best to keep on breathing, I opened and closed my eyes several times, afraid he was going to disappear. But he was there, he was there, and he was still there. A varied range of emotions took control of my mind. My heart swelled ten sizes, and I wondered how my ribs could contain my growing happiness. Tears wet my face.

The expression on his face changed; he mouthed a sweet *no* with his lips. *No, don't cry. I'm here, I'm real,* I thought he said and finally made a move and reached me halfway. I realized that in Greece he had been in a car both times, so I didn't expect him to be so tall, but aside from that, he was exactly how I had imagined him in all my dreams. His body was slim and muscular but not too bulky. He was tanned, his hair shorter but still sun-bleached and untidy. My memories were so vivid that I could compare details even after so long. He was still walking toward me and then stopped, a few yards from the sculpture, so close to me, but not enough.

"Hi," he said.

My swollen heart, already on the verge of bursting, skipped several beats, and without warning, my stomach became a ball of hot lava. Hearing his voice was something I hadn't been expecting.

It was almost too much to ask, as if seeing him was more than enough.

"I missed you." He spoke again, the sweetest of whispers.

The air was vacuumed from my lungs by a power outside my control. My brain was melting, and my body wasn't responding. The meaning of his words eluded me. It couldn't be possible I had understood correctly.

"I missed you so much." He kept staring at me with his liquid eyes.

I felt the warmth emanating from his body. I still couldn't fully realize what he was saying, not in coherent thoughts anyway. His presence was inebriating, and reality morphed into a beautiful dream. He seemed to radiate light, and the music visibly danced about his body, swathing mine like a warm blanket. I felt alive like never before and, at the same time, on the verge of fainting.

He moved closer, extended one arm toward me, raised one hand, and slowly traced the contour of my jaw in the air without touching me. Although his fingers didn't make contact with my face, the shivers that ran over my sensitive skin made me gasp as if he had. I closed my eyes to savor the moment, hoping with all my heart that it was going to last forever. When I opened my eyes, he was still there, and I felt reassured.

Unable to do anything more than look at him, I simply basked in his presence, waiting for him to do something. For a few seconds, he seemed lost in tracing my figure on an imaginary canvas, and then he moved away from me. Slowly but inexorably, the distance between our bodies grew until I didn't feel his warmth anymore. The music dimmed to a faint murmur in the dark night. The scent of flowers became too delicate for my nose to sense anymore. I felt paralyzed by the fear of losing him, of not seeing him again, of waking up and discovering I had dreamed everything. I wanted more, but he was leaving, and I hadn't been able to say a single word.

"Wait!" I finally managed to open my mouth, sharp pain seizing my heart. I wasn't even sure he had heard me since my voice had come out as a whisper, nothing more. "Wait, please, don't go." I still couldn't move to close the growing distance between our bodies, but my voice sounded stronger. "Tell me your name."

I felt desperate watching him going away, and I didn't know how to stop him. My legs didn't respond to my frantic commands, and my eyes couldn't leave his while he was backing away from me.

Before he turned to face the other way, he gave me one last smile and whispered back to me, "Give me one."

And then he was gone.

Hyperventilating, I fell down against the sculpture, and I felt all the blood draining from my body. The world around me faded, replaced by an opaque curtain protecting me from a reality wherein he was gone. I needed to believe that what had just happened was real, that I wasn't going insane. I still couldn't see clearly ahead of me, and I was glad for the cold seeping through my bones because I felt on the verge of embracing unconsciousness again, and this time the threat was real. In an awkward moment of lucidity, I surprised myself by thinking that fainting there all alone wasn't a smart idea. I tried to stand up with the intention of walking toward Sam's house, but the task revealed itself to be a bit too grand for my unwilling body. My senses didn't want to awaken, and I was more numb than before. Someone was out there, but I had a hard time sorting out the shapes in front of me.

The shapes were talking. My ears were probably full of cotton because I couldn't make anything out. "Gaia?" Someone was talking to me, but the sound came from far away. "Gaia?" My name was repeated closer this time by a friendly voice speaking Italian. "Gaia, rispondi per favore." *Gaia, please answer.*

I finally embraced reality with a gasp. Coming out of my clouds proved to be a slow process, but Sara was there staring at me. Finally, I found my voice and tried my best to sound nonchalant. "Hey, I didn't see you out here."

"Meditating on the blond surfer, are we?" she joked.

Immediately sober and awake from the stupor, I hugged her and started laughing. "You are the best friend ever."

"Of course I am."

"You saw him too. I wasn't hallucinating."

"I was looking for you, and I was told you had gone outside. Imagine my surprise when I saw you with that guy. Who is he? Anyone from UW?"

"It's *him*, and he said he missed me."

Sara emitted a choked sound.

5

I didn't sleep at all that night, and I didn't let Sara sleep either. Soon after I dropped my *it's him* bomb, she ordered Sam to drive us back to our apartment. "What scares me the most is that you aren't your usual depressed self," she had said in the car and then proceeded to check my temperature. At our place, Sara kicked the door closed behind her, locked eyes with me, and started the inquisition.

"How drunk are you?" was her first question, followed closely by the expected "Are you on drugs?" Then, when she saw I was sober, she finally stated, "You've gone insane."

At that, I couldn't help but laugh.

She gave me one of her famous arched brows. "I knew sooner or later it was going to happen." She left the dining/studio/informal area we called the "main" room to go to the kitchen to brew some tea.

"What would happen?"

"Your forced celibacy has fried your gray matter." Her voice was accompanied by a loud bang. "Nothing broke." She leaned backward to show me the pan that had fallen on the floor.

"So do you want to know what happened or not?" I walked to the kitchen.

"Fine, tell me." Two mugs in hand, she gestured for me to bring the teapot to the main room. She sat cross-legged on the battered sofa we had inherited from the previous renters. "I really want to know." Pallino jumped on her lap, purring and stretching at the same time.

I didn't miss the sarcasm, but I didn't care and shrugged with a smile. "I haven't gone insane. You told me there was a blond surfer with me. You saw him too. What other proof do you need?" If I had stopped and listened to myself talking, I would have found the whole story hard to believe, but I didn't pause to think at all. The only thing that mattered to me was that she had seen him too.

"Be that as it may, what else can you tell me about this Greek guy who appears years later in Seattle, saying he's missed you all along?" Sara waited for my answer. My mouth hung open for several seconds before she said, "That's what I thought."

Outside the window, the dawn was waking up the day with a pink-and-orange shower of color in the sky. Colored leaves, left withering in the chilly morning, were floating everywhere, unhurriedly reaching the ground, ethereal and fragile in their beauty, ready to be pressed between paper blankets to become immortal bookmarks. A bittersweet emotion filled my chest as I compared the tenacity of the brittle leaves to the connection I inexplicably felt for him.

Melancholia was an addictive sentiment, but it still was an inactive state of being, more suited to meditation than action. I rationally decided it would not help me in the slightest.

"I'll find him." A sudden euphoria possessed my heart. "I know what I need to do."

"And what is that?"

"I'll post messages for him everywhere so he can find me."

"Okay."

"It's going to work; you'll see I'm right."

She closed the distance between us and hugged me. "I hope you'll see him again," she said, eyes half closed, exhausted by the sleepless night.

In fact, as soon as the river of words I had unleashed on Sara relented, she gratefully fell asleep on the couch. Stamping a kiss on her forehead, I put a blanket on her and went to my laptop. Technology was going to be my ally on this crusade. The power of the Internet was going to bring him back to me. It took me a moment to write the note I had in mind, and then I posted my little message in a bottle on all the social sites used by the students, asking them to share it. I was confident in a few days it would go viral.

The message was simple and meant just for him. "I have your name; please come get it."

He would understand right away. I just had to add the place where we could meet, and after thinking of it, I decided the anthropology class was the easiest location for me. I was always there, almost night and day lately, so I didn't need to set a specific date.

Any time would be fine. Just show up, please.

Regarding the name, I had decided the moment he had asked which one to give him. It had been an unusual request, but my happiness had gotten in the way of rational thinking, and I was more than willing to accept little quirks if that meant seeing him again and even talking to him for more than a few minutes.

I'd had only glimpses of him, no more than ten minutes combined, two years ago. Ten minutes that had changed the course of my life. The fact that I was so confident I could find him again in a city like Seattle should have scared some sense into me, but I was beyond that. Once I posted my request online, I went on with my life as if nothing could go wrong. I probably wasn't kicked out of the research because I worked more than usual. I was the first to enter the lab and the last to leave. I was the most organized student in the whole room, the one who willingly took any extra work, without complaining, secretly pleased to have reasons to stay without alarming my roommate.

For good measure, and not trusting all my eggs in one *Internest*, I printed several stacks of colored paper and stapled my message everywhere I could put personal ads: in every hallway, at the entry of every dorm, wherever I legally could, and in a few cases, even where I couldn't.

I waited for two weeks without even being bothered by the thought that maybe my plan wasn't going to work. Then, one morning, looking out the window of my lab, staring at the full-blown colors of late autumn, a triumph of lovely ripe red and orange and deep yellow with the hint of some residual green, it hit me hard. It had not happened yet. Maybe he didn't frequent the same places I did, or maybe he just wasn't the type to check social sites, but he lived in Seattle, and everybody in this city lived and breathed technology. He also looked the right age to be in college or maybe slightly older. Maybe I should have posted the note somewhere else as well.

I sprang into action again, which helped me regain some confidence. I doubled my efforts to find physical and virtual places to post my note. I also increased my time spent working on the research. Two more weeks passed with more of the same, delusional happiness and growing trepidation, with a side dish of mild exhaustion.

Winter was looming closely, the autumn winds had covered the streets with tons of leaves, and my mood took the final hit when one morning, walking to reach my department, I got soaked by an icy-cold rain. I reached the lab feeling sorry for myself, drowning in water from head to toe. I felt cold, and a sinus headache was waiting for me around the corner. To add insult to injury, I didn't have time to go back home and change because our group was going to present the first finished part of our research to Professor Rayne. Thanks to our connections with the Etruscan Museum in Tarquinia through Professor La Mora, Sara and I had been able to incorporate into our dissertation some of the most recent findings about the Etruscan society. The rest of the group depended on us for the parts still in Italian. Some of the documents had arrived only the night before, and while I spent hours translating my half, Sara disappeared. When I left our apartment, she hadn't come back yet.

I went straight to the common kitchen to grab something hot to ease my frustration. Sara, who usually lingered there before classes, wasn't there. I had hoped to see her. Half worriedly wondering where she could be, I reached for my cell phone in one of the too many pockets of my lab coat. I finally found it, cursing softly in Italian. The phone was ringing, but Sara wasn't picking it up.

At last, I heard her voice. "Gaia? Yes, I know I'm late. I'm running as fast as I can. Sorry—lost track of time."

I didn't question her about how she could have lost track of time because my heart started racing the moment I sensed the already familiar smell of wet wood and wild flowers. I didn't have to turn around to know he was there. Everything in the little kitchen suddenly looked newer and full of color, inviting—a beautiful place where happy things happened.

I didn't dare to move, I was almost terrified to spoil the moment. I was still facing the window, holding a mug full of hot water with shaking hands, when I heard him moving in the room, coming closer to and then around me. More than hearing him moving, I was sensing the change his body created, shifting from one place to another, as if the air molecules reacted to his presence, resonating in harmony. When he finally faced me, it was like the air around our bodies was electrically charged.

He smiled, and his eyes were laughing. "Hi."

"Hi…" I was in a hypnotic trance, and it felt good.

"My name?"

I smiled back and found I could still breathe. Relief embraced my tired soul. Everything had worked out in the end. Now that he was there with me, the knot in my stomach, which had kept me company the whole time, finally untangled itself. I anticipated with pleasure his reaction to the name I had chosen for him. It had been easy to decide. It had almost imposed itself. We had met in Greece the first time. My name was Gaia. He was my personal sun. There was only one name. I hoped he was going to see the beauty of it.

"Elios." I looked at him, waiting for his response. "Your name is Elios." For a moment, my hopes were crushed, but then he lit up.

His smile became something so lovely, so purely joyful, I couldn't contain my own joy.

"Where are you? I thought I was the one late. The presentation's starting." The voice from the cell phone startled me, and I dropped the mug I forgot I was holding. The sound of the mug smashing on the linoleum floor in scattered pieces woke me up. I bent to clean the mess, but he was already there, reaching out to collect the pieces. Torn between the desire to stay with him and my responsibility to the rest of the team, I mentally cursed the ill-timed astrological position of the entire cosmos and the invention of the cell phone.

"I'm so sorry," I muttered under my breath, hoping with all my heart he would understand how sorry I was. "I have to go, but I'm coming back as soon as I can." I didn't want to leave, but I had enough sense left in me to realize I really had to go, and sooner rather than later if I didn't want to let down everybody in my group.

"I'll wait for you here."

When he smiled at me, my heart skipped a whole chain of heartbeats. From the cell phone, I could still hear Sara's voice questioning my sanity in a low Italian whisper. I ran to the classroom, and as soon as Sara saw me, she snapped the cell phone shut and then hissed between her teeth, "What's happened to you?"

"He's here."

"He's here, *here*?"

I nodded.

Professor Rayne's assistant called our group, and Sara motioned for me to walk to the front of the class with her. "Later, you'll tell me everything."

I nodded again and followed her.

Several minutes later, our presentation already halfway through, she nudged me. "Sleeping Beauty, do you remember you are supposed to participate in the presentation?"

I rummaged inside my backpack, looking for the papers I had prepared the night before. Once I found the stack with all the notes, I looked at my own writing in dismay. "I don't remember anything."

"Thankfully, your cursive is neat enough—" Sara took the notes from my hands and started reading them. "Can you help me with the pictures at least?" she whispered to me, indicating the laptop she had previously put on the desk.

I did my best to click the button and accompany her words with the right images. Some of the pictures had arrived only the night before while Sara was out. She nodded in approval, and I mechanically kept right-clicking, following Sara's vocal cues. One after the other, the pictures of the Etruscan artifacts were shown on the board behind us. A chorus of comments made me turn to look at the board. The sight of the famous couple embracing in the afterlife, in one of the most famous Etruscan sarcophagi, brought me back to the present. My attention lasted that one slide.

Professor Rayne said something that, considering the reaction the rest of the class had, must've been interesting. With my ears full of cotton, I heard only a few scattered sentences. The necropolis in Tarquinia was mentioned, along with an Indian artifact that resembled something else we had found and catalogued at our excavation site in Bremerton. The excitement in the class was growing in intensity, but I didn't care to be part of it. The only thing I really wanted was to run back to the kitchen and stay there forever with him. My skin was still tingling, which made it difficult to concentrate on anything that it wasn't his memory.

Finally, my group finished the presentation. I looked at Sara and excused myself from the room.

She opened her mouth to ask me something, but I was already gone before she could articulate her question.

He was still in the kitchen, looking out the window. Droplets of rain slid down the glass, blurring the outside world. The dim, metallic light of a gray day haloed his curly hair. He slowly turned his head to look at me, and the smile was back on his lips. I wanted to reach for his mouth, to touch the cracked lips. I was still at the door, enthralled by his figure, when he spoke.

"Love my name. It's the best I've ever had."

I couldn't help but wonder at what he had just said.

"Thanks for giving it to me," he said, moving slowly toward me. He reached me but maintained an unusual distance, more space than people normally keep between them when they are talking, though close enough to feel the electricity growing in intensity once again. "And your name is?"

I was amazed I could still talk. "My name is Gaia." My heart was racing so fast that pronouncing every single word was a demanding task. My legs weren't keeping steady, and I was worried he could see how little control I had over my trembling body.

He stood silent for a long moment, and then his eyes brightened. "Thank you. Our names are perfect together."

My shaking abated, and I felt a burst of fiery happiness.

He continued, "In ancient Greek, Gaia is the Mother Earth, while Elios is the Sun. You couldn't have chosen better."

You are my personal sun.

"What's your real name?"

He looked at me in surprise. "The only name I have is the one you gave me." His eyes were a mixture of wonder and innocence. "My name is Elios. A pleasure to finally meet you." He didn't move and didn't reach to shake my hand or express any interest in any other social interaction required by the circumstances. He just remained where he was. "Do you want to go outside for a walk?"

Outside feels like a cold shower. "Yes, I'd love that."

It was the most spectacularly rainy day in Seattle to date, chilly and unwelcoming. And I loved it. I even left my umbrella behind. I didn't want to embarrass myself in front of him since nobody in Seattle seemed to have any use for this clever invention. The moment we were out of the building, we were welcomed by a warm, perfumed shower and a small whirlwind of petals dancing nearby. I didn't know if I was more confused by his mere presence or by this unseasonal and, I have to add, *unrealistic* natural show. I thought my senses were losing grip on reality, since not only wasn't I cold, but I also was happily enjoying the warm drizzle.

He never came too close to my body. I could sense he was carefully avoiding any kind of physical contact. I didn't think he was being rude, but I couldn't help wondering why he was keeping such an unnatural distance.

"May I ask you something?" He was not entirely formal but not colloquial either.

"Sure." I loved the sound of his voice, calm and elegant. I especially liked the way he pronounced the letter *s*, dragging the sound just a bit longer than necessary; even a little defect was so sexy on him.

"Have you ever thought about me?"

I thought I heard a pleading tone in his question.

"I think of you all the time." Maybe I should've been less spontaneous. "I've been waiting for you." My face became a deep shade of red; I hoped he didn't understand what I was talking about.

Instead, he said, "I've been looking for you for so long. I tried to... but I couldn't wait anymore."

I certainly didn't expect that. "You have been looking for me?" He had been looking for me; I barely registered the rest of the fractured sentence, my head spinning hard. It was overwhelming to think he could share my same feelings about us. *Us.* What an incredible little word that could convey so much meaning. It wasn't just me, it was *us*.

"Would you say my name again, please?"

"Elios." I could have repeated his name forever.

"I love the way you make it sound like a song."

I moved closer to him without realizing what I was doing. My only desire was to be cradled in his arms, out there in the rain, without coat or umbrella, forever.

While I was waiting to be swept away, I failed to notice what his body was saying. When I realized that nothing was happening, I looked at him… and I saw.

Every muscle in his body was tensed as if he were preparing to fight an enemy. An invisible but tangible wall had come down to separate us. His expression changed before my eyes; where joy had been, was pain and sorrow.

With an apologetic smile on his lips, he moved his body away from mine. "I can't come any closer to you. I'm sorry."

Frozen on the spot, I stared at him as if he was speaking gibberish. "I don't understand." For a moment, I felt the rain, wet and cold, falling from an angry sky, and I shivered, conscious of the clothes drenched in icy water and clinging to my oversensitive skin.

He looked at me, raising an eyebrow, and then wiped away the wet hair plastered on his forehead. "I'm sorry about this." The cold feeling disappeared, and the warm, lilac-infused shower began again.

Mesmerized though I was, I didn't fail to notice that strange but pleasant things happened when he was nearby. Curiosity was slowly making an entrance into my thoughts when he started talking, and I forgot my questions once again.

"I'll come to your place tonight. I'd like to see you again." After a brief pause, he lowered his eyes and added in a softer tone, "If you want to see me."

"I'm free now. I don't have to go back to the lab." I wasn't ready to wake up.

He moved away from me and crushed my dream. "I must go."

My disillusionment was partially mitigated by the sorrow in his eyes. "Wait." I managed to shout my address while he was disappearing around the corner of the building. He didn't seem to hear my words and never looked back at me. Unable to think straight, I stayed motionless in the rain for a few minutes and then I decided it was just plain wrong to stand under such a deluge.

6

When I finally turned to go back inside the building, I saw Sara waiting for me by the door.

She had a bewildered expression. "Gaia?"

"I need to sit down." Lightheaded, I passed Sara and signed for her to follow me.

Once inside the hall, safe from the torrential rain but not from the despair I was feeling, I finally let my body relax against the wall since my legs didn't want to cooperate. I forced myself to breathe slowly, and when I saw people were staring, I walked toward the lab with Sara at my heels. She kept looking at me silently while I tried to remove water from my hair. I gave it up and twisted it into a long ponytail.

"What was that about, out there?" Sara couldn't contain the question any longer, but I was still fighting to regain some composure, and I didn't answer right away. Keeping her eyes on my face, she added very slowly, "Why was there a lilac smell and flowers flying around?"

Still dizzy, I shrugged. "Not sure."

We sat down on the worn couch just outside the common room. I didn't feel like being with other people. I didn't want to explain to anybody why I was soaked in water for the second time today. I switched to Italian to keep our conversation private. "Era bellissimo." *It was so beautiful.*

"Had no idea it rained flowers in Seattle." Sara patted my knee. "It did look beautiful."

I shivered, my sweater weighing down on my shoulders, my jeans clinging to my legs, my hands and feet cold.

Sara removed her sweater and handed it to me. "Don mine. I'll go brew something hot for you." She gave me one last look and then headed toward the communal kitchenette.

"Thanks." With some difficulty, I managed to pull off the soaked item and put on the dry one. I still felt under a spell.

Several minutes later, I blinked after having stared at the wall before my eyes without a single coherent thought. "Sara?"

"Yes?" She answered from the kitchenette, where she had just poured some hot tea into foam cups.

Sitting down, Sara smiled and offered me the beverage. She relaxed on the couch while I warmed my hands on the cheap cup, inhaling the fumes. I tentatively sipped the liquid and found it was the right temperature to drink. Sara had put all her love and some extra sugar into the tea. I smiled at her kindness.

As soon as the warm, restorative tea entered my system, my brain started functioning, and dozens of questions filled my mind. I had never felt in my life the range of emotions he made me experience, and I didn't know if it was a normal reaction or if it bordered on obsession. I was worried the latter was the right answer to my question, and I felt the urge to talk to Sara and confide in her usually wise judgment. At the same time, I was embarrassed about the intensity of my emotions. I didn't even have an adjective to describe him. He was far beyond any comparison I could make. At last my qualms won over my embarrassment and I had to ask, "Have you ever had the certainty you could leave everything behind for someone?"

She took some time to answer, her eyes locked on mine. I shivered involuntarily.

"No, I can't say I have."

"But if you had?"

"I can't talk about something I've never experienced, can I? Maybe if I had... who knows? I've never been swept away, if this is what you're asking. Have you?"

Instead of answering, I changed the subject. I wasn't sure my answer would please her, and I didn't want to freak her out, so I opted for a safer ground, a topic we could discuss at leisure. "He's coming tonight. To our place."

"Wow, girl, you sure don't waste time." Sara was making fun of me, but I didn't mind. "I thought you would never date again, after Marco."

"I don't know if it's a date." I absently bit my lower lip.

"And what is it, then?"

"I don't know what it is, actually." I wasn't so happy about the uncertainty of our arrangements.

"Would you care to be less cryptic?"

"Not my intention, believe me. I'd like to tell you I have a date with him." I lowered my eyes to the foam cup I was still holding and found it mangled; my nails had left impressions all over it. Sara cleared her throat, and I looked back at her.

"And so?" Sara raised her eyebrow and her tone.

"He's different—"

"Yes?"

"He doesn't react like you would expect. He doesn't do the things other guys would do. He doesn't talk a lot. Actually, he barely does at all, and when he speaks, he says the strangest things—" I noticed that Sara was looking at me with a worried expression, and I immediately added, "But don't worry. I feel perfectly safe when he's around." I paused to think about what I was saying, wanting to explain myself better without borrowing adjectives from the realm of mythical creatures.

Nonplussed, Sara cut my silence. "So, is he different in a good way?" She waited for an answer then added, "Sweetie, I know how difficult it is for you to talk about things. If you aren't ready, it's okay. You don't have to say anything."

I shook my head. "I can't stop thinking about him, like he belongs to me and I to him. I can feel him hugging me even if he doesn't come close to my body. I feel he is the one for me. I feel I could follow him to the end of the world. The only thing I can think about is tonight, and I hope that he's really coming, that I understood what he said, that my mind didn't play tricks on me, because I want to see him again and I'm worried sick it won't happen—" I said all in one breath without emerging for air.

Sara looked taken aback by my words, or maybe it was the way I uttered them with my heart racing violently in my chest. On cue, I felt fever coming to conquer my tired body, and I was almost grateful for the headache blurring my vision because I didn't want to think or talk anymore. I felt exhausted; showing my naked sentiments to Sara had been good, but I wasn't used to baring my soul.

"You look like something Pallino has dragged inside the house." Sara showed me the car keys.

"Thanks a lot." I was actually grateful that she had taken charge of the situation.

She raised one hand. "Don't mention it." She went to stroke my hair and had to dry her wet hand on her jeans. "I'll give you a ride home, I'll cook something for you, and then you'll sleep the rest of the day."

I nodded.

The first thing Sara made me do at the apartment was to take a long, steaming-hot shower, and then she personally dried and combed my hair like I was a little kid. I loved being pampered. She cooked something, as promised, and then she went back to the lab, but not before making sure I had eaten. Still feeling physically and mentally beaten, I decided I wasn't going to endure the rest of the day wondering and worrying if he was coming or not. I had to sleep.

Once in my bedroom, under my favorite quilt, which my grandma had made for my dowry, I finally allowed myself to think about what had happened that morning. The warm temperature in the room and, probably, the fact that I was dry for the first time that day eased my headache, and the act of thinking benefited from that. The dreaded process of relaxing came more easily than I expected, and my anxiety was soon replaced by a soothing peacefulness. I dozed to sleep without realizing it, feeling cradled and enveloped in warm, gentle arms.

I dreamed of colors and perfumes and flowers dancing around me as if I was immersed in a clear pool of warm, scented water. I felt strong arms caressing my muscles and delicate fingers softly stroking my temples. Sweet thoughts nudged respectfully at my sleeping mind, and beautiful images filled my closed eyes. When I woke up, I was a different person, fully rested and smiling. I felt good, relaxed, at peace with everybody, loved. Outside, the late afternoon was dark and teeming with the city life, cars and people hurrying to their homes. The rain was the icing on the cake of my positive feeling; I was inside, warm and dry.

Inside my backpack, slung over the back of one of the kitchen chairs, my forgotten cell phone rang. I walked to the kitchen, reached inside the backpack and checked the ID displayed on the phone. Sara was calling.

"How are you feeling?" She was somewhere crowded.

"Much better. Sleeping helped."

"Do you need anything?"

"No, thanks."

"Are you sure?"

"Yes, I am sure."

"Then, I'll be coming back late tonight. Got things to do." Sara's code for "I met someone."

"See you later." I closed the phone and then threw it back inside the backpack.

I put on some music and prepared some tea. Then, I danced slowly, sliding my bare feet on the dark, polished hardwood, the black bergamot tea already in my system and the scent from the tea leaves lingering in the air like a pleasant afterthought. I untied the braid Sara had combed earlier and let my long hair free to dance on my shoulders. I kept moving in the room to the rhythm of an Irish melody, dreaming of my knight in shining armor. I was lost in my imaginary paradise when the doorbell rang.

The consideration that I was wearing just a plain pink t-shirt and matching shorts quickly brought me back to reality. I went to answer the door while trying to fix my hair blindly, overly self-conscious of my outfit and lack of makeup. Pallino had beaten me to it and was loudly purring at the door, rubbing his body back and forth against it.

I looked at the door and knew he was outside, waiting for me. I swore I could see colors seeping through the solid wood of the door. Already dizzy, I opened the door, and Elios was there, smiling at me. It had sounded so bizarre naming him, but now that he was there, I could see he was my Elios, my personal sun.

"Hi." His voice was sweet and relaxing.

Images from my dream came back, and I smiled. "Hi. I'm glad you came. I wasn't sure you got my address."

"Sorry I had to leave that way, but I couldn't stay. May I come in?"

"Please," I answered immediately. I didn't want to give him any reason to bolt this time. The mere idea he would leave made me feel sick to my stomach. Meanwhile, Pallino's purring had grown loud and persistent, and I couldn't ignore his presence anymore. "I'm sorry. I don't know what's gotten into him."

"No worries. I love animals." Elios smiled and then bent to pet the cat. "What's his name?"

"He's called Pallino." I watched as he stroked the cat's fur and felt jealous. "Do you have pets?"

He shrugged. "No, I don't."

Hoping Pallino wouldn't embarrass me by spraying on him, I set out toward the kitchen, which was the last room at the end of the hallway, making sure he was following me. I didn't find anything smart to say during the small walk, so I preferred silence. I'm one of those persons who hate small talk with a vengeance. The truth is, I was already tired of this social charade. I had been waiting for him more than two years, and somehow I knew him more than I possibly could have. I was entitled to be tired of going through pleasantries just for the sake of it, but I didn't want to give him the wrong picture.

I was itching to jump to the next stage, when couples sip warm cups of chocolate together at the end of a very busy day spent running errands, warming their bodies in the light of the fireplace. I was going crazy trying to act normal, but I didn't feel our situation was normal in any way, which contributed to my speech impairment. At last, I managed to say something that wasn't completely idiotic. "Would you like something to drink? I brought my moka from Italy. I could brew some real espresso for you." *Maybe he doesn't care for coffee. I should've cooked some cake instead of slumbering.* "Or a cup of tea if you prefer. San Pellegrino water, maybe?" *Or maybe we can just sit down and talk until our tongues fall on the floor.*

"I'd love to try your espresso. It's been a while since the last one I had in Rome," Elios answered and sat on the first chair he found.

I involuntarily smiled at the fact that even the lame topic *because you are Italian I'm going to try to impress you with all the things I know about Italy* sounded so cute on him.

"You lived in Rome?" I played along while tinkering with the moka. All of a sudden, I couldn't remember how to prepare coffee. After a moment, I remembered where the espresso beans were and reached for the last shelf of our cupboard, packed with Italian snacks.

"Si, per quasi due anni."

I knocked out a tin with the last of our tea cookies, Gentilini biscuits fresh from the factory in Rome, a special delivery from my mom. "Oh, really." And suddenly, I realized he had answered in perfect Italian, *Yes, I did, for almost two years.* "Wow, I'm impressed. You don't have any accent." I forgot about the cookies. "What did you do in Italy? And do you mind if we keep talking in Italian?" I finally reached the Illy can and then retrieved a spoon to scoop a handful of coffee beans for the coffee grinder on the counter. While moving in the confined space of the kitchen, I stole glances at him. Under the table, Pallino was still purring, his furry body seemingly one with Elios's leg.

"Not at all. Italian is one of the languages I like the most. And, to answer your question, I worked on a personal project." Elios's voice was rhythmic and slow. I wanted to ask how many languages he spoke—just trying to think in English gave me a headache, but he kept talking. "I also collected some data about the political situation in Europe. I've been working on it for a while."

I spilled some of the coffee I was trying to fill the moka filter with all over the counter and hastily cleaned it up. "This is what you were doing in Greece?"

"Yes, and before that, I was in France and in England."

I placed the moka on the stove but had to try twice to turn on the gas. The small espresso cups and the sugar bowl were already on the table. Sara liked to set the table that way. I grabbed two spoons and sat at the table opposite him, my back to the stove.

"I'm part of a worldwide organization that collects statistics about the growth of and equilibrium between societies." He paused for a moment. "I travel a lot and take up different jobs in every place, to be fully immersed in the culture I'm studying at the moment."

"What a coincidence that my field of study is the same but related to ancient civilizations. Well, I don't travel that much—" I was going to add something else, but I stopped. There was something odd about what he had just said. "It takes time to study a culture, and you seem very young to have traveled so much already." I knew for a fact that the data he was talking about weren't taken in two months.

"I look much younger than I am."

I made a face.

"You don't like the idea that I'm older than you?" He waited a few seconds for my answer and then said as an afterthought, "I never thought that age was going to be a problem."

"I don't mind if you're older than me. I like you." I grabbed the edge of my seat with both hands.

He smiled. "I like you too."

Elios stared at me with such intensity I felt flames burning my cheeks. When I also smelled a burnt scent, I realized the moka had been making sounds for a while, and the espresso had spilled all over the stove. *Not now.* My cheeks turned bright red, for real this time, and I went to turn off the stove and wipe up the mess. He moved silently with me, around me, making me feel hyperconscious of his presence so close to my body but never in contact with it.

"I like you. More than you think," he whispered, sending shivers through my spine and making it hard for me to concentrate on the ruddy business of cleaning the burnt black coffee from the white stove.

"I…" Uncertain of what to do, I decided we could use a little walk back to the living room where a couch was conveniently located for sitting purposes.

Elios followed me, seemingly lost in his train of thoughts. "I'd like to find a way to tell you more about me." Pallino had loyally followed him.

"I'd like that."

The smile he had been wearing dimmed. Still keeping his eyes on me, he added, "I can't now. Maybe one of the next times."

I was starting to get annoyed by all the half sentences. I liked clarity and greatly disliked when people weren't direct. I felt that since we already had a connection, we could skip a few steps. Nonetheless, I loved the sound of the last part of what he had said. *There will be next times to hear whatever he has to say.*

Elios interrupted my thoughts. "Do you mind if we just listen to some music?"

I looked at him, and for a second I read something more in his words. There was a tinge in his voice that matched my own entangled emotions, uneasiness and a subtle hint of frustration. "Sure. What kind of music do you want to listen to?" I was glad he had found another topic to avoid the enormous conversational rut we were slowly sinking into.

"The kind you like."

I went to the stereo system, a gift from one of Sara's many long-gone boyfriends, and I ran my fingers through the untidy stack of CDs waiting for my verdict. I finally found the one I wanted and skipped tracks until one specific song started.

He had sat on the couch and Pallino was now on his lap, as if he belonged there. I sat by him and couldn't help but noticing his rigid posture despite his petting the cat. Then, he leaned his head on the wall behind and just kept his eyes on mine. He didn't move and didn't reach for me, and his arms didn't try to touch my shoulder by mistake. He seemed content enough caressing Pallino, and I didn't dare sit closer to him. I tried to relax and let the music speak for me.

I had chosen an Italian singer with a husky, non-melodic voice whose song lyrics were sensual. The song we were listening to was about a man talking on the phone with the woman he loves, counting the minutes before their next encounter. The words were so evocative my skin started to prickle.

I almost gasped when Elios started singing along, word for word in the same non-melodic tone, in his perfect Italian. Seattle disappeared outside the windows of my apartment; only his voice and his eyes existed. Suddenly, the air in the room changed, tinted with the now-familiar fragrance of wildflowers. Even the light dimmed, and a beautiful shade of violet was cast on every object in the room. Reality became dreamlike. I didn't pause to consider what was happening. I accepted the unreal qualities of what I was sensing without questioning them, exactly like I did before in his presence.

The music, the scent, and the colors led me to another dimension. I allowed myself to relax, and I opened my mind to the experience. My eyes lost focus for less than a second, and when my vision sharpened again, I saw clear images of him driving to reach me and of me waiting for him in a bedroom that wasn't mine. I felt the warmth from the fireplace caressing my skin. He was furiously driving in the pitch black of the darkest night, unable to stand another moment far away from me, devouring the road at an unsafe speed. His only thoughts were on leaving the rest of the world behind us and letting the dawn find us sleeping, embraced. I was pacing the room, listening to his voice in my mind, worried about the way I knew he was driving and lingering on the thoughts of the last time we were together. I sat on the bed and slid under the gray silk sheets, feeling the smoothness of the rich fabric on my bare skin.

I gasped, trying to breathe. I blinked my eyes once. I wasn't in a fireplace-lit bedroom, and I wasn't wearing silk sheets for clothes. I looked around, sure I'd scared Elios with my trancelike episode, but he was still immersed in the singing, looking at me. Apparently, not only hadn't he noticed my trip to Neverland, but he also hadn't moved, not even an inch. I felt immensely relieved I didn't have to explain my behavior, mostly because I didn't know what I had done during the vivid dream.

I was totally shocked when Elios spoke again, ever so slowly, making each and every word sing a love song for me. Burning with a new level of intensity, his eyes locked mine in a steel grip while the rest of the room disappeared again in the dark. "I'd give anything to be that man."

You can't imagine what you just did to me. "Elios..." I wanted to say so many things, ask how we had possibly shared the same illusion, when I remembered that, all along, he had been singing those lyrics depicting exactly the scene I imagined.

"Yes, my Gaia."

My Gaia.

It sounded perfect, like a sunset on a deserted beach, with not a single tourist to ruin the picture. "You make me feel things I can't put into words." I didn't add that I had visions every time we were together.

"You make me feel emotions I shouldn't have." He never released the lock he had on my eyes.

Elios didn't elaborate further, leaving me thirsty for his words. I was starting to dread the apparent impossibility of talking about something at length once we started a new topic. We both seemed incapable of finishing a conversation.

After a moment, he changed expression and position on the couch, again very cautiously avoiding any contact with my body, and then smiled at me. "Would you rather do something else?"

"I just want to stay here with you, listening to some more music and talking, if you want to." I went to the stereo system and stopped the track.

"I can do that," Elios answered in his soft, melodic voice.

I rummaged through the pile of CDs, looking for a band with a different style so we could talk without being sidetracked by the lyrics. "What about Lions and Lambs?" It was the little-known, local band that had played at El Corazon.

"I like them." Elios sang the first verse of one of the group's songs. "'Caterpillars' is my favorite."

"Mine too." I looked for that song and played it. A sudden question popped into my mind. "Are you from here, from Washington State?"

"I'm not from here. Actually, I'm not American."

The answer was surprising, like everything about him. "And you aren't Greek." That I had figured out already.

"No, I'm not. I've been living in so many places, I feel that I'm from everywhere. And nowhere." He rearranged his body on the couch.

I longed to sit by him, but I settled for sitting on the same couch instead. "A true citizen of the world."

"Worlds," Elios absentmindedly corrected me, but I didn't have time to dwell on that remark because he was already asking me something else. "Do you like it here? Seattle is so different from Rome."

"Oh, I like it way better now." I blushed, unable to contain my reaction.

"I agree." Elios laughed, a mixture of little pebbles rolling around on a sandy beach. His luminous eyes were shining at me, and I felt attracted to him like a nocturnal butterfly to the warm light. "I love everywhere *you are*."

The combination of what he was saying and the way he was saying it was almost too much to bear. I couldn't believe I wasn't dreaming, and I tried to concentrate on the music. It wasn't a great help, considering that the band was singing about finding love when you least expected it. I stood up to breathe. I couldn't sit anymore on the couch. It was so unsatisfying being close to him that way. "Since I ruined the coffee, do you want some water?" I needed an excuse to walk, even for the few seconds it would take to reach the kitchen and come back.

"Yes, please."

Pallino followed me to the kitchen. "Are we hungry now?"

He purred in response and rubbed himself against me.

"Unbelievable." I opened one of his cans and poured the exotically named kibbles in his bowl by the sink. "You better give me some privacy now." Pallino let out a satisfied meow and then attacked the bowl with gusto. I went to the fridge and grabbed a San Pellegrino bottle, then I opened the cupboard, looking for two matching glasses. My hands were shaking badly when I put the loaded tray on the coffee table in front of the couch. "Please." I gestured for him to take one of the two glasses filled to the rim. After he chose his, I took mine and accidentally dribbled water on my shirt. At least the cold water had some effect on my system. I sat down, slightly more in control. "You don't talk a lot." A string quartet was playing now. I saw the open CD case lying on the floor and smiled in approval. I liked those classic versions of modern songs.

"I'm not used to interacting a lot with people."

"I can hardly believe that." With his looks, it didn't seem plausible he wasn't a social person.

He stood silent for a moment and then frowned. "Am I boring you? I'm not sure how to talk to you."

I let out a chuckle. "You are definitely not boring me. I just wish you were less cryptic."

"We wish for the same thing." Elios smiled before adding, "I love when you laugh like that, such innocence in your face."

For the second time in his presence, I did something without thinking and moved on the couch toward him.

At first Elios didn't react, just kept looking at me, but then slowly closed the gap between us.

Music played around us. I heard the string quartet as if it were there. I closed my eyes, expectantly. I could feel something warm and sweet reaching for my lips, and...

Nothing happened.

I opened my eyes, and Elios was standing before me. Tears wetted his face.

"I don't understand." I didn't want to cry, but the disappointment was too much. Elios had just refused me. How could I have misread the situation so much? "I was sure—"

"I shouldn't have contacted you. I didn't stop myself even though I knew better."

I gasped. Elios's words slapped me into the cold reality of the moment; the dream was slowly but inexorably changing into a nightmare. I felt betrayed and angry.

"I want to explain to you." His eyes were pleading for something. My comprehension?

"So do it." I startled him with an uncontainable rage shaking my voice.

"I'm not allowed to interact with you, physically." Elios looked at me with a tenderness that made me feel even worse.

I couldn't believe that after two years, so many months, uncountable hours, and a lifetime of seconds passed waiting for him, *those* words were the only consolation I got. "What. Are. You. Talking. About?" I deserved a better explanation. "I know you like me. You can't deny that." I didn't scream the last part, but I was on the verge of breaking down.

Elios stood still a few seconds, probably thinking of what to say, and then he decided with a sigh. "I'm not going to deny the truth, and for what it is worth, I'm going to try to be honest with you."

Finally.

"I've been following you around since Athens. I've been in Rome because of you. I'm in Seattle for you. I'll be wherever you want me to be. Away from you if you so decide. Although I hope not."

Elios had been following me around.

I don't think I really grasped what he was saying because my mind clearly registered the words, yet I remained there on the couch listening to him.

"I can't do any harm to you, and neither would I."

He was saying things that should have scared me, but his voice was so sweet and sad, and his eyes so innocent. I could only linger on the positive meaning of his words. I didn't want to read what I didn't like.

"Don't worry. I'm not dangerous. Just stupid."

"Okay." A stupid stalker was much better than a smart one.

"I need to tell you something about myself that might be easier to understand."

Easier than what? "I'm listening."

He looked at me again, and he was crying. The overpowering need to console him struck my body, but my mind knew better this time.

"I was born to a society that doesn't utilize touch as a form of social behavior the same way you are used to."

He was from some strange religious sect.

"We do touch each other mentally, and some of us will experience the act of physically touching others in our lives, but it is reserved for special unions."

Emotions were fighting to take control of my soul, and I still couldn't decide whether kicking him out was a better option than listening on.

"Remember what I was saying about my job?"

I nodded.

"I'm part of an elite guard, and I made a vow of physical abstinence."

This was getting worse than the usual "I am gay/married/dying" speech. The night had fully become the nightmare I had so much dreaded.

"I'm what you probably can define as a… monk." His calm enraged me more than any insult.

"You are a monk?" I was going to lose it this time. Just the sound of it was brutal, and I felt my stomach lurch, and a staggering ache enveloped my body. "What kind of monk are you?"

"A soldier monk, who's forbidden to even hold hands with you."

I heard Elios talking, but I couldn't stand to look at him anymore. I was devastated. I'd had enough of this. "This is a cruel joke, and it's time you leave. Now."

"Gaia—"

"Get out." When I looked at him again, I saw he was miserable too.

"I'm sorry."

Not as much as I am. I felt only pain, but I knew I would give him the opportunity to keep cutting my soul if I could just have him with me a moment longer. For that, I felt like a pathetic little thing, and all I had left was my dignity. So I used every little bit of it to stand up for myself. "I can't understand what kind of kick you get from hurting me, but there you have it; that's the door." I turned my head the other way, I didn't want to look at him anymore.

He left the room and without a sound closed the door behind himself. Only then, I slid to the floor, holding my head between my knees.

"Never come back," I whispered through angry tears and shaking hands. "Please. Never come back."

When Sara came home, I was in bed, silently crying my eyes out, pretending to be asleep.

7

Life went on without my noticing it.

I kept working on the project; our team made good progress in finding similarities in artifacts coming from different cultures. In my attempt to fill my time with helpful activities, I even made a discovery. Studying the pictures of the Italian artifacts, I found that a vase fragment unearthed in the Tarquinian necropolis had a design similar to a ceremonial plate fragment coming from the Native American tribe. On the pottery shard, half-erased by time and neglect, there was the drawing of a person, more a stick figure than the complex depiction of human anatomy the Etruscans were famous for, and closer to Native American art in style.

I buried myself in the research, wishing that time would heal me. I simply didn't want to think because doing so was painful. I couldn't cry anymore. After Elios left, I spent the next two weeks in bed, curled in the fetal position, hoping to wake up and be free of the hurt. The moments I feared most were at night, when I knew I was alone with my thoughts and my defenses were at their weakest. Sleeping was torture because I didn't have any control over it.

Every night, I tried to stay awake as long as I could, to tire my body and my mind. I wanted to surrender to sleep only when I could avoid dreaming. Every night, I endured the most peaceful dreams. As soon as I unwillingly closed my eyes, soothing images of a perfect life swept my soul away. I was happy in my dreams. I had an alternative life in which everything was normal. No nonsense, no pain. Elios and I spent our lives happily ever after cradling each other in eternal blessing. I woke up every morning to reality.

I felt betrayed and stupid, having waited two years for my dream to come true, and then when I thought miracles could exist and I wasn't crazy, this. He'd said he'd been looking for me, and then once he found me, he broke my heart with some idiotic lie. Maybe

I was crazy. *I imagined everything.* That was the explanation. It could not be real, anyway. People don't fall in love after just a glance, and most importantly they don't follow the object of their desire across oceans. Love conquers all, but only up to a point. How could I have been so childish, naïve, irrational to believe even a single part of this nonsense?

I wanted to believe it so much I had opened my heart, closing my mind to harsh reality. I had wanted to believe his charming words because he was my dream come true. I wanted him to be the same guy I had seen in Greece. He had probably played with my own words, leading me to understand whatever I wanted. And I had wished my fairy tale to be true, more than anything else in the world.

What an idiot.

Could I be so desperate? Could I have been such a bad judge of character? But Elios had seemed so real, so innocent somehow. And the things he knew. How could he know those things? I confided only in Sara. He couldn't have listened to our conversations. But Elios spoke perfect Italian. He had lived in Italy—of that I was sure. He couldn't have faked that.

Our conversations had been sketchy at best. I could've simply committed the error of connecting the wrong dots. Elios had never confirmed or denied what I was fabricating in my mind. It didn't make any sense, but the first moment I saw him in Queen Anne, I knew with a frightening certainty that he was the guy from Athens.

For every answer I found, I had other questions I couldn't even voice out loud. Something in my mind told me I had to react—and quickly. I was smart enough to understand it wasn't rational to pine over a story I had built out of a few stolen glances and a few hours spent with a guy for whom I had an insane interest. But all things said and analyzed, I couldn't get over Elios.

Weeks passed in self-torturing fashion, without a single moment of freedom from the pain that kept constant residence in my broken heart. I put myself to work with an intensity that had Sara worried for my health. Every night, I went to the common gym and ran until I was so tired I could go to sleep without thinking and hopefully without dreaming. Sometimes it worked. The unfortunate times it didn't, Sara took care of me until I could be of some use to society again.

Life went on. Time passed.

For Christmas, Sara and I went back to Italy for three weeks. I didn't want to worry my parents and let them know how alone and sad I felt, so I put on a good show for their sake. The corners of my mouth cracked from the constant travesty of smiling.

Since our lead researcher at UW knew we would go back for the holidays, he asked us to look for anything Etruscan that could have some connection with the discovery I had previously made. We took a break from our families for a few days to check on the artifacts from the Etruscan Museum in Tarquinia. We also took full advantage of our newly received clearances—a most appreciated Christmas gift from our professors—to take better pictures of another two fragments with similar painted images. The little design in both fragments looked similar to the one on the Native American piece. It also had something in common with an Indian pottery fragment where the same sketched figure appeared. The only problem was assessing the similitude with certainty, for all the pieces we had found were nothing more than fragments. Similar designs could be found across different civilizations, sometimes even geographically spread apart, as in this case. However, the fragments we were studying indicated that we might be in the presence of the same exact subject, and this was something new and of such magnitude we couldn't even start considering it.

We didn't want to jinx it, just in case. We wouldn't dare write down any conclusion until we were sure of what we really had. Our professors, both Italian and American, had begged us to be cautious. The two universities had lots to gain if we were right but even more to lose if we were wrong. The prestige of La Sapienza and the University of Washington were on the line. We couldn't afford a wild goose chase.

Once back in Seattle, the pressure of the task helped me get through the months. I still missed my family, but pretending to be happy had proved to be a harder task than I had thought. Three weeks had seemed more like three years to me, and eventually I was relieved to fly back to Washington State. At least, far away from Rome, I was free to be miserable.

More time passed.

A few days before spring break, I had a spectacular meltdown. The idea that we had to stop working was something I dreaded like having a serious illness. Being in the apartment without a series of tasks to fill the hours was something I didn't want to consider. Sara was already worried for me, and she was trying her best to provide entertainment.

She started her crusade by proposing blind dates. Our conversations soon became a repetition of the same words.

"What about going out with Mark's friend?"

"No."

"Lewis just came back from London—"

"No."

"Elise told me there's this friend of hers—"

"No."

After a while, she changed her strategy. I refused all of Sara's suggestions without giving her the opportunity to elaborate. I knew a date was planned in all her activities.

"There's this charity thing tonight—"

"Not interested."

"I just read about the new exhibit at SAM."

"No, thanks."

"But it's Gauguin. You love Gauguin."

"Already saw his works in Rome."

"Then what about Sakura Con?"

I almost said yes to that. The three-day anime convention interested me because it promised to be a fascinating people-watching experience. Then I saw the glimmer in her eyes. "Not in the mood."

The day before spring break started, Sara was contemplating the outside world from the safety of our apartment's windows. "I wish it wasn't raining so much. We could have a picnic in the park."

I absentmindedly nodded while watching pictures of Mount Rainier on my PC.

She walked to me and looked at the screen. "That's a pretty sight. Maybe we could go hiking?"

The field in full bloom resting at the foot of the dormant volcano was indeed a pretty sight, and for once I thought it was a good idea to get out of that apartment. But I shook my head. "The park is still closed. We'll go in the summer."

It rained for the first part of the week, ruining spring break for everybody who liked open-air activities, had a social life, and wasn't from Seattle. The locals didn't seem to notice unless they actually had to swim instead of driving cars. And they would've found something funny about that too.

Closed in my apartment, with no possible escape from my reality, all the progress I had so slowly made disappeared in a single moment. The painful routine of dreaming beautiful dreams at night and waking up to crude reality started again, as if not a single day had passed since the last time I'd seen him. My face changed color from the constant crying and my attempts to not sleep at night.

I lost some weight, but not in a good way.

It was Wednesday afternoon, and Sara was checking the weather to see if we could finally go for a hike somewhere nearby. I was trying to focus on something on TV while Pallino had decided to sleep on my lap.

"Spending a few days away from Seattle is going to help you reconnect with the rest of the world," Sara said.

"Is that so?"

"Yes, it's been proven that open air is beneficial for the health of the gray matter. In your case, there isn't a lot left to save, but still."

Suddenly, the doorbell rang, and I jumped, surprised because we weren't expecting any of our friends. Pallino woke up, irritated by my lack of manners, and then unexpectedly ran toward the door, purring as he went.

Sara followed him. "Stay, I'll get it."

Is that when I felt him?

I knew exactly who was behind that door before she reached the other room. I sat down on the first chair I found because I couldn't stand up, couldn't breathe. I just wanted to scream. I was having

some sort of out-of-body experience because—I don't know how—
I found my way to the other room. I heard Sara whispering harsh
words, and I saw him while I was peeking from behind the corner.

My voice left me, and my strength went the same direction.
Elios's eyes were searching for me, and he only stopped when I
stepped out. My heart racing, I looked at him, and he seemed to ask
me permission to enter.

"Do you want to talk to him?" Sara's voice was cold.

"Yes, please." I wanted Elios to stay more than anything else.
My resolution to forget him was already forgotten.

"I don't think it's a good idea."

"It's okay, Sara."

Sara shot me a look and then walked toward me, holding a
struggling Pallino against her. "Are you completely sure you want
to spend any time with him?"

"I'll be fine. Don't worry."

"I don't think you're in your right mind." She raised one hand to
stop me from answering. "I'll be in my room if you need me."

"Thank you." I put a hand on her shoulder while she walked
away. Then I looked at him and blanked again. My body moved,
but my mind couldn't register anything else but his presence. I sat
down on the same couch, in the same room. It felt like déjà vu. The
only difference was this time he had not dared to sit on the couch
with me. He was kneeling on the floor like a penitent asking for
grace.

He was beautiful, but a sad expression was painted on his face,
and his eyes looked tired. Maybe he had also lost weight, but not in
a good way.

For a moment, the idea he had missed me as badly as I had
missed him gave me solace. And then I realized I didn't want him
to suffer, to feel pain. What I was seeing in him was real. I knew he
had suffered, and I didn't like it. Still, I couldn't say a word to him.

He finally started talking, his voice hoarse. "Gaia, I know you
told me to leave you alone, but I can't."

He lowered his eyes to the floor, and I saw his struggle to
continue. I was concentrating on his words, trying to breathe and
not faint.

"I want you to know why I said what I said."

He paused once more, and I nodded, hoping it was enough to keep him talking.

"Last time we spoke, I didn't lie, but I wasn't completely honest either. I edited bits and pieces. I did it mostly for me; it would've made my life much easier, and for that I apologize. It caused more pain than good to the two of us. But I'm not sure you're going to like the truth—"

Part of me was just happy to see him, to hear his voice again. I didn't care if his words hurt me. Someone who's stranded in the desert and finds a pool of clear water just doesn't question the quality of the unexpected gift.

"I can't stay away from you."

My heart slammed against my ribcage.

"I know you feel something for me. Maybe not exactly the same, but I can read you better than you think. I want to find a way to make it work for us. I *need* to find a way to be together, but I still don't know how. I can't become something I'm not, but I'm not who I was before meeting you in Athens."

I was still dreaming, and he was kneeling at my feet. I had to wake up. I couldn't stand another beautiful, hurtful dream. "You are still a monk then?"

He hesitated a moment. "In certain aspects, I am what you would define as a monk, yes. I made vows to keep my mind pure and to treat the body I wear with the utmost respect."

He wouldn't keep lying about such a serious topic. But it felt so wrong.

"I'm studying your society, and as an Observer, I can't interact with the object of my research. I must maintain scientific neutrality."

I felt anger bubbling inside me and grabbed one of the beaded pillows Sara had bought for the couch. I used it as a shield and pressed it against my stomach. "Stop now. This scientist-monk nonsense is making me sick. You're talking like I'm part of a guinea pigs' colony." One strand of beads slipped off between my fingers, and the beads fell on the floor one by one. The sound they made when they hit the hardwood unnerved me. "Give me a single reason why I shouldn't kick you out right now. Why should I listen to all the crazy things you're saying? I don't understand why you even bothered coming back here, and in the middle of the night."

He stood silent, lowered his head to touch his knees, and then looked at me again, and I could barely hear what he was asking. "How much do you think you want to know?"

"What kind of question is that?" Of course I wanted to know everything; why was he even asking?

He reached for one of the fallen beads, his fingers almost brushing my ankle, and then froze. "I'm going to ask you again. Please, listen to what I'm saying and then decide. I'm begging you to consider your answer carefully."

I hugged the pillow tighter. "What could be worse than not knowing?"

"Please, Gaia, I need to be sure you understand what I'm asking you."

"I want to know." I wanted to end all this pain. If it had to end anyway, better it be quick. I felt the strain in my arms as I kept pressing the pillow against my body.

"As you wish." He looked away for a moment. "But before I start, I want you to remember I care for you in a way I wouldn't have thought possible. Even if you're going to reject me, to reject *who* I am, I'll still have your memory. And it will be enough for me."

My head and my shoulders were starting to ache because I was clenching my jaws to maintain a composure I wasn't feeling.

"Our encounter in Athens wasn't meant to be. I shouldn't have felt anything for you. It happened though, and you can't imagine how glad I am that you're in my life even if you don't want me in yours. I've lived for so long as a well-trained soldier. I've spent my life in the most absolutely ascetic way. I never longed for anything material. I never longed for a companion. The mental communion I had with my close friends was enough."

I was finally listening to what he was saying, but his tale didn't make any sense.

He must've read my expression. "Stop me if you want to ask me something. Anything at all."

I shook my head. "Keep going."

"You can't imagine what it means to me, having the opportunity to explain my situation."

"Again, please, keep going because it's getting late." *Don't do this to me again.*

"When I met you, something changed in me. For the first time in my life, I had feelings I didn't know existed. I even forgot I had a human body to care for after I saw you again here in Seattle. I think I can't survive, at least not in this form, if you decide not to be with me. But I can't leave. I have responsibilities toward your... my research."

"I don't understand." I released the pillow but kept it by my side as a shield.

He shifted slightly on the floor. "I want to be with you, but I can't stay without ruining the objectivity of my research. The consequences of my negligence could be disastrous, and my conscience could not bear the result should I fail."

I realized I had been chewing a nail and stopped.

"I need you to understand I'm looking for a way to make it right. But I'm torn. If I stay with you, I'll compromise my research by letting you know things you shouldn't be aware of. If I don't tell the truth tonight, I'll lose you forever, and the pain will impair my capabilities and cloud my judgment. In this second scenario, I'll be removed from the mission and demoted immediately."

His last words threw me off, and I felt anger building up again. "So, what you are saying is that you are worried about losing the job over me?" I hugged the pillow again.

"Losing the job over you is not what worries me." He looked at me with pain in his eyes.

Cold fingers reached for my heart and squeezed the air from my lungs. "And so what is it?"

"If I am with you, I'll want to save the object of my research, no matter what. If I'm not with you, I won't be sure if I can trust myself with the best decision." He smiled sadly. "I thought I was stronger, that I could manage this situation, and that I could remain objective. At least, I thought so at the very beginning, two years ago." A long pause. "After I left you, I realized I wasn't that strong anymore. I'm still trying to obey my commandments the best I can. But it isn't easy anymore. I don't regret it, though."

"I want to believe you, Elios, or whatever your name is." I don't know why all of a sudden that detail bothered me. I stood up, unable to contain the anxiety anymore. "I need something to drink." I walked toward the hallway, and he followed, two steps behind.

"Please, stop."

I helplessly waited for his hand to reach my elbow to make me turn to face him. The disappointment when it didn't happen was too much. I stared at the deserted hallway ahead and willed the tears away.

"I told you, my only name is the one you gave me."

My heart fought against my mind and won. I did turn to look at him. "I want to believe you because it'd be easier on me, but..." He gave me another of his deep looks, and I shivered, forgetting the rest of the sentence. Barely noticing I had walked back to the couch, I rested one hand on its back for balance and forced myself to focus. "But I'd be delusional."

"What we share is real. It's different from any other human relationship. But it's real, and I want to prove it to you."

I sat and waited for the rest of his words, but he didn't say anything else and closed his eyes instead. Something happened in the room, to the room. We were there, but we weren't anymore. Suddenly, we were listening to my favorite Rondò Veneziano string quartet concert. I closed my eyes too. The air was warm and dry, and I was bathing in rose petals. Hundreds of silky pastel petals were dancing around my body, swirling this way or that, softly touching my skin and falling to rest on my lap.

A sweet, citrusy smell lingered in the air, and my senses screamed, fighting with my brain, or what was left of it. I felt closer to him, even without physical contact. Everything that had happened in the last two years made sense again. For once, I didn't mind losing my mind; my heart was so full of joy I didn't care about anything else. I felt my skin charged with magnetic energy.

My senses were supercharged with all the stimuli, and I finally remembered to breathe. I emerged from the apnea gasping for air but not wanting to go back to reality. "Who are you?"

He smiled, and his eyes lit with joy. "I'm not human."

8

We were alone in the universe.

Just Elios and I were there, sharing something bigger than us. I believed him. In a strange way, everything made sense again. The truth sounded impossible, but it was just out of this world. The lights and music in the room subsided enough that I could breathe again. At last, the perfumed petal flowers fell to the floor, creating a multicolored organic carpet, a potpourri sweetly inebriating my senses.

"Questions?" He went to sit on the floor by the couch while I perched on its edge.

I laughed joyously. My heart was skipping beats, but my hands were finally unclenched. "Yes, definitely." I didn't know where to start. "How long can you stay?"

"I have all the time in the world for you."

"Where are you from?" I looked at him expectantly and was pleased to see my eagerness mirrored in his eyes.

"I'm from Solo, a planet geologically similar to Earth. My species is older than the human race. We also developed in a different way. Humans rely on their physical senses and live physically separated. We rely on mental senses, and we used to share our souls with no separations between individuals. Eons ago, after an unknown cataclysm, we lost that ability and got separated. The separation caused the loss of our inner equilibrium as a race. We simply forgot what we were. The population was decimated because they lost the willpower to keep on living. A few individuals, our strongest ancestors, worked hard to rebuild our society, or at least tried to keep together what was left of it. After several millennia, when the situation had been stable for a while and the suicide rates had slowed to the point of disappearing altogether, the council of the Wise Ancestors decided that our pain and sorrow could be put to work to help other civilizations so they wouldn't have to suffer our agony."

It wasn't my intention to interrupt him, but I couldn't help saying, "That's a lot to digest."

He raised his hands in the air. "You asked me for the truth."

I smiled at his reaction. "I want to know more, please." I would've begged him to keep talking, if necessary. His voice would be mesmerizing even reciting a grocery list. Listening to what he was saying was worth not sleeping for several days.

"And you'll definitely have more." Contrary to what he had just said, he started and stopped a few times before looking at me with troubled eyes. "It isn't easy—"

"It's okay. I can take it."

He slowly shook his head. "From now on, my story gets difficult to tell because it involves us. It's about if we should stay together after all is explained or if we should try to look at the bigger picture."

Not again. I refrained from expressing my frustration out loud. Whenever we moved a step forward, we backed up another two, right away. I didn't like this pattern, but I had to know. "What about us?"

His sad smile gave away his worry. "Let me explain again who I am and what I do. It will help you understand what I meant." He paused, his eyes on the floor for a moment, and then looked back at me.

"As I told you before, I'm part of an elite guard called the Army of the Observers. Our only task is to protect other civilizations from falling victim to our fate. If a world proves its worthiness, we are bound by our credo to protect its memory. In doing so, we give them the gift of living in another state of existence, a metaphysical one, but only when their physical existence is at the very end. In several human religions, there is a similar concept; you would loosely call it *heaven*. The main difference is that our version is meant for the race as a whole, not just for single individuals. To establish if a civilization is meant to reach the metaphysical state, we have to collect as much data as we can. To collect data, we physically descend on the inhabited planet we are studying and live through the life span of the planet itself. We also have to incarnate in a body to better comprehend their way of life. Every intimate social contact is strictly prohibited. In order to maintain absolute objectivity, we can't fraternize. It's a matter of salvation or damnation for the species we are observing. We can't interfere in any way. We can't sympathize or hate because, one way or the other, we might misjudge."

One thousand different questions crowded my mind. "Wait a second. Did you just say that you follow the entire life of a race?"

Elios waited a moment before answering, "Yes, from beginning to end."

"Are you saying that you're older than Earth?" I almost choked on the last word.

For some reason, in a conversation full of crazy concepts, this was the one I couldn't digest.

It took another long, uncomfortable moment before he answered, "Actually, I'm way older than that. Earth is my second mission, and before my first mission, I spent quite some time at the Academy studying."

I could feel the room moving sideways. He was old in a way I could not quantify. I had noticed he hadn't even tried giving me a number. That answer triggered a related question. "How long can you live?"

"I'm not immortal. I was born, and I have parents, siblings, and friends. My life has a span like yours. It's just longer."

"It doesn't sound like mine at all."

"It's just a matter of perspective."

I raised one eyebrow, then I remembered something else I needed to ask, even if thinking about it was still painful. I looked for the throw blanket Sara and I shared when chatting late at night and found it stuck between the cushions of the couch. I covered myself with it and mustered the courage to speak. My voice broke again. I tried to steady it, breathe, and go on with my question. "Last time… you didn't want to come closer to me." Elios's rejection still stung, and tears filled the corners of my eyes. It had been the first time in my whole life I had taken the initiative.

Before him, I had never had to encourage anyone to kiss me. I knew I wasn't ugly, but I had never taken advantage of that. On the other hand, I never had to beg for company. Then two years ago, I had suddenly become the equivalent of a nun. I had tried to change that with Marco and ended up in Seattle because of that.

Before he could answer, I had a sudden doubt, and my knuckles became white as I squeezed the life out of the cushion by my side. "Is there something about me that prevents you from…?"

Living in Seattle had taught me about a multicultural environment, how every culture has different habits, and how something normal for an Italian like me was not okay for someone from another part of the world. "We are from… different cultures after all."

"I wanted to touch you." His voice was soft, but I could barely raise my eyes to meet his. "I want to touch you."

His words sent my heart into overdrive and at the same time intensified my longing for his touch. "But?"

"There isn't a single thing about *you* that could prevent me from getting closer."

"Then, why not?" The longing was rapidly morphing into ache.

Elios changed position on the floor. He was still sitting on the hardwood but didn't seem to mind. "Gaia, what I want and what I can do are two different things."

"I don't understand."

"I'm going to say it again; I've been raised in a way different from what you're used to. The human race depends on physical contact more than mine. Humans normally convey emotional messages with touch. A newborn needs his parents' touch to grow mentally stable. A lover needs his or her companion's touch to be reassured of their mutual affection. Lust is conveyed by touch, and so is hate. My species expresses something more than emotional messages with physical contact. We share our selves completely. My whole entity is transferred with a simple touch. All my memories, all my experiences are shared with the other being I establish a physical connection with. Before the Dark, we lived in total communion. We were single entities living in harmony with no possibility of miscommunication.

"We lost that, and we almost ceased to exist in the aftershock, but we managed to retain at least a spark of that precious gift. We partially regained this ability, but we also learned that in order to accomplish our task as Observers, we could not use it at our whim. I was trained to refrain from any physical contact if I wanted to remain impartial. As part of the Observers Army, we can still share our lives, but we have to ask permission because it's the most intimate thing you can ask of another being. Once you do it, you are linked forever to that being, altering his or her life."

"It sounds intense." I paused, looking for the right words. "You don't want me to know you… in that way?" Maybe it was still too early to share something more. I couldn't believe I was in the position of having to wait for him. *There is definitely always a first for everything.*

"Oh, no, no." His eyes grew wider. "No, it's not like that. It's beyond me and you actually."

I braced myself waiting for the bad news, but I smiled to encourage him to speak.

Elios obliged me, attempting to smile back, but he hesitated—in that way of his I was starting to dread—before saying, "I want more than anything else to share all of myself with you. It's the most beautiful experience you can imagine."

"Is it harmful for my species? Could I be damaged by this experience?" I instinctively looked for the pillow I had used earlier to ease my nerves and found it behind my back.

"No, no damage of any kind could be done to you or to any other species. At least, not that I know."

"Then why can't we…?" I looked away from him and dug my nails into the soft surface of the pillow.

"Because a great deal of damage can be done to your race."

"By us touching?" I blushed at having to ask that out loud. I left the couch and went to look outside the window, taking with me my soft shield. Outside, the sun was shining. Morning had come already, and it had stopped raining. I wanted that to be a good omen. I knew he had silently followed, and my body betrayed me once again, and I turned, unable to resist his call. "Elios—"

I could not continue; my lungs stopped receiving air for a moment. My face was on fire, and my hair was flowing around my head like it was underwater. Elios had simply raised one hand to put it close to my lips, and the turmoil he had created didn't let me finish. I barely remembered my name. I also let go of the pillow.

"We're already attuned in a way that isn't normal, not even for me."

My heart was dancing at the sound of his words, and then everything was normal again.

He had lowered his hand, and now it was resting by his side. "I have never experienced this range of emotions and physical reactions before, with anybody of my race or with someone from another race. There's something in your soul that reacts to mine. This could be the reason why we found each other. But it's also the reason why it complicates our staying together. I can have casual physical contact with almost anybody, but since we are not just acquaintances, I can't stop the process with you. If I touch you, we will be one, and we'll share everything we are completely because of the feelings I have for you."

The intensity of the experience Elios was describing frightened me; I couldn't deny that. But it also seemed something pure, something worth trying.

Elios looked out the window, seemed puzzled by something, and then started talking again. "If I touch you, even once, my already insane dependence on you will become so strong I'll lose the ability to analyze data the way I should. My objectivity will be compromised, and I'll feel the need to save your planet because I'll want to be sure that you personally are going to reach the next phase even if Earth shouldn't be saved."

"I don't like what you're saying." I wanted the music in the room and the petals dancing around my body again. I wanted the magical part of the truth. That I liked a lot.

He shook his head. "We don't have a choice in the matter. No contact with you can be casual. We're on the same spiritual channel. Even the slightest touch of your skin would initiate the process."

His words painted the image for me, and I shivered. "I don't have to like it."

74

"I hate the fact I can't touch you." He sighed, raised his fisted hand, displayed his fingers, and let it hover a few inches from my heart.

If a moment earlier I was shivering, now I burnt. I melted at the mere idea he would close that gap.

Breathing hard, he blinked and brought his hand to his chest and covered it with the other. "It's taking all my discipline not to."

I couldn't escape the spell he was creating by biting his lower lip. "Would it be so wrong?"

"I've been trained to follow my ethical code of conduct to the full extent of my possibilities. I told you already that you could think of me as the equivalent of a monk."

"I hate when you say that." The word *monk* sounded wrong applied to him. Not because the word itself had a meaning I didn't like—on the contrary, I personally knew monks I had a great deal of respect for—I just didn't like to think of the restrictions the name brought with it when applied to the two of us. "How can you live this way?"

"My morality is what has kept me going all these years. The certainty I was doing something right, even when I couldn't interfere in the human struggle, was the only way I could manage to collect data impartially. Can you imagine having the power to change a wrong and making it right but being denied that freedom in the name of a bigger picture? What would you do if you were able to save someone but your hands were bound by an oath to just observe him dying?"

A different kind of shivers ran down my spine, and I felt goose bumps all over my skin. "I can't imagine having to bear that kind of responsibility." I had to avert my eyes for a moment. A loud honk was followed by the noise of a car braking, and my eyes went to the window. "I'd go crazy." The smell of baked goods from the coffee shop below reached my nostrils, but it felt wrong. "I couldn't just let kids die."

"There are moments I must repeat to myself that what I do is right. I can't let doubt into my heart. I have watched the horror of war and famine and let it be because I knew I could bring a different kind of solace to the dead and dying. The preserved memory of a race is more important than its individuals."

Images of recent atrocities committed in the name of religion came to my mind. "But what if you save a race that doesn't deserve it?" I turned.

He looked at me with haunted eyes, as though he was remembering something. "It's a possibility. When I became an Observer, I accepted the responsibility to decide another race's fate. It was a decision I made out of love."

Elios raised his hand again, and a gentle breeze caressed my face. It felt like he was touching my skin with a brush. The assault on my senses was intensified by my emotional state. I wanted to hug him close and kiss his worries away, but even this little consolation was denied us. He never stopped looking at me when he said in a lower voice, "And love is what is giving me ethical problems now."

Noises from the kitchen startled me. "Sara?"

"Yes?" She appeared at the door with a fake surprised look on her face. "Oh, you're here. Good morning to you." She gave Elios a nod followed by a grin. "Did we have a party?"

I was immediately conscious of several things. Elios had clearly stayed the whole night. Rose petals were lying on the floor, on the couch, and I was sure even on my hair. Automatically, I combed a strand with my fingers.

"I could hear some Rondò Veneziano last night. Very romantic."

"Good morning to you too. And it's not what you think. At all," I hissed, and blushed before a very amused Sara. I made a face at her, trying to send the message that I would explain later. What I was going to explain, I had no clue. Elios stood up, smiled at us, looked outside nonchalantly like he had just realized what time it was, and then moved to the door.

"I'll come back later; I think we need to sleep after last night."

Sara's grin became obnoxious. "See you later."

I still had so many questions to ask him, but he was gone already. I immediately felt his absence from the room and a strange bittersweet ache radiated from my stomach to my chest. I caught his lingering scent fading rapidly, and for a moment, I thought I had just seen some kind of light coming from outside, through the door Elios had just closed. My head felt too light to remain anchored to my body. I was too tired.

"So?" Sara raised one eyebrow. "Nothing to say?"

I smiled back at her. "Forgive me if I call for the interrogation later. I'm too tired and in need of sleep."

"I can imagine."

"No, you can't. I promise to talk to you later." I left her standing by the hallway door and went to my room.

"I'll remind you of your promise." Her voice reached me from a few steps behind.

"Do that," I answered, already in my room, and closed the door behind me to prevent her from entering. As soon as I put my head on my pillow, a sweet feeling embraced my body, and the moment I closed my eyes, I was already dreaming of him.

9

I slept for only a few hours; the sun was too bright to stay in bed, and I was too excited. I felt invigorated by the short sleep and happy to be alive. While I was waiting for Sara to join me in the kitchen to eat something together, I thought about the inconceivable conversation I'd had only a few hours earlier.

I filled a pot with water to cook spaghetti and then poured the tomato sauce and the extra virgin olive oil in a pan. I sprinkled the sauce with salt and then added a few more teaspoons of oil. Mechanical movements governed my body while I thought about what I was going to say to Sara. How could I say anything to her at all when I didn't know what to think myself?

A few minutes later, she appeared at my side with a smile, her sunny disposition something I could always count on. She was ready to go out, well dressed as usual, makeup in place, with straightened hair matching her innate glamour.

I pointed an accusatory finger at her. "Sara, you are not letting me eat alone, are you?" I had already dumped into the boiling water the equivalent of four servings of pasta.

She walked close to the stove, peered through the vapor coming from the pot, and laughed.

I hastily submerged the uncooked spaghetti sticking out with a wooden spoon which I then brandished in front of her. "Don't judge. I'm starving."

"I'm sorry, but I'm late—"

"You know it's contrary to Italian Laws." It was true. Italians avoid eating alone at all costs. Peer pressure works miracles to keep waists lean.

"Okay, okay, I'll stay a bit longer, but only because I'm a great friend." She sighed loudly and then sat down on the chair by the window, crossing her long legs. She touched her perfect, unmoving golden-red hair and let me know she was dying to ask me about my night. We had been friends for so long I could recognize all her telltale signs.

I set the tomato clock on the table to nine minutes, three fewer than the instructions on the spaghetti pack asked for, and then I gave Sara an appraising look. "New top. Who is he?" I was curious too, and I loved teasing her.

"Sam, but enough already about my love life." She realized she had been tampering with her hairdo and hastily straightened the strand she was playing with.

"What do you want to know?" I couldn't stall her forever.

"You know what I want to know." Her blue eyes were shining under the subtle line of brown mascara. Her smile was contagious as always.

"Sorry to disappoint you, but nothing happened." Actually, lots of things had happened, but none of them were what Sara was thinking. I smiled at her impishly.

"I don't believe you, young lady."

She looked so happy for me that I almost told her. I couldn't stand the idea of keeping secrets from her, and yet I added, "Not a thing whatsoever." I even shrugged.

"You call that," she waved toward the general direction of the main room, where I was sure there still were petals on the floor, "nothing?"

Now, I could appreciate Elios's words when he said that in our previous conversation he had never lied, but he had never told the whole truth either. He had found a way to be honest, painting only bits and pieces of the whole picture. No wonder he had waited so long to tell me the truth.

Finally, I found what I could safely say. "We didn't even hold hands." The truth. "I wish I could tell you more, but there isn't anything else to say about *that*." I looked in the same direction she had just indicated.

She tapped the table with her manicured finger. "So, the music and the blanket of petals were all for nothing?"

I shrugged again.

Her eyebrow shot up. "Really?"

I schooled my face into a neutral mask. I was on the verge of cracking up. "Really."

Fortunately, Sara's expression changed, becoming sweet. "It looked so romantic."

"It was." Just thinking of it made me shiver. "He makes me feel *things*." Suddenly, as if I had summoned Elios's presence, I sensed the air transforming around my body, and a change in temperature made my skin prickle. I struggled to maintain my composure, not wanting to explain myself, but she was looking outside the window and didn't notice my shaking. I kept talking. "Feelings I didn't think I'd experience, ever. I always thought it was just nonsense, but I now have the proof you can be sure of someone at first glance."

"Well, that's intense."

The timer went off and startled me. I reached for the strainer we kept on the first shelf of the cupboard and put it in the sink. I looked for the pot holders, but they weren't in the usual drawer, and the pasta was overcooking. I hastily opened a second drawer, but it only contained clippings from coupons we would never use, and then I precariously grabbed the pot by the handles with my bare hands. The spaghetti almost didn't make it to the strainer.

Sara passed me the aloe cream always handy on the counter.

"Thanks." I massaged my red fingers with the ointment.

"So I guess yesterday was just too early, right?" She looked at me from under her mascara.

I nodded. "Definitely too early." I sounded out of breath. I needed to cool down.

"Your beau had some time to spare. He sure put some thought into the little concert-in-the-park scene he created for you."

"I guess he's the romantic type." I remembered to transfer the pasta from the strainer into a ceramic bowl. Careful not to burn my fingers again, I checked first that the pan's handle wasn't hot and then poured the tomato sauce on the pasta before it became a solid block of spaghetti.

Sara gently touched my shoulder. "So, he's truly the one you were waiting for...?"

"Incredible, isn't it?"

"It's hard to believe, yes, but—"

"But, what?"

"But nothing. I'm just happy for you."

"Thanks."

Sara took my hands in hers, careful not to squeeze my sensitive fingers, and smiled.

"I'm happy, finally happy after so long," I said, looking at her, and saw that her eyes were wet like mine.

"I know, sweetie. I can read your mind, remember?"

I'm so glad you can't.

"I'd almost lost hope for your cause." Sara laughed softly and then glanced briefly at her watch and gasped in horror. "I'm so late. Sorry, but I have to let you eat alone."

"Go. Don't worry. I'll make you pay for it later." Leaving me alone in the kitchen with a bowl full of spaghetti was a hideous crime, and she knew it.

"Oh, look, he's coming. I'm sure you prefer eating with him, anyway." Sara was looking out the window. "See, you won't have to eat alone after all." She stood up, placed her chair back under the table, and then walked out of the kitchen.

"You're off the hook for now. Have fun with Sam." I winked and followed her through the hallway to the door. Pallino, who had been sleeping in his bed in Sara's bedroom, shot through the house, and I almost tripped on him when he passed through my legs in his haste to reach the door.

Sara laughed at the cat's antics and then gave me one of her looks. "*I* will." One foot already outside, she turned to say one last thing to me. The expression on her face was unusually serious, almost pensive. "Please, have some fun; don't let the petals dry." And she was out, not leaving me time to say anything back.

The door didn't have time to close behind Sara, for Elios was already reaching for it. She whispered something to him, and I heard them laughing. Pallino greeted him loudly, and I couldn't help thinking I had serious competition in this cat.

"Hi, Elios."

He was handsome in his rugged way, as if he had just left a surfboard after hours of riding waves under the sun.

"Hi, Gaia. You look radiant." He bent to pick up the wretched creature who wouldn't stop crying for attention.

I felt that way. The few hours I slept had been enough. Dreaming of him had helped. Especially because I had woken up to a brighter reality. A reality where he was still there.

"Would you like some pasta? I don't like eating alone, and I'm hungry." I walked back to the kitchen and then stopped to face him. "Do you eat?"

"Yes, I do." He had gracefully managed not to collide into me when I made the one-eighty without warning.

"Good." I felt the now-familiar electricity in the air and hugged myself to hide the goose bumps on my bare arms. He stepped back to put more distance between us, and I had to hide my disappointment. I could swear I saw a glimpse of satisfaction in Pallino's round face. "Let's eat, then, while the spaghetti is still good."

"I'm embarrassed to confess I'm hungry too." He looked almost shy when he added, "I forget to eat sometimes." On cue, his stomach rumbled, and we both laughed.

Once in the kitchen, I promptly served some food to Pallino, then when he was done and left us for his afternoon nap, I set the table and served the pasta in two colorful bowls. I used what Sara and I called the "Sunday dishware" for the occasion. We ate in silence, our eyes locking between bites.

He started to say something and then shrugged.

"What?" I made sure I didn't have a piece of spaghetti dangling from my mouth.

"Nothing." He smiled.

Butterflies wreaked havoc inside me, and I found it difficult to swallow and breathe at the same time. I drank two glasses of water to no avail.

He opened his mouth one more time, and I hoped he would say something, but he didn't. When I thought my pasta had glued his tongue to his palate, he finally sighed and said, "It's a beautiful day."

"It is." I raked my mind for something else to say, but nothing smart came to me.

He placed the fork on the napkin and then pointed at the window. "If you don't mind, I'd like to go out today."

"No, I don't mind at all. Let me grab my jacket." I left everything on the table for Sara to clean afterward, knowing she would forgive me this one time, and I set out toward the door. I stopped halfway to the closet in the hallway because I felt the familiar gentle breeze against my lips and nose. I pivoted on my heels. He was slowly moving his right hand in the air following the contour of my face without touching it, his eyes closed. All my senses reacted, and I was left breathless one more time.

Instinctively, I raised my hand to mirror what he was doing, and Elios gasped and opened his eyes, looking at me quizzically. The breeze ceased, leaving me disappointed.

"What did you do?" he asked.

"Just what you were doing. Why?"

"What you did… you touched me in a way that was different. Not something I expected."

"But I didn't touch you at all."

"You reached something deeper than my skin."

I shivered. Then the thought occurred to me that his senses probably worked in a different way. "Do you feel the same way I do?"

He frowned. "Never thought about it before. I guess so since I have a human body."

"But we aren't going to find out…?"

He grimaced at my words and led me outside the apartment without saying anything else. Once on the street, we started walking toward a sleek, dark car I recognized from my dad's car magazines, and he pointed at it. "That's my car."

I could have said I knew what his car was: a brand new Alfa Romeo Brera, in shiny black anthracite. I debated whether Elios would be impressed by my extensive knowledge or not and then decided that maybe he didn't even care since he wasn't a normal guy. Or a human one.

Another awkward silence ensued. I tried my best to act smart, which meant not tripping on the tree roots all over the street. Thankfully, I didn't fail that onerous task.

Elios pressed on a keypad, which unlocked the car with a beep. "So…" He smiled at me. "As I was saying, this is my car, and that's the building where I'm living." He pointed at the building standing side by side with mine with a mock regal gesture.

His voice contained a note I couldn't decipher, but I was so surprised by his statement I didn't think much of it. The irony of it made me laugh. "You've been living here the whole time?"

"Well, I've been looking for you for so long, once I found you I couldn't stand to live away from you. I wasn't sure I was ever going to contact you. I knew I shouldn't have, but I wanted to, so I looked for a vacant apartment facing yours. I was happy catching glimpses of you from the window." Between one sentence and the next, Elios checked my reaction, giving me nervous glances. "I have to admit I did it anytime I felt I was going crazy."

I looked up where my window was and then straight ahead at the window on the building facing mine. "I felt your presence."

"I know." He opened the passenger door and kept his eyes on me for one long moment. I automatically sat on the comfortable black leather seat.

He didn't move but stood there looking down at me. "I know your face so well. I could draw your features anytime. Even with my eyes closed." He raised his hand to trace the line of my nose, then my lips, and finally my chin.

I did the same to him, to see if it would work again like before. It did.

Elios whispered, "Thanks… thanks for this unexpected gift."

By the time he reluctantly reached the driver seat, I had already forgotten my previous thoughts.

"Do you like Alki Beach?" he asked.

"I love Alki Beach." *I am willing to go to the end of the world with you.*

I hadn't visited Alki Beach yet, but I knew of it because it was Sara's favorite place to go on a date. I couldn't wait to tell her Elios had taken me there.

Elios started asking questions while driving. I knew all along he was controlling the temperature in the car. It was just the right amount of cool and fresh air but completely different from air-conditioning. "Do you mind if we talk about you today?"

"Not at all." I did mind, but maybe it was a good thing to talk about something else that wasn't him.

"Tired of listening to me?" Elios laughed, and the sapphire and gold in his eyes became so brilliant it was hard to look at them without feeling the impulse to kiss him.

"You gave me lots to think about, but I'll never tire of listening to you." I looked outside for a moment. "I love Seattle." The sun colored the city in shinier shades of green. "So, what would you like to know about me?" I gave him a sideways look.

"You're still a mystery to me. There're so many things I want to hear from you, what you like, what you hate. Any little thing that makes you, *you*." Elios looked at me and smiled his smile, and I felt even happier than before.

Between smiles and small talk, we had reached Alki Beach. The place was crowded, as usual. "Rain or shine" is the Seattleites' motto. I finally couldn't keep it in anymore, and I blurted out, "By the way, nice ride. My dad would be begging you to let him drive this car. Love the color."

"Do you know a lot about cars?" Elios raised one eyebrow.

"Not about cars in general, but my dad is an Alfa aficionado and, strangely enough, never cared for soccer. My sister and I grew up watching more car shows than we ever cared for."

Elios seemed pleased by my answer, and I felt my smile grow brighter just because of that. We cruised for a few minutes, looking for a parking spot. Every time I looked his way, he was looking at me. More than once, he stepped on the brakes to avoid hitting roller skaters and bikers zigzagging through the traffic.

"Maybe you should look ahead." I blushed.

"I certainly should." He laughed but kept his eyes on me a moment longer.

I had to look away. "There. There's enough space to park between those two cars." I pointed ahead of us at the right side of the road.

He effortlessly slid the car between the other two then got out and went to open my door.

Once on the sidewalk, I realized the parking spot I had selected was barely bigger than the Alfa. "My dad would be proud." Memories of my father teaching me how to park in the crowded streets of Rome came to mind.

After that exchange, we walked in silence for a while, watching the colorful crowd merging and moving constantly. Skaters, bikers, joggers, runners, casual walkers like us, everybody was enjoying the sun and the view of the Seattle skyline. He bought us two cups of hot American coffee, and we sat down outside a small coffee place overlooking the beach promenade, bathing happily in the sun.

"I'd like to know something more about your studies. You seem to enjoy that a lot."

"How do you know so many things about me?"

"Not human. Remember?" He smiled. "And lots of time on my hands." He removed the lid from the cup and tentatively sipped the coffee. "So, about your studies?"

I tried my coffee, but it was still too hot for my liking. "I'm studying the artifacts from an archeological dig in Bremerton where, just recently, an ancient Native American village was found. The climatic conditions, the composition of the soil, and a series of fortunate accidents actually helped preserve the site way longer than usual, like the Ark of the Patriarchs on Mount Rainier. My job is to define what kind of social structure they had and find affinities with other cultures if there are any." I played with the cup sleeve.

"Our jobs are similar; we both study societies," Elios said.

I almost knocked over my cup but steadied it before I spilled coffee on my lap. I placed both hands on the paper sleeve. "My team discovered that we could have a match between two different pieces of pottery. The first one is a Native American piece that was found in Bremerton. The second comes from Italy, and it's Etruscan. We also have a third one with a similar picture coming from India, but we need better pictures, so we sent someone there. Sara and I took care of the Italian piece when we went for Christmas…"

"I felt lost when you left. I worried you weren't coming back."

"I couldn't stay here any longer." I finally drank my coffee, but it was bitter.

He commanded my attention by raising his hand and air-caressing my jaw. "I'm sorry. I should've handled things better."

I burnt for his touch. I closed my eyes and imagined his fingers on my skin, tracing circles along my neck. I made an effort not to purr and drank the remainder of the coffee, now cold. "Something good came out of my Christmas vacation. At least we could take good pictures of the Etruscan piece." I threw the empty cup in the bin just beside me and then stretched my hands on the table. "The fragments are small, so we are hoping the archeologists will discover something bigger and possibly with the same painting on it."

"That's interesting." He finished the coffee he had been sipping, crushed the paper cup, and then reached for the bin. In doing so, he leaned forward and came dangerously close to me.

I heard his intake of breath the same moment my heart slammed against my ribcage. His mouth was not even an inch from mine.

He moved away. "If they do, what would it prove?"

I stared at him while I tried to steady my labored breathing.

His eyes went to my mouth for a moment. "If the pieces are similar…"

I looked elsewhere, focusing on the people walking by. "Depending on how similar the pieces are, a correlation between cultures separated by oceans and time could confirm the theory that different civilizations grow in predictable ways."

Meanwhile, the sun had descended on the city like a golden veil covering everything. His face was kissed by the sunrays, and his eyes exploded in thousands of reflections. I tilted my head to avoid being blinded by the sunlight. "I like this."

"What?"

"Just this. You and me. Silly, little things."

"I like them too." Then he went inside the coffee shop to buy two bottles of water. He came back with two San Pellegrinos.

I felt silly, but I had missed him the few minutes he was gone and rejoiced when I heard his approaching steps. "Thanks." I took the bottle he offered me and then clinked it to his. "Cheers."

"Would it be possible to take a look at the pictures of the pottery pieces?" Elios sat back and relaxed, every movement of his body graceful.

I could watch for hours the way his lips turned upward when he was focusing on something. "Right away. I have one of the Etruscan pieces on my cell phone. I usually take backup pictures of anything important." I rummaged in my purse and took out my phone then looked for the picture in archive and turned the phone toward him. The image was clear enough to show the little fragmented painting on the black Etruscan ceramic. "Look, isn't it curious that they draw a human hand with six fingers? Etruscans were highly skilled when it came to—"

"A six-fingered hand?" Elios asked, corrugating his brows.

I nodded. "For being a cell phone camera, the resolution isn't half bad, don't you think?"

"May I?" He took the cell phone from my hands, and I couldn't help but notice how carefully he avoided any contact with my skin. It hurt.

The comment he made on the picture brought me back to reality. More than the words, the tone of his voice snapped me to attention. "What did you just say?"

He looked at me with a wary expression and then repeated, "I have seen this drawing somewhere else."

10

Elios was lost in his thoughts, and I didn't dare interrupt him. He was half in the sun and half in the shadow, like a beautiful black and white picture of a worn-out blond surfer. The white shirt Elios was wearing was casually open, and the sleeves hung unbuttoned on his tanned golden arms. He was sitting loosely on the small plastic chair, his long legs stretched under the table. I told myself to bring paper and pencil next time we were going out.

Drawing and painting were still my favorite hobbies, but it had been a while since the last time I had found a subject I liked so much. While Elios was still contemplating the picture, I passed some time dreaming about painting his portrait. I imagined drawing his body; with my eyes, I slowly followed the contour of his muscles under the white cotton that seemed so rough against his sun-freckled skin. The jeans Elios was wearing were dark blue and faded on his thighs, cut in several places, long enough to cover his flat tan shoes.

I raised my head to sketch his face in my mind. With my imaginary pencil, I traced his nose. It was straight and curved almost imperceptibly upward at the point. The corners of his mouth were not turned up as was usual. The skin of his lips was permanently cracked and a shade of pink so light it got confused with the rest of the skin. The line of his jaw was soft, aristocratic.

His eyes were my favorite feature. I decided his eyes alone were worth at least several days of practice before I could grasp that exact shade of blue and green. Still kissed by the sun, they were sparkling like rising stars, a triumph of warm, happy colors, always smiling. But not now. I stopped my mental exercise and tried to read his expression. "Something wrong?" For no reason at all I shivered.

"Something I can't explain."

"So, I'm curious, where did you see that painting before?" Talking eased the cold that was slowly but inexorably growing inside me.

"I have looked at this figure so many times I've lost count."

"Where? Do you know of other places with similar pieces? I thought we contacted pretty much everybody working on similar archeological excavation sites."

Elios shook his head. "I didn't see them here."

"Was it in China? We're still waiting for Beijing's anthropological museum to get back to us."

He shook his head again. I couldn't think of any other plausible place.

"It wasn't here on Earth," he finally said.

At first, I thought I had misheard and waited for him to say something else.

He silently hugged himself and changed position on the chair several times, his eyes on the ground. He followed the progress of two ants carrying bread crumbs until they disappeared behind the leg of the table.

"Where did you say you saw it?"

"On Solo," he whispered.

I started tapping my foot against my chair.

He finally raised his face and looked at me. "I saw the same figure on an ancient fragment preserved on my planet, guarded in our equivalent of an archeological museum." He leaned toward me, and my heart skipped a beat. "I need to ask you a favor."

"Anything."

"I need to see the pictures of the other pieces you have in your department. Is it possible?" Elios's face wasn't giving away anything other than an intensifying discomfort.

I realized I had been holding my breath. "Sure. It's not like you're going to disclose secret information to anybody—" I smiled, trying to be funny, but it hadn't sounded right.

Elios showed me his imperfect smile, his Mona Lisa look back on his faded pink lips. "Nobody on Earth."

I stood up. "If you want, we can go to the lab now. The Native American artifact is still there. We got permission to study it and take as many pictures as we wanted before returning it to the tribe who's claiming it for the proper burial."

"Perfect. Thanks. It means a lot to me."

"It's nothing." The sun was sinking slowly and would disappear in a few minutes.

While we were walking back to the car, I realized I had thousands of questions that didn't concern archeology or sociology at all. I wanted to talk to him in the car, but his mood prevented me from doing so. I started humming some songs from the radio, my mind busy formulating a detailed questionnaire. I wanted to know how he did the things he had showed me. The tricks involving a combination of weather-manipulation, flowers, and perfumes were quite pleasant. And incredibly romantic, as Sara had rightly stated.

I was curious about his daily life. He had told me something about keeping jobs to cover his mission. He obviously had some source of money that wasn't coming from whatever he was doing here and there. The car Elios was driving was proof of my theory.

As I told Elios, thanks to my dad's obsession, I could recognize an expensive Italian car when I saw one, especially if I took a ride in an Alfa Romeo Brera. Italians in general being crazy about elegant cars—my father crazier than most—I knew a lot about that brand. My father still proudly drove his beloved red Alfa 75 as if there weren't any other means of locomotion available on Earth.

Somehow, I liked that my father and Elios shared the same taste in cars. He was also a skilled driver. Even then, when he clearly had his head elsewhere, the car glided effortlessly through the streets. He never seemed to accelerate or brake, using the manual gears with a competence that even my father—like every Italian man under the delusion of being a Formula One driver—would have appreciated.

My thoughts were interrupted when Elios parked the car, and I finally raised my eyes, realizing we were back at my apartment. Sensing he was on pins and needles, I suppressed all the questions I wanted to ask and went to pick up my lab key, and in a matter of minutes we were back on the road, heading for the UW campus.

As I expected, the campus was deserted, but I was still surprised to see how lifeless it looked without the students. It didn't seem right with nobody running around or shouting or drinking the tenth cup of coffee of the day. I led Elios straight to the artifacts lab. He must have done something with our bodies' temperature and humidity because the thermometer in the room didn't change. I made another mental note to ask Elios about it later. My list of questions was reaching a considerable length.

His concentration was absolute, and I felt a sort of reverent fear that prevented me from asking anything. I looked for the Native American artifact I had mentioned to him and found it right away. "Here it is." I was very proud of my research and liked the idea of sharing it with him, but there was something I couldn't define lingering in the air, which made me feel uneasy.

He bent his head over the table and took a good look at the little piece. I anticipated his smile becoming wider at the sight of the little piece of pottery. Finding some kind of link between his planet and mine was probably something worth a celebration.

Then Elios looked at me again, and I saw something in his eyes I wasn't expecting at all. I don't know what he was thinking, but apparently he wasn't in the mood for celebrating.

"Is there any chance you also have a picture of the Indian artifact?" he asked.

"Yes, in there." I indicated the room opening at the other end of the lab and set out in that direction. In the corner of my eyes, I saw Elios following me. "I'm the one in charge of the archives, and I file everything carefully. I know exactly what it's under." I went to the file cabinet and opened the third drawer from the bottom. I extracted the folder I was looking for, and once I found the picture of the Indian artifact, I showed it to him. "It's not a great picture." I shrugged. "But it's clear enough to see the details."

Elios looked at me for one brief moment, his eyes troubled, and then he reached for the picture in my hand. He let the picture glide out of my palm and into his without touching me. When he glanced at the picture, his face darkened.

"What is it?" I didn't like his reaction. The day had started so well at the beach, but now that seemed very long ago.

His eyes were cheerless when he answered, his face a blank mask I almost didn't recognize. "I'll tell you everything. I promise. But if you don't mind, I need to drive."

More driving wasn't going to bring more talking, of that I was sure, at least judging from the way Elios had said it. In fact, he drove slowly through the city and didn't say a single word. I didn't dare ask anything, worried about asking the wrong thing. I had the feeling the things I wanted to know probably weren't going to be revealed at this time. He turned on the radio, and I knew it was just for my sake.

Several songs went by with me quietly humming and him obstinately staring outside, his eyes facing away from me. Finally, Elios left the main road and parked the car. We were at the Magnolia viewpoint, one of the most romantic spots for couples—according to Sara. He led me to a bench facing the sea. Every one of his composed gestures was a cold reminder of the fact our skin had never even brushed by accident. Elios made sure of that in his calm and fluid way of moving. The moon was shining, and the sky was full of bright stars. I knew Elios was looking at me because I felt a suggestion of warmth on my face.

I looked back at him and decided it was finally time to talk. "Can you explain to me why your mood has changed so much?"

And still Elios wasn't talking. I couldn't bear one more second of silence. It broke my heart for us to be so close and so distant at the same time. "I'm getting worried, and your silence is not helping. I don't know what to think." I could only hope he was listening to me because Elios looked distant and withdrawn.

"You won't like it." The humidity of the night had taken a serious toll on his already hoarse voice.

I hated the sound of that. It had a cold quality even though I felt only regret in his voice.

Elios was tense, the relaxed image of the afternoon gone. "That little piece of pottery you showed me is connected to my lost progenitors' history."

"That's great news."

He let out a choked noise. "It could help us uncover the truth behind our long-lost civilization. I don't know what kind of link exists between the human race and ours, but there's something."

I kept looking at him, at his profile, and then I turned because it hurt me not being able to touch him. The moonlight made his face ghostly. His eyes were shining brightly. The white of his shirt made his face even paler. I needed answers, but I was afraid of them, so I repeated, "This is great. Isn't it?" His silence was killing me. "Elios, please tell me; what's going on?"

He finally answered, "Not sure." The sadness in his voice was tangible, a physical twinge that was hurting us both. Elios couldn't even look at me when he said, "I'm sorry—"

"For what?"

"I have to report it personally. This is an extraordinary finding, and it's mandatory for me to present the proof in front of a council of Superior Observers. We have never before found links to our past on another planet. After I've talked to my superiors, a court of Wise Ancestors is going to study my memories to analyze the details of what I have seen."

Elios was giving a detached technical speech. I wanted to scream, *Look at me! Please look at me now! I need you so much.* "Who are those people you're talking about?"

Elios looked distant, like the brilliant stars in the dark night. He was staring straight ahead. "The Superior Observers are my direct superiors."

"And the others?"

"The Wise Ancestors are a group of elders—" He paused for a moment. "They're the depository of our knowledge. They're our fathers."

"You have to go to report to them, right?"

"Yes."

"Well, I understand why you have to. But then you're coming back." *Just tell me yes.*

The tension was palpable, and I had never felt so uncomfortable before. I was startled when he answered, and his voice broke.

"No, I won't."

This can't be happening. Still, I had enough breath to keep arguing against his words. "But you told me how important your mission is here on Earth. You said it. It's against your moral code of conduct to fail... us."

Something in my voice made Elios flinch. He turned his head and finally looked at me, really looked at me with his intense eyes and his sad smile. The air around us warmed up, and I noticed I had been shivering. My shivering didn't get any better when Elios indirectly answered me.

"The moment my memories are shared with the Wise Ancestors, they'll also know about us. I'll be demoted. I won't be allowed to come back to my mission… to you."

"Why?"

"Because I've broken my vows—"

"But you haven't touched me. Not once."

"It doesn't matter anymore. I developed feelings I shouldn't have. It's beyond you and me."

"There must be a way."

"It's the only thing I've been thinking since you showed me the figure. I've tried to find a way, but there's none."

"Maybe those people will understand you haven't done anything wrong."

"But I have, under the Wise Ancestors' laws."

"Then they can't be that wise if they're ready to punish you for doing the right thing."

"I'll be punished for falling in love with you."

"What kind of monsters are they?"

"Don't say that. You don't know them. The head of the Wise Ancestors, Lex, is like a father to me."

His words shocked me. "What father would be so cruel?" He was startled by my outburst, but I didn't let him talk. "Stay with me." I didn't care about his planet.

"I can't. I must go back to Solo. I can't betray my race." Elios's words had a tone of finality—nothing to add, no room for a reply, just a cold statement.

It was a death sentence for us, and the realization of it struck me immediately with devastating force. "I don't want to lose you."

"I can't bear to lose you, and yet I must."

I stared at him, furious, angry at those Wise Ancestors, angry at the whole universe, but most of all, angry at him. "Take me back to my apartment."

He recoiled at my request. "Please, not now. Not like this." His eyes were on mine, unwavering. A single tear fell down his cheek.

Just like that, my anger was defused. With a simple plea from him and the sadness in his look, I realized we didn't have time to waste in lovers' quarrels.

We stood there the whole night, not daring to talk and ruin the spell. We focused on each other with a sweet intensity. Every single breath we shared was a gift. His hands air-traced the contour of my face while I did the same. Violins played all night for us. We never stopped shivering. We never unlocked our eyes. I was losing the love of my life.

We had never kissed.

11

Soon after he accompanied me back to my place, I ran to my room, buried my head in my pillow, and cried for hours.

The sun was high in the sky when Sara's voice penetrated my despair. "May I come in?"

She entered my room before I could say "no." I raised my eyes and looked at her. "I must convince him not to leave."

"Gaia?" She took in my disheveled look.

"He can't leave. Not now."

"What happened?"

"He's leaving me." Without knowing what I was doing, I was out of the apartment and inside the elevator.

Sara followed me. "Where are you going?"

I stared at the gray wall before me, my focus on the floor buttons coming to life one after the other in descending order until we reached the first. "To Elios's."

"To Elios's?"

I nodded, stepped out of the elevator, and ran to his building. The main door was closed, and nobody was around to open it for us. I rang one random apartment on the intercom and yelled, "Pizza delivery!" Sure enough, the door buzzed open, and I went for the elevator. I didn't know for sure which one was his apartment, but I knew it was on our same floor. Once I reached the corresponding landing, I knocked at the door of one of the two apartments whose windows would face our building.

"Yes?" A sleepy redhead opened the door, her mascara plastered on her face.

"Sorry, wrong apartment." I walked to the other door. "Elios!" I accompanied his name with furious knocking.

"Who are you looking for?" The redhead stepped out of her apartment.

"Elios! Open up! I won't leave until you talk to me."

"Gaia—"

I felt Sara's hands on my shoulders, but I kept knocking on the door.

"Hey, listen, I don't think your friend lives there." The redhead walked closer to me. "I've never seen anyone leaving or entering that place."

"Sweetie, let's go home." Sara tried to move me away from the door.

"Elios, please, come out." I refused to move and stood before the wooden surface, waiting for him to open the door. After a while, I tuned out Sara's voice while reality blurred behind my tears. Eventually, I had to accept the truth. Elios had already left.

Time passed. People, events, and places came and went. Life unraveled before my eyes like a silent movie, fast and slow at the same time.

Sara and I finished our research in Seattle, and we were sent back to Italy one year earlier than planned to study Etruscan material for a conjoined investigation. La Sapienza University was still collaborating with the American counterpart, and my group was the bridge between the two institutions.

Leaving Seattle was my salvation. I could not stand the sight of the pottery piece depicting the six-fingered hand. That image was forever associated with my misery. I saw it when my eyes were closed. I saw it when my eyes were open. The little figure with the golden halo and six-fingered hands was always there to haunt me. Sara and other people from the group covered for me because most of the time, I was useless.

As soon as I was back in Italy, however, I longed to be somewhere else. With Sara, I could be my desperate and sad self; with the rest of my family, I couldn't. I should've gotten my act together, but I didn't even try. Instead of staying in Rome where I had to fake being happy, I went to visit Giulia and Marcello, family friends who had a summer house in Pantelleria, a small island closer to Africa than to Sicily, to which it belonged. It helped my cause that in August every office is closed, so I couldn't work on my research.

The dry heat of the Sicilian sun welcomed me to Pantelleria as soon as I stepped out of the small plane I had taken in Palermo, coming from Rome.

"Oh, sweetie—" Giulia said as soon as we disentangled from our embrace while Marcello, her husband, relieved me of my luggage. They were my parents' age and didn't have kids. The couple had been in my life since I had reached the age of reason, and I considered them my extended family, the cool uncle and aunt who came back from exotic places with their luggage full of trinkets for me and my sister, the adopted relatives I ran to when I had problems.

"How was the flight?" Marcello asked, giving me a look but managing to suppress any comment on my unhealthy sheen and pallor.

"Turbulent, as usual, but the view from above is spectacular." The dry sun hit my skin, and the sharp blue of the sea made my eyes water. I was glad that I didn't have to explain my sudden tears. "I forgot my sunglasses," I commented, blinking several times. The color of the sea had just reminded me of the color of Elios's eyes. I barely repressed a sob.

"I'll give you a pair of mine." Giulia hugged me again. "When did you lose all this weight?"

She wasn't expecting an answer, and I smiled a sad smile back at her.

"I'll take care of you," she said and looked at her husband, who nodded.

"Let's go home so you can change." Marcello led us to the car parked just outside the small airport.

Marcello and Giulia had a beautiful beach house, a typical restored *dammuso* sitting on the edge of a low ridge overlooking the sea. I was there to spend the whole month of August with them.

"What about a swim to cool down?" Marcello proposed once I was settled in their white guest room with arched windows framed by light-blue plantation shutters.

I looked outside one of the open windows and inhaled the breeze coming from the beach below, the sound of the waves crashing on the pebbles music to my ears. I closed my eyes and opened my other senses.

"You'll have a private view of the sunset every night." Giulia stepped closer to me, one arm circling my waist.

I let my head rest on her shoulder. "I can't wait." I opened my eyes to look at the warm, salty Mediterranean Sea. "Yes, a swim is what I need," I finally answered Marcello.

Sixty-two miles from Italy and forty-three miles from Africa, Pantelleria is a volcanic paradise of wild flowers and inebriating perfumes. Swimming was exactly what I needed to recharge my batteries and avoid conversations.

* * *

"I just bought some lemon granita and sweet, soft *grissini* breadsticks. Do you want some?" The morning after, and every morning after that, I woke up to similar treats. Every day, Marcello went down to the bakery to pick up the bread fresh from the oven and then to the *gelateria* for the Sicilian lemon granita or the more exotic mulberry sherbet. Every morning, we had breakfast outside on the veranda facing the sun, the blue sky, and the azure sea shining like a jewel.

It took some time for the mornings to become tolerable. At first, I went through the usual pattern of beautiful dreams at night and horrible awakenings in the morning. Then Pantelleria's out-of-time atmosphere and Giulia's cooking eased my pain to the point I could smile once in a while, and I started enjoying my imaginary nights with Elios. In my dream life, I was happy again, and some of that happiness rubbed off on the first hours of my mornings. I knew my mind had just found a safe, though delusional, way to deal with reality, but I would've taken anything.

From spring break to August, I had felt numb at best. Even changing continents hadn't really made any difference. After almost six months, the sadness and grief were still there; I was still mourning for him, but against all odds, I was still alive. With a cynical attitude, I had listened to an old CD of a famous Italian songwriter. In one of his songs, he had said, "Che non si muore per amore e` una triste verita`." Loosely translated, this meant: "The fact that love pains don't kill is a really sad truth…"

The songwriter was right; surviving love pains was almost an insult to my sorrow, a sad joke. But survive I did, despite myself. My mind and body were shattered by a confusion of real memories and wishful fantasies. I honestly didn't care to discern between dreams and reality, as long as it kept me alive.

Marcello and Giulia made sure I was busy with menial tasks every day. I was the one in charge of picking aromatic herbs and succulent capers from the garden outside the kitchen. I liked sorting tomatoes by color in the little pea patch blessed by the sun and the dark, volcanic soil or staining my fingers with the vivid green bleeding from the cut parsley.

One day, after lunch, I noticed Giulia had left pencils and papers by the stone bench facing the sunflowers' row.

"Do you still paint?" I asked. We were drinking an espresso under the pergola.

She nodded. "I come here mostly to paint. I'll show you my latest drawings." Giulia went inside and reappeared a moment later with a thick stack of papers. "Here, take a look."

I leafed through the drawings, mostly black-and-white representations of the view from the house, a few of them architectonic details of the *dammuso* itself, a column, the archway, terracotta vases. "They're beautiful."

"Pantelleria is beautiful." Giulia turned to look at the sea for a moment. "Do you still paint?" she repeated the question to me.

She was the one who had gifted me my first set of professional colored pencils. I was eight at the time, and I used to pester her to draw all the characters from my favorite cartoons. Somewhere in my room, I still had a stack of the drawings we had made together. "Not like I used to." My eyes went to the caper flowers cascading from the trellis, their alien shapes begging to be sketched.

"Let's do it." As if reading my mind, Giulia passed me colored pencils and paper.

We spent the rest of the day walking around, looking for objects to immortalize. The night came, and I had filled a whole sketchpad with prickly pear cacti and bright-yellow broom fields.

The morning after, Giulia found me still drawing. The first light of dawn had wakened me, and I had come down for a cup of espresso. The sea framed by the wooden window was picture perfect. "I had to draw this." I smiled at her and pointed outside with my pencil.

"What do you think about touring the island on my Vespa? There are plenty of interesting spots." Giulia went to the moka to fill her red-and-white polka-dot espresso cup.

"On one condition."

"Which is?" She turned to look at me, the cup hovering before her lips.

"Only if you let me drive."

She finished her coffee in one gulp. "All yours." Giulia tilted her head toward the dusty-pink Vespa, anchored to the wall just outside the kitchen door.

I dropped pencil and paper on the table and went to check the Vespa. "Always wanted one of those. How old is it?"

She shrugged and then reached for the bowl of fruit on the table. "It was my aunt Tina's and then my mom's. It's probably fifty years old."

"It's a beauty." I removed the chain and the rusty lock and straddled the seat. "Are you coming?"

Giulia took a bite of a succulent persimmon already in season on this warm island, wiped her mouth on a napkin, and followed me outside. "Let's get off the beaten path." She sat behind me, and we left. "I'll show you a place where tourists never venture."

"Cool." I followed her directions and drove the Vespa unhurriedly, toward a winding road that looked more suited for goats than wheels. "Are you sure?"

"Park here, and we'll go down by foot," Giulia instructed me.

I stopped the Vespa under a tree and secured it to the trunk.

"Be careful where you walk; the gravel on the road is treacherous."

She hadn't finished saying it when my flat-soled espadrilles slid on the gravel, and I fell on my butt. Giulia looked at me and started laughing. "Care to help me?" I asked but couldn't help laughing along. It felt good. The beach was worth the pain.

* * *

In the following days, Giulia and Marcello drove me around the island. Gadir Bay and the Arch of the Elephant were among the many places we visited. Giulia was never in a hurry. "Don't you think this is just too beautiful?" she asked before the sight of the bay from the lookout.

I had to agree. "Do we have time to take a sketch?"

"We have all the time in the world," Giulia answered, already taking out the sketchpad and the colored pencils from her leather satchel. Marcello patiently waited for us to finish.

The scene was repeated several times in as many days, but he never complained, just took out a book and started reading under the shade of the closest tree. "I'm used to Giulia's flights of fancy," he explained with a smile when I told him he was quite organized.

One afternoon, on our way back to the house, we ended up roaming just across the main road, and Giulia showed me a pristine, isolated beach just a few minutes away from the *dammuso*.

"One last swim before dinner?" she asked.

I was already on my way to the shore, removing clothes as I went. As usual, the crystal-clear water of the Mediterranean Sea, with colored rocks beneath the surface, reminded me of something else light blue with sparkles of golden and green. Tears rolled down my cheeks as I jumped off the low cliff where we were standing and dove into the water. I let the seawater wash away my pain. That night, I went to sleep with the feeling of being rocked back and forth by gentle waves. I dreamed about soothing colors.

"You can't live without having seen the Sesi of the King," Marcello commented the next morning.

"He's right. It would be such a pity if you were here on vacation and never saw the ruins." Giulia passed me the orange marmalade. "We can make sketches of the tomb."

We were having breakfast under the pergola, my earlier melancholia subdued by the night's sleep. I looked ahead, avoiding eye contact, a new pain swelling in my chest. It was entirely my fault, though. When gently asked a few days earlier if I had a boyfriend, I had told them I met someone in Seattle and fallen in love brainlessly. They assumed from my mood the story hadn't ended well, but I never bothered with details. And now, I didn't feel like explaining why visiting ancient ruins could be a cause of sadness for me. "Sure, I'd love to."

With me in tow like a sacrificial lamb, we went to see the Sesi of the King, a megalithic funerary building, a rocky monument to an important family who had lived on that blessed island five thousand years ago. We arrived late in the afternoon, hoping for a reprieve from the blazing heat. Marcello parked under a tree, and then we reached the site by hiking the pebbled trail that wound through the rocky terrain. The cicadas' soporific chirping was accompanied by a warm, dry breeze.

"Look, the guide is starting the tour." Giulia, who was several steps ahead of me, came back to take my hand, and we sprinted toward a small group of people gathered before one tall boy who had his back to the ruins.

The boy, who wore a vest with the word "guide" stenciled on it in bright colors, gave us a brief nod, waited for Marcello to join us, explained he was a volunteer, and then resumed his tale with an enthusiastic voice. "Pantelleria's Sesi are funerary structures shaped like truncated cones. Of the fifty-eight Sesi found by the archeologists at the end of the eighteen hundreds, only a few remain intact. All around the perimeter of the tomb are two to eleven entrances which lead to a circular cell, where the dead were buried—"

After a few minutes, despite the boy's enthusiasm, his voice became a blur that blended with the cicadas' buzzing in my ears, and I tuned out. Being there, looking at the rocks that formed the steps covering the elliptical tomb, created a familiar pang in my stomach. I felt a connection with Elios through that ceremonial place, ancient but not forgotten. He had already been living on Earth when that powerful royal family had lived. Maybe he had even known them. It surprised me how easily I had come to accept his words. Then, while I was trying not to let my emotions out, a thought slowly emerged above the chaos in my mind: *I must continue my research.*

I didn't have to hate the six-fingered figure. I could study it. I could find something. Maybe the key to understanding what had happened on Elios' planet was in front of me. I had to do something. I needed to feel him closer in whichever way worked.

"Don't you love this?" Giulia asked.

I felt her eyes on me, but I didn't turn. I kept looking at the tomb, composing myself before answering, "It's an unforgettable sight." I reached inside my leather shoulder bag for the sketchpad and my number two pencil and hard eraser. "Deserves to be immortalized."

Giulia followed suit, and Marcello opened his paperback. If they saw the tear I had hastily wiped from my face, they didn't say.

The vacation came to its end. The sun, Giulia's cooking, and Pantelleria's beauty all helped me recover. Looking tan and a little bit heavier suited me better than being skeletal and ghostly. Still, I wasn't ready to confront the rest of the world. At the little hybrid military and civil airport in Pantelleria, I hugged my friends, not really wanting to leave.

I looked better though, and that had been the whole point of exiling myself there. In reality, my new resolution to go back to work on the research just for the sake of finding clues scared me a bit. In my twisted mind, I needed those clues to bring Elios closer to me.

"Remember, sometimes it feels like the end of the world, but it's not," Giulia whispered to me, with one last hug before I entered the gate.

"Thank you." I hugged her tightly, already missing her radiant smile.

12

The month of September was a constant blur of people hugging me, kissing me, and asking me questions about my experience in the United States. Cousins, aunts and uncles, grandparents, and friends visited my house almost daily. I was grateful that I had no time at all to think—lots of questions to answer quickly.

Did I like it there?

Was the weather really terrible?

How about the social life?

Did I meet someone there?

Did I like the boys there?

Yes, no, no social life, yes, I can't say...

And so on and so forth for the whole month.

I always answered honestly; it didn't cost me anything. Finally, September was over. After my specific request, I was assigned to the team that was going to study the artifacts coming from the archeological sites, both in Tarquinia and in Cerveteri, once known by its Etruscan name of Caere and famous for its well-preserved necropolis.

I spent October and November preparing for two exams I needed to pass to be part of the archeological team. The weather was particularly mild for that time of the year, and I was mostly outside the house. I wasn't a good liar, and I didn't want my parents to be worried about a problem that didn't have any solution.

I tried to slip back to my former routine to give my days a purpose of some kind. I had friends in Rome who used to hang out every afternoon outside a historic caffè bar in Piazza Vescovio, and I started joining them there whenever I had time. I felt normal again, not happy, not well, but alive, barely surviving but still breathing. It was a big victory for me. Sometimes, Sara joined my group of friends at the coffee place, and we spent time together just talking about silly things while eating our favorite *tramezzini,* the white-bread sandwiches I had missed so much while in the States. Other times, we drove our scooters around the Trieste neighborhood. Sara even tried to set me up with some guys, whom she swore were handsome. I never got their names straight. After a few botched attempts, she declared defeat and never suggested dating again.

Finally Christmas arrived, and I had to don a mask to fake a happiness I didn't feel. I couldn't help but notice the ironic and cruel symmetry with the other Christmas I had spent in Italy the year before. I was still in pain. Nothing had changed. *Everything had changed.*

Christmas was another blur of family and friends, hugs and kisses, and more questions. When I received an email from Professor La Mora asking me if I needed housing in Tarquinia, I thought I'd won the lottery. For my research, I had to follow the new excavation site in Tarquinia on a daily basis, and even though Rome was just around the corner, avoiding one-hour commuting sounded perfect. I only had to convince my parents to let me go again.

I waited a day, thought about what I had to say, and when my speech was ready, called my mother, "Mom, can you come here a moment?" Her steps stopped outside my bedroom.

"What is it, honey?" She was busy sorting the laundry and delivering it to everybody's rooms. I could smell the lavender scent she added to the detergent wafting through our apartment.

"I got mail from Professor La Mora."

"What does it say?"

"He's asking me if I need housing in Tarquinia." I let it out, hoping to sound casual.

"Hmm." She left a pile of folded clothes on my bed and walked closer to my desk.

I pointed a finger at the opened email. "Here."

She hovered behind me, leaning to read the professor's words on my computer's screen. "But you just came back."

"I know… but I'm supposed to be at the excavation site first thing in the morning." It didn't actually say that anywhere, but it could've been true. "I'll have to wake so early every day and drive late at night to get back home." I sighed at the idea.

"I hadn't thought of that. No, no, of course I don't want that." My mother straightened up and affectionately kissed the crown of my head. "Sweetheart, I prefer you in Tarquinia safe and sound."

"Thank you, Mom." I almost felt bad for deceiving her so easily. Almost. I had to run away from Rome; my acting was getting tired, and more than once my mother had asked me about my love life. I couldn't have that kind of conversation with her. Actually, there was nobody I could really talk to. So I had run away from Seattle, and now I was running away from Rome for the second time. I hoped I was going to find some peace in Tarquinia.

* * *

"Let's take possession of our mansion." Sara had followed me in this new adventure and was now looking at the big old door of a building in the historic center of Tarquinia. The gray-stoned, imposing structure was from the early nineteen hundreds, modern if compared to the rest of the city.

Five flights of stairs later, I handed her the keys to our new apartment. The smell of Clorox, recently used to clean the floors, reached my nose. The marble tiles in the hallway were shiny and worn. The wooden door opened loudly, and we entered. Coming from the darker hallway, I was immediately aware of the light surrounding the place.

"Well, it needs some restoration, but has a decadent charm, high ceilings, and enormous windows. We can work with all this white..." Sara commented once inside.

I let my eyes get used to the brightness and then looked around. Everything was white, the walls, the ornate metal radiator with lion's head–shaped legs, the heavy wooden doors, the elegant window frames, and even the two couches that came with the rent. "I'll work with that."

I didn't break that promise. I saw the white walls as a challenge. The same day, I went to the small but well stocked artists' store just around the corner from our place and bought canvases in every size, acrylic colors, and brushes. I started painting that night. Soon, the apartment's walls became my personal showcase. Crimson-red wild poppies, strawberry fields, sunflowers, hydrangeas, and blue skies populated the unframed canvases I hung everywhere. Sara bought heavy deep-red cotton curtains and red pillows for the couches. In no time, the apartment looked like an art gallery. All our friends started stopping by and staying at our place. Everybody liked to spend time there.

The very first day, even before buying my art supplies, we had already decided where to have our cappuccino and *cornetto* in the morning, where to have our slice of wood-fire-oven-baked pizza in the afternoon, and where to buy our groceries.

The American team was stationed between Tarquinia and Cerveteri, and we were happy to see them again, Sara more than I, but I did my best to help them get around. After a few days in the city, we were assigned our portions of the research. Sara was sent to Cerveteri to help the American team translate Italian documents. I was sent to the new excavation site in Marina Velca, just outside Tarquinia. My job was to translate into English the documents the archeologists were producing.

Several months passed. Every morning, I arrived at Marina Velca, punctual as clockwork, sat at my desk in the small office overlooking the camp, and translated the documents the archeologists passed me. After a while, once the monotony of my task set in, I executed what was asked of me, but without real enthusiasm. I was almost losing hope of finding something useful for my personal research when one afternoon, I complained to Danilo, one of the archeologists, who had come to pick up a document. To the usual question, "How's it going?" I honestly answered, "I'm starting to get bored. I wish I could be in the camp with you guys and uncover something interesting."

"Actually, if you have a minute, there is something…"

I was wasting time, double checking a few items in a list I had already checked the day before, waiting for the clock to hit five before I could drive back to Tarquinia. "Sure." I followed him outside. "Where to?"

"To the Ark."

The archeologist called the artifact tent the Ark. It was their inside joke. After a minute of brisk walking through the camp, we reached our destination. He opened the fabric curtain enclosing the tent and let me in. "We've just uncovered a tomb. It's already been looted, but the thieves left something behind among the rubble. Nothing more than fragmented scraps of terracotta, but one has an interesting design," Danilo said, looking over his shoulder at the pile of artifacts on the table where all the findings were placed before being catalogued.

We walked to the table covered in pieces of broken pottery and bronze items. Danilo's eyes scanned the items for a brief moment, and then his face lit in recognition. "Here it is." He reverently picked up a fragment and showed it to me.

I looked at the shard, and my heartbeat quickened. "May I?" I reached out my hand.

"Be careful," he said, handing me the fragment.

"Thanks." I automatically smiled. Then I looked down at the small piece of terracotta lying weightlessly on my hand. It was even smaller than the ones I had already catalogued for the University of Washington, but there wasn't any doubt. Before my eyes was a faded drawing of a six-fingered hand. It was just the hand; nothing more had resisted the invasion of the looters.

"So, isn't it remarkable?"

"Remarkable—" I repeated trancelike.

"Etruscan art was so sophisticated that this must've been done on purpose." Danilo went on and on about it, but I was elsewhere already.

Driving back to our apartment, for the first time in months I noticed the color of the sky; it was the lightest shade of blue. My lips curved up. I was going to solve the puzzle, and then I would find a way to reach Elios. *Step by step,* I kept repeating to myself. I knew my mind wasn't following a rational path, but I was beyond caring.

That night, falling asleep was easier than usual. Later, I remembered feeling relaxed and weightless, almost floating on the bed, unusually light-hearted. Pleasant warmth enveloped my body, and I closed my eyes. Soon after, one of the most vivid dreams I ever had started. Out of the blue, as if I had opened a window into a different reality, I saw Elios.

He was meditating with his legs crossed, reciting some kind of mantra over and over again. His face was illuminated by pale light, and his features were all sharp angles. He was sitting in a puddle of water, the strange-looking kimono he was wearing was soaked, but he didn't seem to mind. Plants I had never seen before dotted the nocturnal landscape. In the dream, I called his name several times before he raised his head and smiled at me. "Elios, come back to me," I had time to say before his image disappeared as though it had been erased from a canvas. I was left with a sweet taste on my lips and a peaceful sensation.

When I woke the next morning, I felt some semblance of happiness returning to me. Instead of staying in bed like I usually did, trying to summon the power to confront the living, I went to the kitchen to have some coffee. I started the day with an energy I didn't know I had anymore. Sara, already pouring the black nectar from the moka, noticed and gave me a big smile.

"Good morning, sweetie, how do you feel?"

"I saw him."

"You dreamed of Elios again?"

"No, I saw him; he has lost some weight and looks paler, but I think he's okay." I hadn't meant to say that, but now that it was out of my mouth, I believed it.

"Do you want me to check your temperature?" Sara smiled at me, serving hot espresso in our white teacups. We still had to buy proper espresso cups.

"I remember lots of details from this dream. I mean, more than I usually remember from any dream. I normally forget almost everything as soon as I wake up."

"I know I lose my time arguing with you, but I want to humor myself today and do it anyway."

"Please, feel free to ruin my sweet mood." I smiled back at her while sipping my reinvigorating drink, munching on oatmeal cookies we had prepared the night before. "You were right; the ceramic jar maintains the cookies better than the tin one." I tapped the aforementioned jar with my index nail.

She rolled her eyes. "Do not change the subject." She accepted the cookie I was offering her. "You, my friend, are seriously delusional. It would be a great idea for your mental health, and mine, if you would voluntarily go see a good neuropsychiatric specialist. You know my dad could ask one of his colleagues here in Tarquinia."

"Ha, ha. You're so funny."

"As a matter of fact, I am." She showed me her pink tongue. "Anyway, seriously, I'm glad you're finally in a more cheerful mood. I was honestly starting to think you'd lost the ability to smile." She came closer to me to give me a hug, and then released me from her tender embrace. "Whatever makes you happy."

"I know I'll find him again. We got separated for two years, and he still found me on another continent. We can do it." Something deep inside me made me say the words again, and as incredible as it sounded, I was sure about every single one of them, as I had been before.

"Your faith in him is so out of this world."

Interesting choice of words. "He's the love of my life. I can't imagine my life without him. Is it so difficult to understand?" It felt so good to embrace the truth. It was strangely liberating not having to act anymore and accepting I was unhappy without him, without hiding it.

"*Your intensity* is impossible to understand. Sometimes, I think you've developed an obsession with him only because you've never had any physical contact whatsoever. I can't think of any other explanation."

"There's so much more between us. I can't explain."

"Of course you can't; nobody could." Sara took another cookie from the jar and ate it in two bites. "Anyway, like I said before, I'm glad that some part of the Gaia I knew has come back."

"You know I love you too."

"I'm sure you do. Nobody else would put up with such a melodramatic, sleeping beauty act."

I laughed at her words. "You're right. I'm still waiting for my first kiss."

"Can you believe this?" Then Sara looked at the clock on the wall and gasped, horrified. "We're so late, there isn't enough time to buy *maritozzi* at the bar," she said, displeased by the idea of going the whole day without the sweet pastry filled with whipped cream. Sara had her priorities straight.

In the days that followed, Danilo and the other archeologists at the excavation camp found a new tomb containing a full set of kitchen potteries. Unfortunately, expert thieves had already removed anything in gold, but the ceramic pieces were abundant. None of them showed the six-fingered figure, but some of them were drawn in the same abstract style. In two weeks' time, I was asked to help catalogue the new pieces; there were too many of them. The Ark had been filled with three tables full of artifacts. Some of them held special interest for me.

Although I wasn't an archeologist, for a while I was being asked to act like one, which more than suited me. I found a way to become essential to the group by being the most enthusiastic when it came to cleaning the pieces and writing detailed descriptions. The majority of the male archeologists preferred the digging, and the girls in the group didn't want to be treated like girls and went along. I was out of my small office almost daily, helping the field team, and finally I was given an official task: I had to establish the periods the abstract-painted potteries belonged to.

It was a nice challenge after the tedium of the clerical work. The abstract drawings were an interesting riddle to solve. As Danilo had said the first time, the Etruscans had been a sophisticated society. They were skilled in the art of painting, and their knowledge of the human anatomy was evident in the frescoes they had left inside the tombs in the necropolises they had built both in Tarquinia and Cerveteri.

When the six-fingered figure had turned up in a Native American archeological site in Washington State, nobody had thought anything about the whimsical anatomical detail. It looked like any other Native American drawings. It had been an incredible coincidence that months earlier I had made the connection with the Italian equivalent. For that, I had to thank Professor La Mora, who had been collaborating with Professor Rayne, who in turn had been working on cataloguing the artifacts from a newly discovered Etruscan tomb. Professor Rayne thought that one of the persons buried in that Etruscan tomb was a young boy, and therefore the pottery with the abstract drawing could have been one of the child's belongings.

Although the normal custom was to bury objects representing daily life with the deceased, the archeologists couldn't agree unanimously on whether the objects had actually belonged to the dead, or they were new ones made especially for the burial and representing his or her position in the society. This last point was crucial to understanding whether the abstract figure was a child-like drawing of a human being, or it meant something specific about the people buried inside the tomb. The connection between the two drawings was a mystery. When the third drawing of the same six-fingered figure was discovered in India, at an Indus Valley civilization archeological site, our professors could barely contain their excitement.

The Indian team was working with us, trying to solve the puzzle. After a moment of uncertainty, I was able to date all the Etruscan artifacts with the abstract humanoid drawing from the same period, around the end of their civilization, just before 90 BCE when they became Roman citizens. The Indus valley civilization that had produced the similar piece was comparable to the Etruscan one. Both at the end of their primacy, both polytheistic societies, both were advanced in several fields.

Dionigi of Alicarnasso had described the Etruscan language as unlike any other. Even the bucchero, the black Etruscan earthenware, was still a mystery. If the similarities between the two populations, the Etruscan and the Indian, could mean they had been somehow related, it remained to explain how the same figure was part of a Native American ceremonial site, dating at least a thousand years later.

The real question, for me at least, since I was the only one who knew about it, was how the same design had appeared outside the Solar System. The more I researched, the more I grew entangled in the apparent conundrum. Meanwhile, I kept seeing Elios every night in my vivid dreams. The location where our encounters took place was always the same or a variation of the same landscape. The sky was pale green with cloud-like formations in brilliant shades of azure blue and violet. Sometimes, it rained silently, and the drops of water had a silvery quality, which created little mirror pools in the short grass. I could see a body of water and luscious green hills far away. The landscape reminded me of the rice fields in the Chinese region of Guangxi but with an altered color palette.

My dreams never lasted long; after a few minutes in the relaxing meadow, Elios usually disappeared, whispering something I couldn't hear. Seeing his face, even in a fictitious context, helped me get stronger. Sara knew that my happiness was the result of a particularly eye-catching delusion, but she was my friend and let me have the solace of it without judging or commenting out loud.

"How was your date?" she asked me more than once before our morning espresso.

It became our inside joke. I enjoyed it because I didn't want to let it go, and I needed to talk about it, even if Sara was going to make fun of me. I could have sworn that at times I distinctly heard Elios's voice. Once, he recited poetry to me. Or so I thought in my delusion. I even had the courage or, better said, the insanity, to describe how beautiful it had sounded to Sara. Elios was present in my mind all day long as well since the only purpose of my research now was to find clues to solve his puzzle.

Meanwhile, I was disappointed by the way the research was being conducted. When the two universities found the Indus Valley civilization piece had something in common with the Etruscan, they immediately followed the most plausible theory. From one civilization of travelers and merchants, two different societies had originated. The theory was self-explanatory. Nobody wanted to take into consideration the third, younger piece coming from the United States. In their opinion, it didn't fit the story they wanted to write.

I had an advantage on them that I couldn't reveal, and that was the cause for my frequent headaches. I had proof the Native American piece wasn't just a coincidence, but it was part of a pattern. It killed me, not being able to talk, but I felt that nothing good would come from saying out loud what I knew. I resorted to biting my nails and went on with *my* research in total secrecy.

Both Professor La Mora and Professor Rayne dismissed the Washington artifact—which among the students was affectionately called the "little piece from the rainy land"—as one of those odd things in life. In their academically oriented minds, that little piece of pottery couldn't be part of the grand theory explaining the mysterious Etruscans. Therefore, it was nothing more than a pebble in the glorious path toward archeological heaven. The two colleagues were hoping to finally be on their way to cracking the cryptic Etruscan language, and since the "little piece from the rainy land" wasn't useful, it had been released to the Bremerton tribe who had claimed it and was now resting in peace in its proper burial place.

But I knew better, so I went on looking for clues nobody else knew existed during the day and dreaming my dates with Elios at night.

One day, a beautiful warm morning in May, I was waiting for the archeologists to finish digging what looked like a promising tomb. Sara had stopped by to bring me a fresh *maritozzo*, and I left with her to take a break at the Belvedere, the scenic lookout just outside the camp. Sara and I were sitting under the cool shadow of a secular Italian pine, enjoying the view. The calm Tyrrhenian Sea shining under the sun seemed to smile at us while we slowly ate the sugary pastry, biting away the dough to find the whipped-cream core.

Feeling sinfully satisfied by the treat I had just consumed, I was in full relaxation mode, idly crushing pine needles to smell the refreshing fragrance. I threw my head backward to contemplate the blue sky and the heavens above, lost in my reverie while slices of light filtering through the pine branches were playing tricks on my peripheral vision. Shadows danced on my eyelids, and I closed my eyes to shield them from the intense light, when I felt something both familiar and alien.

Sara raised her head at the same moment I did. My heart started beating faster, and I stood up looking for something, for someone. After a minute or two, someone climbed the little stone wall behind the tree and approached the two of us. A pang of dark disappointment wrapped my heart. It wasn't him.

I didn't know who he was. He wasn't one of the archeological team; I knew all of them by then—if not by name, then by face for sure. He spoke before I had time to give him a better look. Once I had decided he wasn't Elios, his face had become one with the landscape. This was the way I looked at guys nowadays, which never failed to exasperate Sara.

"Hi, Gaia," he said in Italian, his voice warm. "You don't know me, but I gave my word to a dear friend of mine I was going to look after you. I hope you don't mind." He stared at me with his dark eyes.

For the first time after so long, a guy finally had my full attention. Too bad that didn't last a single heartbeat. My head felt light, and I passed out before I could say anything back. Under the shade of the Italian pine tree, with Sara, the dark-eyed guy, and the Tyrrhenian Sea as witnesses, I lay on the ground in a peaceful and dreamless slumber while my body gave my mind time to recover from the shock.

13

"Gaia?" Sara was looking at me with worried eyes.

As soon as recent memories flashed back, I fought the urge to flee reality again. Sara's concern didn't let me escape, so I stayed awake to face her and the guy also staring at me. We were under the tree's shade, I sitting on the ground, Sara by my side, and the guy standing a few feet from us. A gentle breeze from the sea had brought me back from the fainting spell and was now ruffling my hair. I felt embarrassed and also had problems connecting thoughts.

First things first.

"Who are you?" I looked up at the guy.

He seemed relieved to hear my voice and walked closer to us. "I'm so sorry I scared you. I really am. Please forgive me, it wasn't my intention." He had big almond-shaped black eyes.

"It's okay. Don't worry." I still didn't have a clue about whom I was forgiving, but I needed to know. "Let's try this again. Who are you? And how do you know my name?"

"I'm Areel. I know Elios." He stared at me and then turned slightly toward Sara as if asking if he could talk before her.

My head started swinging again mercilessly. Deep inside me, something had stirred in his presence, and I'd sensed his closeness to Elios. Sara hugged me to support my limp body and angrily whispered something I didn't hear, but I got the gist from Areel's answer.

"Please, let me talk to her in private for a few minutes, and I promise I'll leave her alone."

I straightened my back and pushed my heels on the ground.

"Don't think so," Sara spat back.

"I've traveled a great distance just to meet her. Please?" Areel's voice was low.

Sara hissed, "Only if she wants to talk to you; otherwise you can go to hell!"

"I'll be fine." I softly squeezed her arm.

She didn't move and kept looking at him. "I *really* don't think so."

"Sara, I promise I'll scream if he touches me even with one single finger." I smiled at the irony in my words. Sara didn't get my joke of course, but she heard my tone.

She relaxed and walked away toward the stone wall. "You have five minutes!"

"Now tell me whatever you came to say," I said to him as soon as she was out of earshot.

Areel crouched in front of me. "Gaia, I had to meet you—"

I raised one hand.

"No, no let me finish. Elios is like a brother to me, and I wanted to help him, but I couldn't do anything."

I grabbed a handful of dirt. "Did anything happen to him?"

Areel talked over my words. "I know everything about you. I know how important you are to Elios because I had access to his memories before I was sent here to finish his mission."

I made an effort to open my fisted hands and release the dirt. "Is Elios alive?"

"Yes, he's alive." He looked down at the pine needles covering the ground. "Elios is alive, but he'll spend the rest of his life in solitude. The Council of the Wise Ancestors exiled him on a planet where he can't communicate with anybody else." He paused for a second and then looked at me and shivered. "It's beyond torture. It will drive him insane."

It will drive him insane. Even if I hadn't remembered all the things Elios had said about his species and their need to be in mental contact, I would've been horrified anyway at the idea of him spending all his life alone. An eternity of solitude. The horror of it slapped me violently and made me scream back, "It is not true. I saw him. Elios is getting better. He's going to be fine. Why did you come here? You shouldn't have come. You're a liar. Go away. Go. Away. Now."

"Gaia, please listen to me. I didn't come here to make you suffer. I came here to tell you that Elios never had a single regret and that he wanted more than anything else to keep you safe. He wanted it that way. I felt what he felt… and it was so beautiful. I had to tell you he would've done it again. I'd never felt sentiments so untainted before. Your memory was pure."

I registered his words about the sacrifice Elios had committed for his planet and for us at the same time, and I kept thinking of him kneeling on the grass, smiling at the sound of my voice. "I see him every night. Elios is getting better. He's meditating and regaining some strength." I looked back at him in defiance.

He shifted on his bent legs. "I don't understand what you're saying."

I didn't care if I sounded crazy. Meanwhile, Sara was coming back after the five-minute truce. In reality, she had conceded Areel more than that, and she didn't seem inclined to let him talk to me any longer without supervision.

"Okay, time's up. You can leave now." Sara looked straight at Areel, and he stood up.

"I'm sorry I've disrupted your day, but I had a moral task to attend to, and it couldn't wait any longer." Then Areel did something unexpected. He gave Sara his hand to shake, a polite practice between people meeting for the first time, and I was completely disconcerted. "A pleasure to meet you, Sara."

Then he helped me stand up, and I couldn't help backing away from him as though he had some sort of illness.

"You can't touch us," I stated.

Sara frowned in confusion.

Areel shrugged. "It's just a handshake."

Sara tugged at my elbow. "Let's go," she whispered.

I nodded. "I'd like to go eat something."

"Sure." Sara let go of me and started walking in the general direction of the camp.

I followed her and then turned to face Areel, who had stayed behind. "You can join us."

His eyes lit up. "I'd love to."

Behind me, I heard Sara's sputtering and then her hurried steps.

A moment later, she was at my side. "Gaia—"

"Please, allow me to invite you and your friend to eat in a little trattoria I just passed while I was driving here," he hastily said.

"I really don't think that's such a good idea." Sara turned her back to Areel and faced me with weary eyes. She silently mouthed, "What are you doing?"

"Trust me," I mouthed back.

Sara opened her mouth and then closed it.

"It's going to be okay."

She closed her eyes, pinched the arch of her nose, sighed, and then turned to address Areel. "Go ahead. We'll follow you to the restaurant, okay?"

When he started to talk, she cut him off immediately, "There is only one restaurant on the way to the camp." And then she whispered to me, but loudly enough that he could hear, "We would never get in a car with a stranger, would we now?"

Areel smiled and led the way back, commenting once or twice about how beautiful the Maremmana countryside was. Sara didn't seem to appreciate it. On the other hand, I thought that sometimes reality is crazier than my own dreams. And that said it all.

Sara didn't want me to drive, so we took her car. The little family-owned restaurant Areel had mentioned stood on the road bordering the brown sand of the beach and was therefore permanently dusty and shabby outside. Inside, the small trattoria was a good example of simple, country-beach style: whitewashed walls, light blue shutters, and recycled furniture from decommissioned ships. The smell coming from the kitchen made me feel better immediately.

We were waiting for the owner to greet us when Sara's purse started ringing. She fished out her cell phone and then swore softly. "I hate it when there is no reception… Gaia, it's my mom."

"News about Grandma Rosa?" Lately, her grandmother wasn't feeling well. I considered her a putative grandmother. Rosa had always treated me as her own niece, and I was as concerned as Sara was about her.

"Yes."

"Go. Don't worry." I nodded calmly, and she gestured it would take just a few minutes.

As soon as Sara was outside to take the phone call, Areel leaned closer to me to speak. "Does she know about Elios?" he asked, looking outside.

"No."

"What does she know?"

"Only what I could say. Elios and I met. He broke my heart twice. He left." I was looking outside too. Sara was on the phone, and she looked worried, but she was well aware we were talking.

"Good." He was pleased by this information.

I wasn't. "What? That he broke my heart or that he left?"

Areel looked at me in horror. "I told you I shared his memories. How can you think I rejoice in his pain?" He raised his voice at the end.

"She can hear you." I smiled at Sara, but I felt Areel's eyes staring at me.

"It's *good* that your friend is not involved in this. Elios has enough problems as it is. Had you said anything to her, I would've reported it. I was sent to check on you, not only by Elios's wish. I was also commanded to do so."

I stared back in shock. I had been so focused on my misery that I had never thought about the consequences of *knowing*.

"I care deeply for Elios. He's like a brother to me..." His eyes went far away for a moment, then he shivered and focused back on the present. "I'm just glad you didn't do anything that would force me to act against Elios's last requests."

"And if I *had* said something?" I asked lowering my voice.

"My orders *were* to wipe your memories and everybody else's involved." He paused for a second and then added, "Elios doesn't know it. He would've gone crazy with grief."

Why, I wanted to ask, but I could see that Sara was almost at the end of her phone call. Instead I asked, "*Were?*"

"Elios's memories changed me. More than I'm comfortable admitting. What you two have is too pure to be tainted. If you promise me that you won't say anything to anybody else—"

"Sorry, it took longer than I thought." Sara came back, and Areel couldn't finish what he was going to say.

He looked at me though, and I mouthed back a heartfelt, "Don't worry."

I wasn't going to put anybody else in danger just because I needed a shoulder to cry on. And even if I were so selfish, who would've believed me?

I realized at the moment there was only one person who could understand me. I needed someone I could talk to. Although I wasn't sure of Areel, I needed him. He was the last one who had talked to Elios and seemed sincerely affected by his friend's fate. The shared worries made us traveling companions in my madness. It was enough for me to take the risk.

During lunch, Areel was extremely gracious to Sara, but she remained suspicious. We ordered three pasta dishes and two bottles of sparkling water. The food was delicious, and with her belly full, she relaxed and even said a few polite sentences.

After lunch, it seemed the most natural thing for me to ask, "Would you like to have coffee at our place?"

"Seriously?" Sara gave me a reproachful look, her words hissed between clenched teeth, good manners forgotten.

I shrugged. "We aren't expected at the excavation site until later this afternoon."

Areel stood and didn't give Sara the option of changing my mind. "I'll follow you."

"Get in the car." Sara led me all the way to the parking lot with her fingers firmly holding my right elbow. She silently drove the whole way back to Tarquinia with the single-mindedness of someone intent on losing the enemy behind.

During the ride, I looked back once or twice only to see Areel still behind us, a small smile on his mouth. His lips were still upturned when he reached us outside our building, but soon flattened at Sara's glare. My friend's mood didn't improve during his stay, and she stood vigil the whole time he was with us. I had so many questions I wanted to ask him, but eventually I realized inviting him hadn't been a smart idea.

Still, when it was time for us to go back to work, I said, "Come back any time you want."

"I will." Areel left with that promise, and Sara had the good grace not to say anything back.

This time, she drove unhurriedly, which gave her a few minutes to try to extort a confession out of me before we reached the excavation site. I knew what was coming before she started talking.

"So, what was that all about?" She kept her eyes on the road.

"What?" I needed some time to come up with a convincing half-truth.

"You know what."

"Do I?"

She rolled her eyes. "I'm glad you feel much better. Being obtuse on purpose is the first sign you're in good health."

"You're right. Sorry." I wanted to tell her everything, and I remembered with dismay how many times I'd been so close to confiding the truth to her. Now I couldn't anymore.

"What did he say to you?" Sara seemed to be very interested in the landscape outside, but she didn't fool me.

I didn't answer.

"When I was out, at the restaurant. What did Areel say to you?" Sara patiently repeated.

"What do you want to know, exactly?" I sighed, collecting my thoughts.

"Who is he, really?" She looked in the rearview mirror, slowed down even more, and finally looked at me.

Could it be that Sara had understood something? That morning, I had felt him coming before seeing him, and that is why for a split second I hoped for the impossible. Maybe she had felt something as well.

"Areel knows Elios. They're good friends. He wanted to let me know Elios is in trouble."

"What kind of *trouble*?" Sara decided to let the first question go, even if I could see in her eyes she wasn't satisfied by my answer.

"The kind of trouble you don't get out of." I turned toward the window, staring at the sunflower fields rolling by. Any other time, the sight would've given me great pleasure. I often went out there to sketch, but now I barely saw anything.

"Is Elios in jail or something like that?"

"Something like that." A few tears caught in the corner of my eyes while I tried to keep my voice steady.

"What did he do?" Sara pretended she hadn't seen my moment of weakness and kept the conversation going.

"He broke some laws." I wished he had broken all of them.

"So, you're saying that Elios is a delinquent?" Now Sara's eyes were back on me. She stopped the car by the side of the road and waited for my answer.

"Elios didn't break any of our laws. He couldn't be with me. Because of me, he broke an oath." I knew my words didn't make any sense, but what else could I say without revealing the whole truth?

"Gaia, what's going on here?" Sara was staring at me.

I couldn't stand the look in her eyes. I felt bad; I wasn't treating her right. I lowered my head in defeat. I had to tell her something. "Elios is sworn to celibacy. We never had any physical contact because of that."

"He's what… a priest, a monk?" Sara's eyes were darting at mine.

"Yes, sort of…" I could understand her reaction to my explanation because it had enraged me so much the first time I had heard it. "*I* wasn't supposed to happen. He's paying for his transgression in solitary confinement."

"In which religion do you get in so much trouble for a transgression like that?"

"It's not a religion." My voice was shaking. I was walking a fine line and felt I was going to fall soon.

"Elios is in some crazy sect? I'm so glad he left for good, whatever happened to him. I don't care if he's rotting in hell. I only care that you are free from that fool," Sara said in a rush of heated words. I could almost feel the relief sweeping through her body.

"It's not like that. He left because there was something he had to do, and because of that he got caught. He had to confess our involvement, and he's paying for that." I couldn't resist correcting

Sara's opinion of him. It probably was the first time I tried to put in words what had happened between us, and it was strangely liberating even if I wasn't saying anything at all.

"From what you're saying, I get the idea Elios is involved in something unorthodox. What else if not a cult?" She looked at me and then gasped. "It's a gang? Please, tell me he doesn't belong to a gang!"

"No, not a cult, and absolutely not a gang." I almost smiled at her words. "Just another... way of life."

"Oh, this is what they call it? A way of life?"

This time I felt the urge to laugh, but I didn't. "No, it's the way it is." I went to look back at the yellow fields.

"Did he try to brainwash you?" She put one hand on my shoulder and gently turned me around to look at her.

"No, Sara, he didn't. Give me some credit. It takes a bit more than a pretty face to convert me to the dark side." I forced myself to sound lighter than I felt.

"At least you can still make a joke about it." She looked at the clock on the dashboard and then turned on the engine. "Crap, it's late." She started driving down the road again.

I breathed, happy she had to drop the conversation.

Then Sara bit her lips pensively and said out of the blue, "I know there's something about Areel." She shrugged her shoulder imperceptibly, and I felt cold sweat running down my back. I didn't know what she would say next, and I was terrified of it.

"Never mind, I'm sure I'm imagining things. Being Elios's friend and all." She was too focused on the driving to realize I was trembling. "They have something in common, but I can't point out what. Probably because he's in the same cult."

I decided some confusion could prove beneficial for both of us. For different reasons. But I still had to correct her. "They're from the same place."

Meanwhile, we had reached Marina Velca, and I didn't have to answer any more questions. I hugged Sara and thanked her for being such a great friend. She was late and was gone as soon as I closed the passenger door.

"Gaia! I was waiting for you. Come to the tent, there's something you might find interesting." Danilo, the helpful archeologist, greeted me at the gate.

"What is it?" My mind was elsewhere, but Danilo seemed excited, and I didn't want to sound uninterested. I followed him inside the tent, making small talk. Waiting for me on an immaculate white cloth was a single piece of black earthenware, a small circular plate completely intact. "You are right. It's interesting." I could barely contain my excitement now. I was holding yet another variation of the six-fingered figure. This one had something in its hand, but the object was just outlined, and I couldn't determine what it was.

"Thought so." Danilo smiled at me.

"Can I take some pictures?" I couldn't believe my eyes.

"Of course, just be careful when you handle it. This piece is very brittle." He passed me some gloves and a soft brush.

"Thanks. Do you already know the period it belongs to?" With gloved hands, I gently pushed the piece on the table until it was better illuminated by the natural light coming through the plastic window. I gently brushed off the dust from the piece then took my camera from my purse and shot several pictures.

"No, I don't. The other team is working on it, but they're in a hurry because of the Etruscan exhibit coming up in fall, so it won't take long."

"Let me know when the results are back." I took another look at the drawing, thanked Danilo again, and went to report to my group.

Later that night, I had a relaxing dinner with Sara, who decided to talk about everything but Elios and Areel. Because of that, I felt greatly indebted to her. As soon as I managed to escape to my room without being rude to her, I immediately went to sleep, hoping to dream about Elios. I blissfully spent my night hanging out with him, and I was delighted to confirm that in my imagination he was definitely getting healthier.

Elios wasn't as pale as he had been in my earlier dreams; he had put on some weight, and even his eyes looked more peaceful, less sunken. That night, I took time to make a mental note of the clothes he was wearing, a sort of dark samurai kimono with some details completely out of place. Something about the fabric and the design wasn't right. Even in sleep, I remembered smiling at the conclusion it was a dream after all, and I couldn't pretend things made sense. Elios tried to talk to me several times, but I couldn't hear anything, and there was a precise moment when I saw him mouthing my name. In the middle of our "date," I also thought I should tell him about Areel. At the moment, it seemed important enough to mention.

The rest of the week passed quickly. I had lots of things to do, and with the summer season approaching, swimming and surfing also occupied some of my time. Areel, as promised, came back to visit on a Saturday. Despite having invited him myself, on seeing him at our door my first instinct was to be wary of his presence. After all, during our last conversation, he had revealed to me his orders were to obliterate my memory.

I had to get the issue out of the way and didn't have time for pleasantries; Sara was outside on the terrace playing with Pallino and could barge in at any moment. "Areel, regarding what you said about erasing—"

He raised one hand. "If you're thinking I'm here to harm you, you're mistaken. I didn't like my orders to begin with. Don't talk to anybody, and I'll find a way to leave things the way they are now." Then he silently asked permission to come inside.

I opened the door all the way to let him in. "Welcome back, then."

He had both lunch and dinner with us. Sara never left the premises though, so the conversation was kept on a general level for a while. However, in a serendipitous turn of events, my personal bodyguard actually helped the conversation to a different level. Out of some kind of impulse, she wanted to show Areel a few pictures of the artifacts we were cataloguing, and among them was the little plate with the six-fingered figure holding the mirror.

Areel knew more than what he was allowed to reveal before Sara, but when he saw the little plate, his surprised expression gave him away.

"What's so interesting?" Sara smiled, pleased.

For a brief moment, I had the impression she had done it on purpose. But that wasn't possible.

"The object in its hand is something familiar to my culture. It looks like a ceremonial mirror we use when we are but kids," Areel answered.

Sara didn't flicker at his admission of having seen the abstract figure. The anthropologist in her was immediately interested in the sociological ritual mentioned. "Is it some sort of rite of passage?"

Areel looked at Sara and shrugged. "Yes, I guess you could call it a rite of passage. It's different for everybody, but normally we receive it as a gift when we learn how to distinguish between ourselves and others as separate entities. In our society, kids are raised all together in a communal place."

"You lived in a kibbutz? I didn't realize from your accent you were from Israel. Your name isn't Italian, but you speak Italian so well." Sara didn't have time to continue because Areel stopped her immediately.

"No, I'm not from Israel; we just share some superficial traits with the kibbutz sociological structure, nothing more than that. Our communion goes beyond the material world." He inadvertently stressed the word communion.

"So, I was right that both you and Elios were raised in a sect." Sara looked at me triumphantly, and for good measure whispered, "Told you so."

Areel's onyx eyes lit, mirth showing on his face. "The word *sect* has a negative connotation. We're the good guys, and we don't work for our salvation but for the greater good of everybody else."

"Oh, no! You want to recruit us in your satanic cult of depravation and whatnot." Mock horror showed on Sara's face while a hint of a smile got immediately suppressed.

I was grateful that Sara for once wanted to joke about it. I needed some levity, and judging from how much I was enjoying it, more than I thought.

Areel raised his hands, offering a truce. "I wouldn't dare."

Sara raised one eyebrow, and I could swear I saw a flicker of brief disappointment on her face.

Areel's smile suddenly became a playful grin. "Would you like me to recruit you?"

"Thanks, but no thanks. My own religion is more than enough." Sara openly smiled now.

"Too bad," Areel responded.

The rest of the night went smoothly. Areel confirmed he had been living in so many different places he had lost his accent when he spoke, but he didn't elaborate on where he was actually from. The increasing number of questions Sara was asking prevented him from having to answer most of them completely, or at all.

When Sara asked if he was an "army brat," Areel answered with yes and no nods. When Sara finally and directly asked where he was from originally, he admitted he wasn't from this planet. Sara laughed a lot at this particular answer, finding his evasiveness cute, as she confessed to me later. I found her reaction to him interesting, but I didn't say that right away.

What I told her was that I truly envied her ability to question incessantly. The few times I had been in Elios's proximity, my head had never been clear enough to ask more than a few things. My senses reacted to his presence in a way that was fatal for the neurons in my brain.

While Sara was giving Areel the third degree, I realized with unexpected relief that his presence was going to help me speed up my quest. Areel knew all the things I didn't, and after all, we could collaborate for a common cause.

He could communicate with his superiors and report new discoveries. Maybe I would find the missing link that would explain everything. Maybe Areel and I, working together, could even find a way to mitigate Elios's punishment. Maybe.

I had to provide that discovery and prove it was connected to their history. Even then, my plan sounded childish, but it was the only hope I had. My excuse was that I had an oneiric, romantic nightlife that I'd mistaken for real more than once, so I could not be held accountable for my own acts.

I had to believe I could do something to change a situation that was only causing me pain. The only way the human spirit can survive the most terrifying and painful circumstances is by envisioning a way to make things better. Areel was now part of my idiotic plan to save the love of my life.

Sara was still grilling him when I realized I was late for my "date." I said good night and went to sleep. I had the feeling my friend wasn't going to be too upset about being left alone with Areel.

Elios was there, waiting for me as soon as I closed my eyes. He looked happier than the first time I had seen him in my dreams, his eyes now full of life, not sunken anymore. From the way he moved, I could see his physical condition had improved as well. Seeing him like that made me feel much better. Elios's smiles made me smile during the day; his joy was my joy; his increasing strength made me want to get stronger. Our fates were so intertwined I couldn't believe even for a second I wasn't going to see him again.

In my dream, he said something, but I couldn't hear anything, so I tried to say something back. I found it strange we weren't able to talk. Maybe it was important to understand why. Not that I wanted to talk to somebody other than Sara about my dreams, but a good psychologist could have explained why we couldn't talk.

As usual, our "date" ended abruptly, and once again I sank into the dreamless portion of my night with a satisfied smile on my face.

14

A few days later, I finally had the occasion to talk in private with Areel. He was often at our house now, with one excuse or another, but Sara's presence prevented us from having deeper conversations. While I found it almost a waste of time since I wasn't making any progress on my plan, my friend seemed to tolerate him well. More than well.

"Excuse me for a sec." Sara looked at her ringing cell phone. "It's my mom."

The three of us were drinking an espresso accompanied by my favorite mini pastries. Lately, bad news had been coming on a daily basis for her. Grandma Rosa's health had worsened and was now in critical condition. What had started as an out-of-season flu had evolved into something more worrisome. The whole week, she had watched her cell phone, days and sometimes even nights, waiting for *that* call, and her weariness had rubbed off on me as well.

I couldn't help eavesdropping on her conversation. Her tone had gone from worried to frantic in the span of two sentences. Areel and I were sitting outside under the umbrella when she came back, her eyes already red.

"Is your grandma—?"

"Yes, they had to hospitalize her. I must go to Rome." She looked around as if to gather her thoughts.

"I'll accompany you." I stood and went to grab my purse.

"I'll drive you," Areel offered, walking ahead and opening the door for us.

Sara looked at him, a sad smile coloring her face. "Thank you."

I was grateful. Neither of us was in any condition to drive. Sara was too worried, and I was too tired from cataloguing objects until five in the morning.

We entered Areel's car, Sara in the front seat and I right behind her, my hand on her shoulder the whole time. She made a few phone calls to cousins and uncles along the way, but otherwise the three of us kept silent. The hour it took to drive from Tarquinia to Rome seemed a year.

We left Sara at the entry of the Umberto Primo Hospital, and Areel managed to park not far away. She called me on my cell phone a few minutes later to tell me we had to wait outside. By hospital policy, only one person at a time was let into the room. I told her we were going to have a coffee downstairs at the hospital bar.

I was getting more and more tired. Normally, car trips made me feel dizzy if I wasn't the one driving, so another espresso was the only thing I could think would help at the moment. We sat outside at a table facing the busy street; the droning of the cars driving by was conducive to deep thinking. Something that had bothered me for a while about Areel surfaced, and after considering how to phrase my question, I blurted out, "Excuse my forwardness, but why do you have a name?" He looked at me, a puzzled expression on his face, and I added, "You know, since Elios asked me to name him... Forgive me if it isn't something I should have asked."

"No, it's okay to ask." Areel smiled at me and then sat more comfortably, crossing his legs at the ankles. "Soleans have names. We inherit them from our parents and then we renew them when we become adults. It's a long story—" He passed his hand through his hair. "Our names depict who we are, and we are normally happy with what they stand for. Elios has always been different from the rest of us and never cared for his individual name. He is—was— very old-fashioned and believed in being one with the rest of our race." He smiled again at me. "Then, you came along."

I blushed, pleased by his words. "Oh—"

Areel's expression sobered, and he straightened his back, hands steepled on the table. "Do you mind if I too ask something personal?"

I shook my head. "Go ahead."

"So, what do you mean when you say you see Elios every night?"

I was surprised he remembered what I had said the day we met. Or maybe Sara and Areel talked about me when I wasn't around. "I have vivid dreams of Elios."

"You see him in your dreams?" Areel stared at me, giving the impression he could read through my words.

"Yes, I think I do, but they aren't ordinary dreams. I interact with him. We have conversations although I can rarely hear his voice." I shook my head. "I know that doesn't sound sane."

"Sometimes, our minds can give us what we want the most in our sleep. It happens a lot in human physiology." He slightly raised his voice at the last word as if he were asking a question.

I laughed. "I know; I'm sophisticated enough to know that. But I'm sure we aren't talking about normal dreams here." A slight hint of irritation escaped through a sigh I couldn't repress.

"When we first met, you were clearly under stress." Areel's tone was kind but also resolute.

"Yes, I confess I don't accept life without Elios, but believe me, it's not just that. I'm not crazy." I didn't know why I was reacting so strongly when just a few days ago I wouldn't have. Maybe his words had triggered an automatic response, but I wasn't the kind of person who had to have the last say in anything.

"I'm not saying you should see a doctor. I'm trying to rationalize something that can't be happening for more reasons than you can possibly understand." Areel's tone was even calmer than before, which helped me to find the right words.

"Listen, I know that there probably isn't anything I can say that will make you believe me, but I *know* who I see at night. And it's really him." I finally said it. The more I talked about it, the more I knew I was right. I was having an epiphany of a sort, sitting outside a bar facing a crowded, polluted, noisy street in Rome.

Areel waved a hand before my eyes. "You got it all backward. You don't know how much I'd like to believe you. The main problem is that although Elios is probably the only one strong enough to expand his mind to the point of reaching yours, he simply can't. The planet where he is exiled was chosen for its shielding quality. It's called Silenzio because you can hear only silence on its surface. The magnetic field on that planet doesn't allow any form of mental communication to escape its surface. Elios can't access the astral world, and at the same time, nobody can reach him."

"Maybe we found a way around that." My certainty wasn't going to quiver easily.

"I doubt there's any possibility that even Elios could pull that kind of stunt."

"Areel, seeing him is more than I could hope for. Please, don't kill this hope." I didn't want to hear anything that could prove me wrong at this point—not now that, for reasons I couldn't understand, I was sure we could see each other.

"I'm sorry. I seem to always say the wrong thing to you, but it's not my intention." Areel lowered his eyes to the concrete floor, his shoe kicking cigarette butts around.

"I know you mean well. Don't worry." *Now or never*, I thought. "I want to ask you to help me with something."

"Sure. What can I do for you?" He smiled warmly.

"Join the archeologists' group."

Areel raised one eyebrow in surprise.

I stopped him from interrupting me by adding right away, "I know you can find a way to sneak in. I need help deciphering the meaning of the little figure. You're the only one on Earth right now that can help me do that." I rushed the words breathlessly.

He seemed to ponder it for the longest time and then slowly nodded. "Let me see what I can do to obtain a temporary job at the excavation site in Marina Velca. It shouldn't be difficult. I can try to apply as a visiting student."

My heart started beating again. "Thank you so much."

He gave me another of his small smiles and shrugged slightly. "But why? I can't see how working on this is going to help *you* in any way. To be honest, I only see grief coming from it."

I breathed slowly and took my time answering. "I meant to talk to you about *my plan* for a while. I know it will sound childish, but here it is: I am trying to find enough proof to solve the mystery of your ancestors."

"Why?" Areel's body went rigid.

"I want to help Elios." I steadied my voice.

"How?" Areel looked at me, and I hoped I could be convincing because his body language told me he was going to dismiss me as crazy.

"He was the one who made the connection and reported the finding back to your planet. I'm sure that whoever is in charge would show some leniency toward him if the truth behind what happened to your race is found, considering that without him it wouldn't have been possible at all. You could appeal for him. I'm sure your society has something like that, right?" I was trembling. I hadn't realized how much I wanted Areel's support until I finished speaking.

"What do you want me to say?" Areel looked at me with his big black eyes opened in disbelief.

I felt like falling down. "Just that you're going to help me. I don't care if you only do it out of pity." Maybe I had too much caffeine in my system already, and the fact I was shaking didn't help, but I had to turn my head toward the noisy street to hide the sparkling wetness in my tired eyes.

"I will."

I faced him again. I almost couldn't believe what I had just heard. He was looking at me, and compassion radiated from him. "Thank you," I whispered. I was too happy to ask why he had decided to give me a chance. I didn't care.

Instead, I showed him the pictures I had in my laptop right away. Lately, I didn't go anywhere without it. Areel went through several images of the artifacts we had found in Marina Velca, commenting on the color similarities to the Soleans he had seen on his planet. He spent several minutes studying the piece that had the little figure holding the ceremonial mirror.

"Can you send me these pictures, please? I think there is another connection, but I don't want to say anything unless I'm sure."

"As soon as you're part of the team. Lately, they're getting paranoid with security. There is a big exhibit coming up."

"I'll work on that as soon as we go back to Tarquinia."

"Thanks, it means a lot to me."

"You know, in a way I'm doing it for me as well—" Areel didn't finish his sentence, his eyes focused behind on something, someone, behind me.

I saw the expression on his face lighten.

"Sara. How's your grandmother?" he asked, and I could swear his tone had changed.

I turned to face her.

"She's going to make it this time, but her heart isn't in a good shape." Tears were rolling down her face.

"Oh, sweetie—" I hugged my friend. Sara hugged me back, and I could see she was exhausted.

"Can we take you somewhere else to eat something and maybe relax?" Areel stood up to offer Sara his seat.

I noted real concern in his voice. His normally serene face was showing unexpected emotion.

"Yes please, we can hang around a bit, if you don't mind, and then we can go back to Tarquinia."

She needed a break, and we were more than okay with the idea. Sara proposed to eat gelato at the Zodiaco, a famous bar where you could see Rome from one of the seven hills upon which the Eternal City had been built.

We had a pleasant night out. Sara relaxed after the emotional rollercoaster she had just gone through. I looked forward to Areel's help. While he drove us back to Tarquinia, I fell asleep in the car, exhausted from the eventful day.

Three days later, I was working at the camp on a translation to send to UW when our excavation superintendent introduced a new student visitor to us. The new guy was going to help in the field during the summer months when almost everybody was on vacation. Although I knew he had the means to accomplish that, I was still astonished at the velocity with which Areel had been able to infiltrate the camp.

Half the camp was surprised by his presence as well, but for a completely different reason. For the next few days, all I heard from the archeologist girls was a constant blathering about how handsome and cool and exotic and kind he was. I heard all about his almond-shaped, pitch-black eyes, his straight corvine hair, his incredible mouth, and his muscles. I even heard about the perfection of his jawline. One of my distinguished colleagues even sketched him semi-naked.

I told Sara the new gossip, laughing at the hysteria that had swept the camp at his arrival, but she didn't find it the least bit amusing. Soon after having this conversation, I noticed Sara's presence at the camp increased. She was there every day, sometimes for no good reason at all.

Summer arrived, and the hot weather slowed down the archeologists' job, at least the job of the few who hadn't already left for some backpacking Euro trip. The camp opened early in the morning and then again late at night. Everybody spent the rest of the day at the beach.

The beauty of working at the excavation site in Marina Velca was that we could walk to the beach. I loved swimming alone for hours while everybody else was busy playing all sorts of aquatic sports or just tanning on the brown sand. Areel had become so dark that when he walked along the shore, lots of eyes followed him. He didn't seem to notice anything. Sara was normally around.

One hot afternoon in July, I spent several hours going in and out of the warm water, trying to cool down my body. After one last swim, exhausted by the constant exercise of the day, I lay down on the sand, enjoying the cooler temperature. I was so tired that my mind drifted for a while.

And here he was, Elios resting beside me. The sand where he was sitting was of a different shade, much lighter, almost golden. His skin was wet like mine. I moved my hand toward his body. I wanted to finally touch him, at least in my dreams.

"Elios?"

His mouth shaped an "Oh!" His eyes were shinier than I remembered. He was tan again, freckles everywhere, his hair longer and blonder.

"Gaia?" Pure happiness in his voice.

He disappeared from my view while he was still looking at me.

Then I realized I had never closed my eyes. I wasn't sleeping at all.

A few steps to my right, Sara and Areel were staring at me with strange expressions on their bewildered faces.

"Is everything okay?" Areel asked.

"Gaia?" Sara exchanged a look with him.

I looked at them, a little confused myself. This time something had been tangibly different. I was trembling, and I didn't know why. My thoughts must have been written on my forehead for everybody to see because almost at the same time both Areel and Sara asked me, "Did you... see him?"

Sara rectified herself immediately, "Were you sleeping? Did you just dream of Elios?"

I could read through the lines. She didn't want to augment my delusion further. I was already deranged; I didn't need help from the outside as well.

Areel promptly followed with his own rectification. "Did you have a nightmare? You seem... disconcerted."

I finally found the strength to say something. "I just saw Elios."

They were still looking at me, but even in my confused state of mind I could see they weren't matching expressions anymore. As expected, Sara was worried I was losing it for good. Areel's expression I couldn't read. His eyes were looking through me; he was there, and he wasn't at the same time.

After a long awkward pause, he blinked and then asked, "What did you see?"

Sara gave him a sour look, but Areel didn't seem to notice.

"Elios was on a beach. I heard his voice." I left out the part where his voice made me weep.

"You think you heard his voice?" Areel's tone didn't give the impression he was correcting me, but his choice of words stung nevertheless.

"I'm sure I heard his voice. I don't *think*." My declaration had a strange effect on him. "Elios was relaxing on a golden-sand beach by the sea." The image was still before my eyes. "The colors in the sky were strange, but other than that, everything else was quite recognizable."

Areel's black eyes focused on my face with a perplexed stare.

"Sara, would you be so nice as to bring me a Fanta? I need some sugar. I feel lightheaded. Please?" I asked.

I saw Sara startle at my request. I knew she was asking herself why would I want to talk to him instead of her. I mouthed a "please," and she went to the beach kiosk to buy the orange soda.

"What is it? Hurry, before she's back," I asked Areel.

"I need to ask you something first." Areel was looking straight at Sara, but his hand was outstretched before me.

I hesitated.

"Please, Gaia—"

"Okay, shoot." I shook my head.

"Do you remember anything specific about Elios?"

"Like what? His face, his eyes, his clothes?"

"Yes, his clothes. Do you remember what he was wearing the first time you *saw* him in your dreams?"

"I remember he looked like a futuristic samurai. His hair was tied. Why?"

Areel gasped. "You can really see him."

Sara was coming back, juggling three bottles of Fanta, sipping from one of them.

"So?"

"I felt something too—"

To my profound disappointment, Areel couldn't finish.

"Here's your sugar fix, and I bought one for you as well." Sara was trying to maintain her hold on the slippery bottles. Areel took one by the neck, relieving her.

I smiled at Sara, who had noticed something but decided not to ask. I drank the whole bottle and then tried to stand up to throw it into a garbage can. My legs didn't cooperate, and I swayed.

Sara was immediately at my side. "You need more sugar. Take mine, here."

I thanked her and sipped from the bottle she offered until it was empty.

Areel gently removed the bottles from my hands and disposed of them and then came back to sit close to me. He let Sara comfort me for a while before asking something again. People were hovering curiously around us.

"Just a mild heatstroke." He waved the crowd away.

Sara looked at our colleagues dispersing to resume their activities and then turned toward us. "I'm going to buy another round of sodas." She headed toward the kiosk once again.

"Tell me," I said to Areel once she was out of earshot.

He looked in the direction Sara was walking and then looked at me again, and his eyes had a light I had never seen before. "You just described what Elios was wearing the last time I saw him."

"So now you believe me." I dipped my feet in the sand.

"I never thought you were lying. I was sure you just wanted to see him really badly."

"It doesn't matter, really. Before Sara comes back, I want to know what you saw, because you saw something, right?"

Areel glanced again at Sara, now coming back with croissants as well.

"I saw him, for maybe a second, probably even less. It was almost imperceptible." Areel paused for a moment and then added between his teeth, "And you're right, Elios is getting better."

Sara dropped on her knees before me and laid the bounty on the towel. "First, you're going to eat this croissant, and then you change."

"Thank you, Mom." But I did eat the flaky pastry, and then I did go to change my clothes as ordered. When I came back from the locker room, I found them deep in conversation, sitting on the same towel. I stopped in my tracks, wondering if I could tiptoe back before they saw me. They looked as though they didn't want to be interrupted. Sara's head tilted toward Areel's, their bodies angled toward each other, without touching. The image evoked a bittersweet feeling in my heart, and I must've made some noise because they both turned at the same time.

Sara spoke first. "Ready?"

I nodded. "Where to?"

Sara stood in a graceful motion and dusted the sand away from her swimsuit. "Areel's driving us back to the apartment."

"Anything for my ladies." He donned a pair of shorts and a white shirt and then, like a gentleman, offered to carry our totes to the car.

Once back at our apartment, I went straight for a cold shower. I needed some time to cleanse my thoughts. When I was ready to come back to reality, I found Sara and Areel sitting outside on the terrace, waiting for me to eat.

Sara had done an excellent job decorating the small outdoor retreat with a multitude of terracotta pots full of plants and flowers. The white cotton umbrella was illuminated by white lights, and citronella candles were scattered on the marble balustrade. At night, Pallino loved to take long naps on the terracotta floor. The brown-red tiles released the heat absorbed during the day, and it was pleasant to walk barefoot and enjoy the refreshing breeze coming from the sea.

Areel and Sara were sipping pineapple juice and looked engrossed in each other's company. Areel was absentmindedly stroking Pallino's fur. The cat's satisfied low purring harmonized with the serene night.

I lingered a moment inside. Once again, I didn't want to intrude. Their heads were close but, as before, not touching. Something in Areel's stance seemed out of place. He looked as he was restraining himself from getting any closer to Sara. I suddenly realized they were often physically close, but I hadn't seen them touching in a while; however, he was still acting careless around me.

I heard a soft chuckle, and I saw Sara's raised eyebrow, her eyes on me. Deep in my own mind, I must have looked like an idiot frozen at the threshold.

"Hey, sleeping beauty, are you with us?" She gestured for me to come forth and join them at the table.

I passed a hand through my hair and grinned. "Yep, I guess I really had heatstroke."

Sara exchanged a knowing look with Areel, and they both laughed.

"Have some." He poured some pineapple juice from the carafe on the table and gave me the glass.

"Thanks." I drank the contents in a few gulps. I hadn't realized I was so thirsty. Then, as if on cue, my stomach rumbled. "By the way, thank you for preparing dinner again, I'm kind of useless lately." I eyed the covered pot whetting my appetite.

Sara raised the lid with a flourish. "You're welcome. I made your favorite risotto."

I clapped my hands, glad my nose hadn't betrayed me. "You know I love you. I smelled the artichokes and shrimp cream from the bathroom."

"Let's eat it now, or the risotto will become glue." Sara started serving us, smiling serenely.

The night was beautiful, the citronella candles kept the mosquitoes at bay, the temperature was finally pleasant, and the company was excellent. I could only ask for one more thing.

Areel probably read my mind, or maybe he was on the same train of thought, because after a few moments contemplating the brilliant light of the stars, he looked at me and said, "Don't worry. You'll see him again."

I needed to hear those words from someone else, someone who wasn't me. "Thank you." I couldn't trust myself at the moment. It was better to say nothing else instead of risking blurting out something before Sara's innocent ears. She saw I was trembling and stroked my hand softly.

"Okay, let's eat now," I said, forcing a smile.

We talked about silly things, and mostly I let them answer each other's questions while I took turns petting the already spoiled Pallino. I realized it was late when I heard the church bells announcing midnight. I excused myself as usual and ran to my room because I couldn't wait to see Elios again.

Since I knew I didn't have to be sleeping to see him, I felt in control, and I tried to call him. I didn't know how to initiate the process, but my desire to see him was so strong I was sure I could make it work.

I concentrated on the memory of his lapis lazuli eyes and on the warm quality of his voice. I added the memories of his constantly upward lips and the halo of his blond hair. Then, I imagined his elegant tanned hands, down to his long fingers. Finally, I combined all the separate details.

All of a sudden, I saw him. He was sleeping, his chest moving rhythmically. Longing possessed my heart. I wanted to cradle his body, to kiss his lips, and to caress his face. I didn't want to wake him up because he looked so relaxed. Something happened on his end, though. He opened his eyes and saw me. The expression on his face made my heart jump. After a moment of shock, he realized what was happening, and smiled at me. I felt lost in his gaze.

I started talking. I wasn't sure if he could understand what I was saying, but I went on and on. I told him about the progresses in my research and Areel's involvement in my plan. After a while, his image trembled a little bit, and worried I was going to lose him, I opted for saying goodbye before it happened.

"See you later." I smiled at him one more time. Elios disappeared right afterward. I fell asleep with the certainty we could make it through this ordeal.

15

From that night on, my life changed.

I worked hard to find new clues. Sometimes, I was the one opening the camp in the morning and closing it in the wee hours of the night. I literally had the keys. The superintendent saw my dedication to the research and decided to trust me to be responsible enough to keep the place in perfect condition.

Areel normally came to help me when nobody could see he was there taking care of business that wasn't exactly his. Sara was part of the team whenever possible, but lately she had often been absent from both camps. Her grandmother was in the hospital again, and she drove back and forth from Rome every other day.

Despite our best efforts, nothing really new or interesting came up for a while.

One night, I was working alone at the camp because Sara had received another frantic phone call regarding her grandmother, and Areel, seeing how distressed she was, had insisted on accompanying her to Rome. They had called me on my cell phone while I was working, just to explain they couldn't come to help me later at the camp. I had offered to join them and support Sara, but they were already on the freeway speeding through the night.

So I was working late, not so much worried about being alone but mostly thinking about Sara and her grandmother. Full of worries, I kept calling them every half hour to find out how the situation was. Areel was the one answering while Sara was with her family. He didn't sound optimistic about the outcome. I tried to concentrate on what I was doing, and I had almost decided to close the camp and reach my friends when I found something that caught my attention.

Putting my cell phone back in my purse for the umpteenth time, I lost my grip on it, and the phone fell inside a box lying on the floor. A loud thud echoed in the silent tent. Unnerved by the noise, I bent over the box to blindly retrieve the phone. My fingers found a cold, hard, pointy surface instead, and I shrieked when I poked my right index finger. Worried I had touched a rusty surface—an ordinary occurrence at the camp—I looked at the box thoroughly. It was one of the several boxes full of artifacts coming from the tomb called The Hunters' House.

Inside that tomb, the archeologists had found plenty of hunting artifacts, and the paintings on the walls depicted only men. The quantity and quality of the artifacts had reawakened an interest in the Etruscan society. The curator of the Capitolini Museum in Rome had immediately seized the opportunity and arranged to recreate the tomb for the much anticipated fall exhibit. The finding couldn't have happened at a better moment, and it had soon grabbed the attention of the media. Every archeologist in the camp was talking about it, hoping to be asked to help the museum.

I gently moved things around inside the box to see what I had actually touched. What I saw made me pause. After several days of cataloguing pieces that were important for the official research, but not so much for mine, I'd finally come across something useful, a bronze spear with an unusual inscription on the blade. I looked at it for a while without recognizing the letters on it. I put it under a stronger lamp to see if I was missing something in the half-light.

A few sentences immortalized in black Sharpie on the box stated that all the objects in it, bronze spear included, were going to be catalogued the very next day to be sent later on to Rome. Time wasn't working in my favor at the moment, and I couldn't shoot a good picture because it was too dark. I tried to use the flash and gave it a try anyway.

I checked to see if the pic was any good, but I had to admit my digital camera resolution wasn't meant for spy business. I couldn't say why, but I knew I had to show the inscription to Areel, and tomorrow was too late since the contents of the box were going to be moved to a safer place away from clumsy wannabe archeologists and indiscreet eyes.

My cell phone rang and I jumped in the dark, my heart beating fast. I knew before I answered what that phone call meant.

"Gaia?" Areel didn't do a good job masking the sorrow in his voice.

"Areel, is she…"

"Yes, Sara just left with the family to arrange *things*."

"I'm coming."

"No, stay put. I'll pick you up. I can't stay a minute longer here at the hospital. There's too much pain. I can't breathe."

I could feel Areel's distress; it radiated through his pauses. I had never thought about the effects of human feelings on their kind.

"Okay, then I'm going back to the apartment." I was relieved I didn't have to drive all by myself to Rome in the middle of the night.

"See you there in about an hour."

I still had the spear in my hands and decided to follow my hunch. My first impulse was to make a rubbing of the inscription, but having worked with archeologists for so long, I knew I couldn't risk ruining the artifact. I put it under the lamp and started sketching the inscription on a piece of paper instead. It was in some language I didn't recognize, and I took my time even if it was just a short string of letters. After checking my accuracy several times, I put the spear back in its box.

I cleaned my station carefully and closed the place. Outside the tent, the air was fresh and the darkness almost absolute. My only companions were the noisy summer crickets singing their odes to the night. When I arrived at the apartment, Areel was already there. I hadn't realized how long it had taken me to copy the inscription.

I parked my car and walked to Areel's. He was hunched behind the wheel, breathing slowly in and out. Through the open windows, I heard him quietly muttering something that resembled a nursery rhyme in a foreign language.

I realized I had never heard the Solean language spoken before. I knew a few scattered things about Elios's culture; he'd only had time to cover the basics. I knocked delicately on the window to announce my presence.

Areel gestured to enter without raising his head from the wheel. "Give me one minute, please." His voice was almost a whisper.

He was in more pain than I had imagined. I waited silently until he slowly turned his head to face mine.

"I'm sorry. Normally, I can control myself better." He sighed. "Lately, it takes lots of effort to shield myself from the feelings around me. I couldn't stay another minute in that place."

I didn't know what to say to make him feel better. I was worried he couldn't keep it together once back at the hospital. "I can go by myself. Maybe it's better if you stay. I'll explain it to Sara." He gave me a worried look. I shook my head in response to his unspoken question. "Don't worry. I'll think of something."

He relaxed for a moment but then shrugged. "No, I can't leave Sara alone. She's so close to her grandmother. *Was* close. I have to be with her. I appreciate your concern, but this is something I can't run from." Areel talked slowly, making every word count.

"Is it unbearable?"

"It's the constant grief. The regrets of mean things said and good things not said when there was time. Mothers' pain, sisters' sorrow, children's tears, husbands' mourning. Nothing can prepare my kind for the full blast of human ache. I'm defenseless. Elios is much stronger than me. Now I understand why he had to banish himself from humankind during wars and famines. We can't interfere, and it's just too hard to watch."

"Elios tried to explain it to me—"

"We're so evolved and strong; compared to many other races, we're the pinnacle of evolution, but we're utterly flawed."

I couldn't believe his words. "You're anything but flawed. You're practically omnipotent. You can live forever."

"We grow old, we die. My current human body goes through the same being born-aging-dying cycle as yours does."

"What do you mean by *current body*?"

"Exactly what I said." Areel finally smiled at me.

I was glad to distract him from his pain, even if for just a moment. "Can you explain?"

"Our spiritual essence transmigrates from one mortal body to the next. It's a rule that applies to our whole race. It has a very long life, but it needs a series of successive bodies. Our aura stays the same the whole time. Our corporeal bodies change from time to time."

"So you are saying you weren't always like this, and that you'll be completely different several years from now... in your next incarnation?"

"What you see now is what I am. Our bodies reflect our inner souls. We evolve spiritually by growing older, so our exterior aspect will depict the change. I'm very young, and so is Elios. We haven't gone through serious spiritual growth yet—"

I stopped him curtly. I didn't mean to be rude, but I had something to ask, "Wait, you are saying that Elios has a frail human body like mine?"

"Yes."

"But he is capable of doing things no human I know can do. He can play with the weather and other stuff. How is that even possible?"

"It's possible because we aren't human. We can inhabit human bodies, but our core is still alien. For example, in addition to the things you already saw, things that Elios probably should have kept secret, we can heal our bodies, we can prevent major illnesses, and we age gracefully. But eventually our bodies will age. And we'll die."

My head was spinning at the number of concepts I was assimilating in such a short period of time, so it came as a pleasant reprieve when he said, "I think I've told you enough for tonight. Let's go confront the inevitable."

I glanced at the car clock and realized how late it was. "We'd better hurry."

"Gaia—" Areel's eyes were serious once again.

"Yes?"

"Thank you so much."

"For what?"

"For letting me vent. I needed a friend, and you were here to help me."

"You have no idea how reciprocal the situation is." I gave him a pale smile.

We reached Rome in record time as the freeway was deserted. It was too late even for the disco-goers. Sara called Areel to let us know where they were having the wake. It was almost five in the morning. The city was awakening, illuminated by an already bright sun, only a few clouds staining the blue sky white, buses and cars already littering the streets.

We brought some breakfast to Sara's family and then waited with her outside the funeral home. The service had been scheduled for the next morning, and I was glad the family had decided not to wait for the distant relatives to arrive from overseas. Postponing the Mass any longer would have been excruciating for Sara.

Sara's parents were professionals with busy careers, and she had spent all her childhood with her caring grandmother. I had loved visiting their house when I was a kid because Grandma Rosa knew how to read stories. Sara and I used to sit cross-legged on a big pillow on the floor and listen to her rich soprano voice for hours.

We sat in the waiting room outside the wake chamber, helping Sara greet relatives who were already arriving to pay their last respects to her grandma. As usual in these kinds of circumstances, we started talking about all the beautiful things we remembered about the deceased. I watched as Areel listened to Sara; he looked completely enthralled by the dozens of anecdotes about her beloved "Nonnina."

I couldn't help but watch them, the way they talked to each other, the way their eyes shone. I knew I was witnessing something beautiful. However, I could see Areel's torment. His body betrayed him, more than a thousand words could. He didn't dare to step any closer to Sara, even when she clearly needed a friendly hug.

I was there to cover for him. He was suffering more than he would confess, and thankfully Sara wasn't aware of what was happening. It was probably for the best; she already had enough to mourn at the moment, and we were just at the beginning of a very long day.

After having met and greeted Sara's family, Areel and I took care of all the little things that needed to be done: driving relatives back and forth, calling the ones who hadn't received the news, accompanying people to eat something, supplying Sara with a constant flow of coffee and sugary pastries to keep her up throughout the day, and other menial tasks.

Finally we found our way to my house since Sara's apartment was overflowing with tired out-of-town relatives. My parents had already prepared dinner for us and were happy to meet Areel. I was glad to have a limited amount of time with my family because I was still hiding my melancholia from them. I hadn't visited in several weeks. I would've loved to see my sister, but Clara was on vacation with some friends. Maybe it was better this way. She would've asked me questions. After a pleasant dinner and some conversation, I went to help my mother arrange the guestroom for Areel while Sara and he were outside in the veranda talking quietly. I was tired, but I knew that after the day we'd already had, an even longer night was waiting for us since Sara was emotionally overloaded and couldn't relax enough to sleep. I joined them, and we chatted until the first light of the new day started shining in the sky. Only then did we manage to find our way to the beds for a few hours of dozing.

The funeral took place in Nemi, a small city that once hosted a famous Roman sanctuary, situated a few miles outside of Rome. It had been chosen by Sara's parents because Grandma Rosa had loved to spend time in their country home in Nemi, and the parish priest was a close friend of the family. Every aspect of Sara's family life had taken place in that little medieval church: marriages, baptisms, first communions, confirmations, and funerals—the full cycle of life.

Padre Carlo knew the family well. The ceremony soon became a celebration of the love bonding Sara's family to her grandmother. It was moving and peaceful. The Mass had a healing effect on Areel's troubled soul. I observed him nodding more than once at the priest's words.

After the ceremony, we gathered at Sara's summer house by the volcanic lake for which Nemi was remembered. Sara, Areel, and I went to sit on the terrace facing the sunset descending on the placid waters. Someone brought fresh lemonade for us, and we relaxed on the comfortable reclining chairs.

I was sitting between Areel and Sara, thinking of Elios, missing him more than usual—feeling frail and very human—when I saw tears on Sara's face. She wasn't wearing any makeup, her eyes were tired, and she looked pale under her sun-tanned skin. I stretched my arm to reach hers, and I closed my fingers softly on hers. Then something made me turn my head the other way, and I saw Areel looking at us. His eyes were shiny, and I could feel his sadness.

And then I realized he was right. For he was flawed. He could do incredible things but not what he wanted to.

Keeping my grip on Sara's cold hand, I firmly took Areel's hand with my free one. Sara didn't notice anything, but Areel understood right away what I was doing and silently thanked me. A single tear escaped his right eye and rolled down his shaved skin. Beautiful music was transported by the breeze to our terrace, and I closed my eyes to imagine my Elios.

"Oh, I can smell the perfume of freshly cut freesias! It is my favorite flower. Nonnina used to arrange full vases of them in my room when I was a child."

I didn't know how Areel knew about that detail. I had a distinct memory of the perfumed flowers in Sara's room, but it wasn't something we talked about often. However, they had been seeing each other a lot lately, without me.

We spent another full day in the countryside, cleansing our souls and lifting up our broken spirits. We went horseback riding by the lake, and we ate at the trattoria by the marina. When we left the little town of Nemi, we were in better condition than when we had arrived.

The bond of our friendship had become stronger. We were a family now. I felt that Sara and Areel were my sister and brother. My relationship to them was the easiest to assess. They were going to have to define the nature of their relationship sooner or later, and it was going to be painful. I knew.

We were back in Tarquinia, and I was sifting through all the little papers and other stuff that found their final oblivion in the bottom of my purse when I picked up the sketch of the inscription I had made the night before the funeral.

Luckily enough, Areel was in the living room talking to Sara, so I went to show him the paper right away. I had a strange feeling and almost hesitated before opening my hand and releasing the folded white paper.

"What is it?" Areel asked me.

"Maybe nothing."

He took the paper from my hand and looked at the drawing for a moment and then at me. He bit his lower lip and brought one hand to his forehead. His eyes went to Sara and back to the piece of paper. He finally asked me, "Where did you find it?"

"It's an inscription on the blade of a bronze spear. It's dated shortly after the other artifacts we have been studying for *our* research."

"Where is it now?"

I gave a brief look at the calendar on the table, thinking idly that I should've hung it in the hallway already. "In one of the boxes being prepared for the Capitolini Museums in Rome."

"Did you find other inscriptions?"

"I didn't have time to go through the whole box."

"Is it part of the new exhibition the arch-guys were talking about?" Sara interrupted our seemingly private dialogue.

"Yes. There were at least other twenty boxes marked with the same museum seal, already locked and ready to go. The only one still open was the one with the bronze spear."

"Do you remember when the exhibit is going to open?"

"I think in October."

"We can't wait that long."

Sara had enough of half sentences. "You can't wait for what, exactly?" Her voice was tired, and I could feel it wasn't just her recent loss that made her look so worn out. Sara deserved the truth, and I fervently hoped Areel could muster some courage.

I missed so much having a best friend who knew everything about me, one in whom I could confide everything, even the things I wouldn't say to anybody else. I missed that Sara, and it was entirely my decision. She had never done anything to alienate me. When at the beginning I started to see Elios in my dreams, I thought that somehow I had built a substitute for Sara.

Meanwhile Areel and Sara were staring at each other.

"I repeat my question, what is it that you can't wait for?" Sara's voice was different now, suspicious.

I tried to save the situation by redirecting the focus of the conversation onto the question I wanted to ask from the beginning.

"Do you know this language? It isn't Etruscan or Greek. I can't recognize any of the symbols."

Areel unlocked his eyes from Sara's and slowly turned his head in my direction.

"I know this language; I can read it. Probably, I can even speak it."

"Is it—?" I didn't know how to phrase it before Sara, but Areel spoke before I could find the rest of the sentence.

"The language on the spear is ancient Solean. Those kinds of pictograms were used before the Dark happened."

I gasped at his statement, one hand covering my mouth. I felt relieved my hunch had been right but hadn't expected him to say it out loud like that.

Sara looked between Areel and me, trying to make sense of what she had just heard. "The two of you owe me a long explanation."

Areel glanced at me and then moved closer to Sara. "I must tell you something."

I got the message and retired to my room. I hoped Sara would believe Areel or at least try to listen with an open mind. He was putting himself in great danger for her.

I sat on my bed, weighing the implications of my last discovery and realized I still didn't know what the inscription said. The distant buzz of the cicadas coming through the open window lulled me. I rested my head on the pillow, closed my eyes, and imagined Elios in my room. I wanted to tell him all about the bronze spear and maybe even show him the piece of paper with my drawing, but I'd left it with Areel, and that wasn't a good time to go back and interrupt.

I closed my eyes for a second, just to relax my tired vision, and when I opened them, Elios was already there, smiling at me. The experience this time was almost surreal; it was like Elios was sitting on my bed. I could almost smell the salt on his skin. As usual, I called his name. I loved the sound of it and the way Elios reacted anytime he heard me calling him.

I told him about the new important discovery, and I went on with the plan to save him and the news about Areel and Sara. Once or twice, I even heard his comments, but mostly Elios smiled at me as if trying to decipher what I was saying. The communication was sporadic the whole time, but I heard his voice again, and that was the only important thing. We weren't supposed to be able to do what we were doing, so I didn't feel like complaining.

The experience ended abruptly as usual, but this time I was sure Elios had understood bits and pieces of what I had tried to say.

Life was perfect. I could only be full of hope for our future.

I went to sleep, silently praying for my two friends. I wished them luck in sorting out their situation.

16

Areel and Sara talked for the next two days, sleeping little and eating less.

I silently moved in and out of their sight, bringing water and food at regular intervals. I didn't go to the excavation camp, and I called to excuse the three of us with some kind of white lie. I stayed in the house, just to be sure they were okay. Mostly, I felt that Sara could use a friend nearby to protect her from snapping.

I was cleaning the dishes in the kitchen, trying to give them some time to rest in the sleepy hours of the afternoon. I went to close the curtain to cut out the bright light when I saw Sara stirring on the couch. She opened her eyes and gave me a sad look.

"I'm so sorry you had to go through all of *this* alone. I didn't know. I couldn't possibly imagine." Her voice was coming with some effort. Sara was trying her best not to cry.

"Oh, sweetie. I've already told you thousands of times, but I'm so glad you're my best friend."

"What happens to all of us now?" Sara looked so small and on the verge of breaking.

"I wish I knew."

"Areel told me about Elios. I'm sorry I judged him so harshly."

I nodded. "I couldn't tell you the whole story. I've been dying to tell you everything ever since."

She lowered her eyes. "You must miss him so much."

"I do, and it's painful. I can't bear to be separated from him. It's almost driven me insane, but I've managed to focus my pain on something useful."

"I want to help you in *this*."

I patted her hand. "You already have. I rely so much on your strength."

"We are both doomed, then." Her smile was finally back, and her happiness woke Areel, who was sleeping on the love seat. He looked at Sara as if she was water in the desert.

I left the apartment for some unnecessary errand. I went swimming, and on the way back home, I bought some freshly baked bread, olives, and prosciutto, just to justify my absence. Not that they would notice.

When I came back, they had already put something on the table. Sara and Areel looked more relaxed, and I was happy to see she hadn't run away. She was taking it better than I expected. I still didn't know what kind of consequences Areel's actions were going to bring on all of us, but for now, I wanted to enjoy the relative calm. Happiness is such a capricious feeling; it can suddenly mutate without warning into something less pleasant. You have to hold it close when you experience it. Savor every second of it because it doesn't normally last.

They looked like a normal couple, talking softly, laughing at each other's little jokes, smiling incessantly.

I had a long cold shower to remove all the sand and salt from my body, and then I joined them in the kitchen. I accepted a fresh coconut juice and finally remembered to ask Areel my million-Euro question, "Before we forget how everything started," I smiled smugly at the two of them positively beaming as if they were radioactive, "would you be so kind as to reveal what the inscription says?"

"I bring you peace."

"Pardon me?"

"*I bring you peace*. It's what the bronze spear says on its blade."

"That is… creepy." Sara shrugged.

I felt cold myself. "It sounds hopeless."

"Yes, it's sad. It's also the fruit of a society that had lost hope. Probably, it was exactly how my ancestors felt."

"I don't understand. How does a Solean artifact end up inside an Etruscan tomb?" Sara brought us back to more practical considerations.

"That is a theory I was already working on when Gaia showed me some pictures, but I didn't want to say anything without having proof. I believe that maybe we can explain why the Etruscans had so little in common with other pre-Roman populations living in the same area."

"Are you saying the Etruscans weren't human?" Sara asked.

I stared at Areel in disbelief.

He raised his arms. "I know, I know. This is why I have kept my mouth shut until now."

Then something hit me that invalidated Areel's theory. "No, it can't be. The chronology is completely wrong. Your ancestors from the Dark period must have lived thousands, maybe millions of years before the Etruscan civilization on Earth. Elios was already here at the time; he would've noticed a colony of his own kind living on the same planet. There must be another explanation for the language on the spear."

"She's right." Sara looked at me and then at Areel.

"I already thought about that." Areel paused for a moment and then added, "I can't explain the temporal gap yet. But regarding Elios's presence on Earth at the time, I do have an explanation for how he could have missed other Soleans. When we observe life on a planet, we move from one place to the other collecting data, but we can't be everywhere at any time. We have physical limitations. We normally tend to study larger conglomerations of life, societies like the Greeks and the Romans, for example. The big civilizations give us more data, and although the Etruscan society was important, it wasn't big compared to others. At the time, Elios could've been in Egypt, for all we know."

I shook my head. "Let's assume that Elios skipped the Etruscans altogether." Among other reasons, I would've loved to have had Elios around to ask him that question. I almost smiled at that thought. "The chronology by itself is enough to invalidate your theory." Areel was still looking for explanations that could fit in his picture, but I needed solid facts. "The Etruscans were never a Solean colony."

"I know I'm onto something." Areel steepled his hands and then brought them to his mouth. "I'll prove it."

I was going to reply when Sara, seemingly following her own thoughts, nodded and said, "Point is, we don't have the right knowledge."

"What do you mean?" I wasn't following either of them.

"I mean that maybe our human minds can't solve this piece of the puzzle."

"That could be true." I looked at Areel.

He smiled apologetically. "Sorry, but my Solean mind doesn't understand it better than yours."

"The missing piece is still hidden in your past. We need something else to put everything together." I was thinking about what Elios had told me about his society. Maybe we could try to look into it and see if Areel had really detected some sort of pattern. "We should compare all the similarities we can find between the Etruscans and what you know about the Soleans before the Dark."

"I can write down everything I remember about the Solean society pre-Dark, but it's not a lot, I'm afraid. And I'm not good at drawing. I'll try my best to describe the artifacts I saw."

I started to say we couldn't ask for more when Sara stopped me.

"Why can't you show us anything? I understood you can share memories."

I watched as Sara's question hit Areel like a blow. Clearly, they needed some more time to talk. Areel had yet to explain what their relationship was going to be.

"I'm able to show you everything about my culture, but I can't do it. I am not allowed. I thought you understood that." Areel looked at Sara with pleading eyes.

The atmosphere abruptly became chillier, and I decided I was the proverbial third wheel. It was time for me to go see Elios.

In my room, I changed into something nicer, put on some makeup, and combed my hair. I looked at myself in the mirror in the new outfit I had bought to complement my tan and my sun-highlighted hair. It was just a tank top and a little miniskirt, but I was happy with my look. It had been so long since the last time I consciously made any effort to look nicer for somebody. It felt good. I had waited all day, anticipating what I was going to wear, what I was going to say, what Elios would think about the way I looked.

I was going back to the chest of drawers to try something else, maybe a sexier little dress, when Elios appeared on my bed without any warning. Each time seemed easier. Even though the process was still trial and error, we managed to at least initiate communication with almost no effort lately.

"Elios."

He smiled. "Gaia."

I made a pirouette to show him all my efforts, and he threw a kiss with his hand. Our date went as usual; I blathered incessantly about the news, looked at him, and tried to concentrate on his words. As usual, I understood a few things and missed the rest. With each date, Elios looked more serene; his face was smooth, and apparently he was content with our visitation arrangements.

It looked like Elios was doing a great job rehabilitating his body and his spirit. I could see he was building up muscles again, and he had gained some weight. His eyes had gotten back that spark I loved so much. The dark lines under his eyes were almost gone, and the skin on his face wasn't stretched on his cheekbones anymore.

Elios scowled at me lightly when I explained again about the plan involving Areel's help, but then he stopped and smiled sweetly. This time, I had time to say I loved him before he disappeared.

While I was half asleep, I thought I heard someone sobbing. Then a door opened and closed softly, but that was enough to wake me up completely. I walked through the dark apartment until I found Sara rocking herself on the floor of the living room, illuminated by a silvery moon. I sat down by her and hugged her sobbing body.

"Shush, it's okay. Don't worry. Everything's going to be fine. You are not alone. I'll always be with you if you need me."

Despite all my efforts, Sara trembled more than before, her eyes unfocused. She didn't seem to listen. I left her to go to the kitchen and prepare some chamomile tea to calm her nerves and mine. To save time, I microwaved the water. The warm tea reanimated her somehow, and I was able to make her focus on my words.

"Listen to me. Everything seems worse than it is." I brought my free hand to my heart. "I know we'll find a way."

"How can you say that?" Sara's voice was cold.

"Because I can't afford the luxury of thinking otherwise."

"I thought I understood before. But now…" Her eyes watered again. "I don't know anymore." She put her cup down, her fingers circling its rim. "How can you accept it?" Sara's eyes were now focused on a pale shadow on the marble floor, her voice breaking.

I wasn't sure about what part she meant though I had a hunch.

"I don't have a choice, do I?"

"I don't know if I can bear it."

"I love him."

"I believe you." She finally looked back at me. "Don't you desire anything else? Something more from him? Something more from this situation you accept so easily?"

I knew she wasn't really asking about me. "I'm human. Of course I want more." Then, all of a sudden, I felt the urge to laugh. "Not only can't we touch, but at the moment we're also separated by the whole universe."

"I'm not as strong as you are."

Sara's face was painful to see. Her recent mourning and now this were taking a toll on her beauty.

"Sara, it isn't easy."

"But you seem to go along with… *this*."

"Abstinence?" I sobered up. "Honestly, we didn't have enough time together to realize how difficult it was going to be." With a sigh, I patted her hand still playing with the cup.

"But don't you desire Elios? Don't you ever think about what you can't have?" Again, it didn't seem Sara was really talking about Elios and me.

"Oh, I want him. I can only think of how our first time together would be. Night and day, I can't think of anything else but him. I can describe to you how many freckles Elios has on his face, the exact shade of his blond hair, the way it curls around his forehead sometimes, and how he tussles with an unruly curl every now and then. By heart, I can draw his long, elegant hands, the way the veins show under his skin, how Elios relaxes his fingers when he's talking to me. I can describe his eyes, lapis lazuli and gold in a sea of brightness. I can keep going for hours and still not be done. This is how much I want him. I would give anything for just a kiss." I stopped because I felt drained. My cup was empty and my lips parched.

"I'm sorry. I didn't mean to upset you."

"It's okay. I just need a second."

I went to the kitchen and opted for another chamomile tea. My heart was beating so fast, I needed to calm down. With my back to the door, I heard her steps coming closer. She hugged me and lowered her head on my shoulder.

"I'm sorry," she repeated in a whisper.

I gently pried her arms away to free myself from her embrace and turned to face her. "Do you love him?"

Her face colored slightly, and she nodded. "I feel... strongly about him. But is it enough?"

I shrugged. "Only you know the answer."

She hugged herself. "I told him to come back tomorrow. I didn't want him to see me like this. I'm not sure of what I want." She laughed, and she sounded a lot like me a few minutes earlier. "I'm not even sure I believe all of it."

Once she stopped laughing, she looked at me with an uncertain expression. I knew she wanted to be reassured it had been just a weird dream.

"Everything he said to you is true. You were ready to accept the whole story until the last part was added to complete the picture. But it's still true."

"It isn't just the abstinence. It's something more than that. It's unnatural for a... human to withhold touch."

We had already discussed it when I was trying to explain that Elios was some sort of monk. It was a known fact that kids raised without being touched could experience delays in their mental development.

"It horrifies me to think we'll never be able to be intimate," she finished.

"Do you prefer not having him at all in your life?"

I saw her eyes widen the moment she had the answer to my question. It would've been better for her if the idea of losing Areel hadn't pained her enough to make her cry. She slowly sagged onto the kitchen floor, and I followed her. After several minutes of silence interrupted only by her soft sobs, Sara finally raised her face from her knees, her hands clumsily drying her eyes.

When she reached for my hand and squeezed it gently, I couldn't help but whisper, "I'm so sorry. I wish I could do something." She smiled sadly at me. I caressed her hair, and we hugged without saying another word. The morning sun found us still on the kitchen floor. We started the day without adding a single word to the conversation.

When we arrived at the camp—as fate would have it, Sara had been asked to help at Marina Velca for a few days—we found Areel already working with the archeologists. He looked tired and silently glided between the others like a ghost.

Sara and I worked inside the Ark, cleaning the pieces just discovered. She had begged me to find something to do that didn't involve crossing paths with Areel. I decided the day was too hot to stay outside. Once or twice, they inevitably met, but Sara avoided him politely and both kept minding their assignments. I felt sorry for them. I hoped that Sara could busy herself with hard work and free her mind for a few hours.

Unfortunately for my friend, there wasn't a lot to do once we finished cleaning the few pottery pieces recently uncovered. The highlight of the day was actually when I was asked to move the boxes for the exhibit toward the entry of the tent. I asked Sara to help me with the task. The boxes were heavy, and it took all our strength to haul them from one corner of the room to the other.

"When are they going to be shipped?" I asked Danilo, who was escaping the outside heat and had decided to linger and help us.

"Tomorrow morning. The curator has called at least five times just today. As if we don't know how to handle artifacts. He has been pestering the archeology team with all sorts of requests. We had to catalogue every piece twice just to make him happy. I can't wait for all of these boxes to be gone so I can start working on my assignment again." Danilo grabbed one of the heavier boxes, took it to the corner with the others, and then came back to check on the smaller box I was holding. "It doesn't have the proper seal."

"What seal?"

"The curator asked for the museum's seal. It has this little fleur-de-lis engrained. Come, I'll show you."

I followed him to the corner.

"This one." Danilo pointed at the box he had just moved. "You must use this tape with the printed fleur-de-lis." He showed me the tape sealing the box and then the roll on the windowsill. "So that nobody can tamper with the boxes. As if!"

Actually, the idea of opening one or two boxes had crossed my mind. I had high hopes to find something else as interesting as the bronze spear. Not anymore, thanks to the curator. And Danilo only left long after he had double-sealed the last box.

At the end of the day, I was slightly disappointed that such an opportunity had been wasted by the curator's zeal and Danilo's sudden dislike for getting tanner. Since I was tired from the night before, I decided to go back to the apartment a few minutes earlier. Sara followed me to the car. She didn't have the strength to propose anything different. I saw Areel waiting for us in the parking lot before Sara did. She was strangely interested in the intricacy of the ground, but soon enough his presence was too dark and looming to be ignored. He was sitting on the wooden fence and looked younger with his shoulders down and his face hidden by his hair. I glanced at Sara to see her reaction, and the look in her face revealed her longing. Sara's eyes were so focused on Areel's face, she looked like a statue.

We were already at the car, and Areel hadn't moved an inch from his position when he finally decided to speak.

"Sara, I need to talk to you." Areel's voice was low and strained.

"I'm going to the beach for a swim." I was already on my way out of the parking lot. The idea of lying on the warm sand for a while was suddenly appealing.

Sara followed me and grabbed my arm by the elbow. "Gaia?"

I looked at her and then at Areel expectantly waiting for her decision. "Just be honest with him." I resumed my exit before she could run away. Sara had to decide by herself.

I reached the beach and stripped to the bikini I wore under my pants. I stuffed my clothes in my little backpack and then took my pink Zune from a pocket—the little souvenir, already out of production, that I'd brought back from Seattle—and went walking in the shallow water. Contrary to what I'd thought, I felt too edgy to lie on the sand and relax. I needed to let out some steam.

I walked for hours, listening to my favorite playlist without noticing time. I realized how late it was only when the darkness of the incipient night surprised me far away from where I'd started. I turned around and tried to hurry to the camp. I started running. Before I was halfway there and already breathing as if I had smoked my lungs away, I saw Sara and Areel running toward me, waving their hands.

At first, I was happy to see them together, but when I got closer and could see their faces, I saw something was wrong.

"You are okay." Sara hugged me tight.

"Of course I am." What time was it? I had no idea.

"We couldn't find you, and we thought that you were still at the camp, that maybe you had gone back to work instead of going to the beach while you were waiting for us, and then you were missing—"

"I was walking…"

I saw people who worked at the camp looking at me with relieved expressions, and then I saw several police cars in the parking lot. Someone said something to me along the lines of being happy that I was fine, and I smiled tentatively.

"What's going on?" I asked Sara, but she was answering someone else. I heard Areel reassuring the superintendent they had found me already.

"Someone got hurt in the artifacts tent, we couldn't find you anywhere at the beach, and we got worried sick," Sara finally answered me.

"Someone got hurt?"

"There is blood on one of the tables, and several boxes are missing."

"Someone entered the camp and stole some boxes from the tent? The exhibit's boxes?" I was incredulous; who would do anything like that? The treasure diggers had already stolen anything of importance before the archeologists had started excavating.

Whatever was going to the museum was only a small percentage of what the tombs had originally contained.

"There was almost nobody left working. Only a few archeologists were outside digging, and only Areel and I were here in the parking lot. We heard muffled noises coming from the artifact tent, and then someone screamed and we saw a flashlight beam. When we arrived, nobody was inside, just a few things out of place and the blood on the table."

Sara was still staring at me as if to make sure the blood on the table wasn't indeed mine.

"Is anybody missing?" the police officer asked Areel.

"We were the last ones in the parking lot. Our friend here was on the beach. Only four other archeologists were working outside, and they all came running when they heard the scream from the tent." Areel kept glancing over the officer's shoulders in Sara's direction.

She walked closer to him, and I followed her. I was presented to the officer and assured him I was fine.

"Did you see anybody else at the beach?" the man asked me.

I tried to remember, but I hadn't seen anybody else from the camp. "I was the only one out there." Then I amended, "Aside from one or two families with little kids."

"Thanks, that's all for now. Please stay in the city in case we have other questions." The police officer left to question the other guys.

"Sure, no problem," Areel answered for all of us.

"We can go now. Police are investigating, and they won't let anybody inside the tent anyway." Sara was clearly uncomfortable.

"Are you okay?" I squeezed her cold hand.

"I can't stop seeing the blood. When we didn't find you at the beach—" She hugged me with all her strength and left me breathless.

"I'm okay. I'm here. Just lost track of time; you know me. I like walking, and I was listening to my music." I tried my best to lighten the situation, without succeeding.

"Girls, let's go. I'm going to follow you home with my car."

Sara went to the passenger door of her car and threw me the keys without saying a single word. I drove back to Tarquinia with Sara anxiously checking that Areel was behind us. We ate something at the pizzeria close to the museum, and then we went back to the apartment. Areel escorted us to the main entrance downstairs and waited for us to be safely inside the hall.

Sara turned around to look at Areel, and her eyes were shining with fresh tears. "Stay. I want you with me."

Areel's eyes widened at her request. "Are you sure?"

"Yes, I'm sure." Sara was crying openly now and didn't care to stop.

"Thanks." He hovered close to her, and the air shimmered with a faint rainbow.

I heard her gasp and felt I was intruding once again. The perfume of cut freesias reached my nostrils, and I vanished inside the elevator.

Hours later, we went to sit outside on the terrace, the pale moon illuminating us—we didn't bother lighting the candles—and the topic of the burglary finally came up again.

"Who knows whose blood it is?" Sara didn't seem to be able to get rid of the image.

"Maybe the thief injured himself?" I asked.

"I'm curious to know what was stolen." Areel had been deep in his thoughts for the last ten minutes.

Sara's cell phone rang at that precise moment and made us jump. She talked for a few minutes and then looked at us with a curious expression.

"Who was it?" I asked her.

"It was Danilo." Sara looked at Areel, who made a face at the name.

"What does he want?" he asked.

"He said we don't have to go to the camp for the next two weeks because the police have closed it for the investigation. Only the people from the Capitolini Museum are allowed in because they can help with the search."

"Why them?" Areel asked.

I felt a shiver running down my spine. I already knew what Sara was going to say.

"Because only the boxes with the Capitolini Museum seal got stolen, nothing else."

17

We spent the rest of the night speculating about who could have been interested in stealing catalogued material with almost no commercial value. I still felt my skin tingling; the whole thing made no sense. The first rays of morning light illuminated the terrace, and one solitary rooster announced the day. I suddenly realized how exhausted I was, both mentally and physically.

Sara rose from her patio chair, covered in night dew. She couldn't help a loud yawn. "Let's get some rest."

I followed her into the house and helped prepare the guest room for Areel. One look at her, hugging the pillow before carefully placing it on the bed, made me ask, "Are you sure this is a good idea?"

"I want him close." She sat on the edge of the bed. "Sleeping in another room but under the same roof is the closest we can get, at night at least."

I personally thought it was a recipe for disaster but kept that to myself. Then again, for me it was simple. I was in no danger of touching Elios. I could understand why Sara wanted Areel close; she was starving, and his proximity was the only fare available. It was either that, meager meal as it was, or sentimental anorexia. I honestly didn't know how they were going to sleep at night, but love can overcome any obstacle. I knew that first hand.

Probably too keyed up to go to sleep, Sara and Areel headed out to the terrace again, and I retired to my room. I had just closed my eyes when someone timidly knocked on my door.

"Yes?"

"We were wondering if you could contact Elios and let me talk to him." Areel's voice was muffled.

I smiled at the ceiling. "Come in."

First Areel and then Sara entered the room. While he remained by the door, she walked to my bed and stood still, uncertain of what to do. "Are you sure you're okay with it? Because if you aren't—"

I stopped her and patted the bed for her to sit by me. "We should've tried this already." I gestured for Areel to sit on the desk chair. "Let the séance begin." We all laughed. It wasn't that funny, but we needed a good laugh.

Still feeling a little giddy, as if I had drunk a full bottle of Spumante, I tried to concentrate on Elios and forget I wasn't alone. It wasn't as simple as I thought. I couldn't open the channel. His image flickered before my eyes for a good three or four seconds, and then it disappeared. Sara gasped. A few minutes later, Elios's voice filled the eerie silence. He called my name, once. Then nothing. I called him for more than two hours without any results.

"I'm done." It was just frustrating, and I was beyond tired.

"Sure, sweetie." Sara squeezed my hand and then gestured for Areel to follow her outside.

"Maybe tomorrow?" Areel asked from across the room.

I nodded, my eyelids too heavy already. "Tomorrow."

I slept until the next day. I could probably have slept even longer if it weren't for the sun blinding my eyes. Nobody was in the apartment. Sara and Areel had left a note saying they were going to the beach and I should join them there and have lunch.

I liked the idea, but I needed a shower and some coffee first, so I went to the kitchen to prepare my fix. I put my Bialetti—the two-cup moka I personally brought from Rome, the same one that had accompanied me all the way to Seattle—on the stove and went to the bathroom for a quick shower.

Five minutes later, I was in the kitchen, in time for the coffee to emerge from my little moka. Cradling the small cup and breathing the caffeine fumes, I turned on the TV looking for the morning news. Here it was, on national television, our devastated camp full of people who didn't belong there. Reporters and police were going to destroy years of work just with their presence. I felt very protective of the place. I had been working for a while with the archeologists, and I knew how long it took to unearth even the smallest of artifacts.

"A thorough investigation is still in progress, but lab reports confirm the blood found at the crime scene doesn't belong to any of the people working at the site." The blond journalist, a petite woman in her mid-thirties, was smiling at the camera as if she had just recounted a soccer game's result. "Nobody seems to be missing."

Still, something bad had happened to someone.

On the screen, the image shifted from the TV studio to an elegant sitting room where an older gentleman sat primly behind an antique desk. The man appeared to have problems answering the blonde's questions. The camera zoomed in, and a caption appeared underneath the now half-length portrait revealing he was the curator responsible for the Etruscan exhibition at the Capitolini Museum. "We are shocked," he said.

I bet he was. He just got robbed of one of the most publicized exhibitions of the last two decades, probably second only to the Van Gogh exhibition for which people stood in line for hours and which lasted months. I hate lines and personally waited three months before I could even hope to enter without having to wait too long outside.

"There must be something about the stolen boxes that made them so valuable—"

The man made a visible effort not to insult the journalist's question. "The content of the boxes is being evaluated by the police as we speak."

Sipping the last drop of espresso, now cold, I thought that at least the Etruscan exhibition would get enough publicity to make it as successful as the Van Gogh one.

I was about to push the off button on the TV remote when the journalist made one last comment.

"Who on earth would want to commission such a heist?"

"I don't have an answer to that." The curator rested his hand on the desk and composed his face pleasantly. "It is true that the collection is literally priceless since it represents the entire content of the Hunters' House tomb. A team of world-renowned archeologists is going to recreate it in a special room inside the Capitolini Museum. But, despite its archeological value, it doesn't contain any jewelry. Normally, private collectors would pay a fortune even for a single earring, but in the Hunters' House tomb, there weren't any pieces of jewelry."

The woman didn't give the curator time to pause before she asked, "Can you tell us something more specific about your last statement?"

The curator raised an eyebrow and then schooled his face again in a display of professionalism. "The tomb was called the Hunters' House because it contains only hunting devices. That is the reason why the tomb wasn't looted and we found it almost in pristine condition. The tomb raiders left it alone because there wasn't a single ornament to be found. It truly is a man sanctuary."

"And spears and knives aren't good resalable items on the black market, are they?" The journalist chuckled.

I turned off the TV, grabbed my backpack, and went out to meet the Etruscan sun. As I was driving my scooter to the beach at a pleasurable speed, my cell phone rang. I slowed down to a full stop by a small copse of cypress trees and answered. "Sara?"

"No, it's Areel. We're starving. Meet us at the trattoria."

"Five minutes." I smiled. The trattoria by the beach had become our favorite spot. When I arrived, they were waiting for me, sitting outside on the veranda facing the blue sea. The glaring sun played tricks on my eyes, and their silhouettes appeared closer than they were. I knew it wasn't the case, but my heart still ached. Areel turned around and saw me.

"We've already ordered for you. Sautéed mussels." Sara smiled at me under a new straw hat.

I was happy to see she looked better already. "Thanks, I hate waiting." A pleasant salty breeze came from the beach and messed up my hair.

"Have you heard the news?" Areel showed me the newspaper he was reading.

The painful TV interview was still in my thoughts. "Yes, just the kind of publicity our camp needs."

"We went to check this morning, but we couldn't even reach the parking lot. Journalists, police, just plain curious bystanders… it's a circus out there. I lost count of the TV reporters. There're cameras everywhere. The arch-guys are frantic, and I really feel for them.

Fortunately, you copied that inscription before everything got stolen." Areel was looking at the seagulls playing with the waves.

I couldn't help but notice how Sara was looking at him as though she were memorizing his features. It felt familiar. I was suddenly interested in the fascinating life of the seagulls. I opened a bag of *grissini*. The thin bread sticks were a bad idea for my diet but made me look occupied rather than morose.

"Probably, the whole city of Tarquinia was there," Sara stated once she refocused on the here and now.

"This is such a quiet place. A robbery like this would stir the news anywhere—but here…" I paused when Gianluca, the young waiter we had befriended since becoming regular customers, brought our food and lingered instead of leaving. He gave us a knowing look, and I knew he was going to stay. I mentally prepared for the gossip.

"My brother, the policeman, is working at the camp, and he told me they don't know where to start. There're no fingerprints; nobody is missing in the area; the stolen boxes were quite heavy; they can't understand how whoever did it made the boxes disappear in such a short time. And there're also other things that don't make sense." Gianluca looked around. "But you can't repeat my words to anybody else. Okay?"

We hastily nodded while the waiter added a few things he had probably sworn not to tell anybody else as well.

"You've got to love small cities where there are no secrets meant to remain such," Sara whispered under her breath.

I couldn't help but smile. The owner, Mario, called Gianluca back, knowing how much his waiter loved to waste time talking to the regulars.

"We don't have time to gossip today." Mario playfully swatted the waiter with a rolled napkin. The usually grumpy restaurateur was in a good mood. "I need you to help me with the oven while I'm preparing more pizza dough."

I looked around and saw that the trattoria was at full capacity, every table taken. Someone was going to benefit from the nearby camp's invasion after all.

We ate al fresco, enjoying the view of the sea and the cool shadow under the veranda, and stayed for coffee and dessert. The owner's wife was a culinary genius, and Gianluca conspiratorially told us she had baked her famous ricotta and amaretti tart. We couldn't enter the camp and were in no hurry to go anywhere else. It was too sunny to stay at the beach, and our apartment didn't have air conditioning. We were lazily debating whether we wanted another coffee when four policemen sat at the table just behind ours. Gianluca went to greet them, soon revealing that one of the officers was the aforementioned brother.

The five of them, completely oblivious that we were sitting so close, started talking about the case. Even Mario, forgetting the restaurant was still full and he had to bake pizza, couldn't contain his curiosity and joined the party. They talked quietly but weren't whispering, and we shamelessly eavesdropped. At the beginning, it was a faithful repetition of Gianluca's words, but then the tale became interesting.

"It's amazing how the thieves didn't leave any trace behind." The older policeman sitting behind Areel dropped his voice on the last part.

A younger man, whom I couldn't see without turning around, said, "They left the place squeaky clean."

"Really?" Gianluca couldn't resist asking.

"No, I mean there aren't any prints whatsoever, not even the prints from the people who work there." The younger man sounded eager to talk.

We were itching to ask questions and were lucky enough that both Mario and Gianluca asked them for us.

"No prints at all? What do you mean?"

"Everybody is Sherlock Holmes in Tarquinia," Sara whispered, and I chuckled.

Gianluca's brother answered, "No prints of any kind. Like the tent had been sterilized with fire and then bleach, locked, and preserved at constant temperature."

The older man raised his voice in excitement. "No dust, no pollen. Nothing we can work with. I've never encountered a crime scene so clean before."

Gianluca seemed to think about something, and then his eyes lit up. "What about the smell—" His brother coughed, and Gianluca hurriedly added, "Everybody is talking about some strange smell by the camp. Some journalist was commenting about that in the news this morning. *"*

I thought Gianluca would pay for his indiscretion later and smiled at his attempt to minimize his blunder. But the other officers didn't seem to mind. Rumors were probably already out of their control.

The older policeman swirled his wine glass in small circles. "Oh yes, the smell is something special, isn't it?"

The fourth man, who had kept silent most of the time, joined the conversation. "We can't decide its origin. It doesn't come directly from the tent, and it started several hours later than the robbery, sweet and acrid, but not entirely unpleasant."

"To me, it smells like a flower essence gone bad, like a perfume that once was very expensive but was left out in the sun." The young man seemed to speak from experience.

"It's more likely the result of a combusted material," the older policeman said.

The fourth man shook his head. "I'm more for the cleaning product theory. It must be something they used to cover their tracks, and it must have reacted with the soil outside the tent when they spilled some of it."

The older policeman asked for a refill of his wine and then added, "We're waiting for the blood analysis to come back. It's going to tell us something. We hope."

"So far, we have found absolutely nothing..." the younger man commented between mouthfuls.

The fourth man intervened, "Oh, that isn't completely true. We do have something—"

The less loquacious one finally said, "And what good is that? We don't know what to do with it."

I was sitting on the edge of my chair, anxiously waiting for one of them to explain what they were talking about.

"Yep, and what about the burnt soil just half a mile south of the tent? Who knows what happened there?" Gianluca asked.

The four men started talking all together.

"We're still interrogating some of the guys working at the new tomb, just to exclude some innocent bonfire."

"No bonfire leaves that kind of color behind."

"Maybe they used some accelerating substance?"

"It's hot, even at night… no, I don't think so. If it were winter, yes, but not now."

"And that smell—it is different. Not a burnt smell for sure."

They probably could have talked all day long, but one of their cell phones rang.

"Yes… oh crap, no… we're coming immediately."

"Mario, we're coming back later."

"Not a problem. I'll reserve a table for you guys," the restaurant owner hurried to say.

"Thanks, Mario. See you later."

They left in a hurry, clearly annoyed and hungry. Before they left, one last piece of incomplete information reached our eager ears.

The older man whispered to the other three, "The results from the lab are back. You won't believe what they found."

Unfortunately for us, that was it. We had idled enough, and after paying our bill, we left. A few minutes later, we reached our spot at the beach. Everybody working at the camp was there. Nobody knew what to do with the unexpected free time. Nobody could leave the city until the police said so.

The archeologists were talking about the mysterious crime, but we didn't feel like joining the debate about the possible techniques used to haul the boxes away. I went swimming by myself while Sara and Areel joined a volleyball match. Swimming relaxed me, and I lost track of time. The water was cooler than I expected, which was pleasant. I closed my eyes and slowly backstroked while thinking of Elios. The sun cast a warm yellow light on my closed eyelids, and the waves rocked my body in a constant and hypnotic motion. Out there with nobody talking to me, I could almost imagine being with Elios. He could have been swimming with me, just a wave apart. "I miss you," I whispered to the sky.

"I missed you too," the sky answered back with Elios's voice.

I opened my eyes and stared at the fast-flowing clouds chasing each other. Disappointed that reality didn't match my hopes, I slowly swam back to join the land of the living. Back on the beach, the now-jobless research team was organizing an unauthorized expedition to the camp. Curiosity was strong, and they knew where to enter without being caught by the police. Rumors of some of the aspects of the investigation had leaked—no wondering how that could have happened—and forced inactivity was a bad advisor. Of course, Sara, Areel, and I were the first in line. After what we had just heard back at the trattoria, we couldn't miss the opportunity to play detective.

The rendezvous was at 2:00 a.m. We could go home, shower, have dinner, play board games if we wanted, and still have plenty of time to spare.

After dinner, Areel and I tried to communicate with Elios, but it didn't work at all. We had less luck than the night before.

Out of stubbornness and the desire to see Elios, as soon as Areel was out of the room, I tried to reach him alone. I only had to try twice before it worked. After greeting him, I asked Elios if he had any clues why it worked only when I was alone in the room. Unfortunately, the audio part of our communication was erratic as usual.

I noticed something different about Elios, and I gestured to him to spin around slowly so I could see him better. Elios was wearing his hair in a different way. He had tied his longer mane with a black ribbon and looked like a knight from another era. I smiled at him to let him know I loved his new look, and immediately regretted I hadn't changed into something nicer. Our date was cut short, and I was left alone with my ever-growing longing. After what seemed like centuries, Sara knocked at my door.

"Still coming to the break-and-enter party? Or are you too tired?"

I laughed. "I'm so keyed up, I should run a marathon to relax enough to sleep. No way I'd stay behind."

Half an hour later, we met with the rest of the "Indiana Joneses" at the beach.

"This way." One of the archeologists, a guy named Saverio who had already stated twice he worked closely with the Capitolini Museum curator, appointed himself leader. "Watch your steps. There're holes everywhere."

It turned out he was right, but fortunately for us, a full moon was out. We hiked through the sand dunes and soon reached the edge of the camp by following a hidden trail that ended up just outside one of the new tombs. We could see some of the policemen, but they couldn't see us hiding in the lower portion of one of the tombs.

That part of the camp didn't have any barrier, for the archeologists had just started working on it and they needed full access to excavate the entries to the inner chambers typical of the Etruscan tombs. It was quite fortunate for us because we could hide from the police without having to jump safety fences in the dark, possibly trashing them. I have to admit it was quite exhilarating. We acted as if we knew what we were doing, and from the easiness some of my respected colleagues showed, I had the impression that for some of them, it might've been true.

We reached the place where the mysterious bonfire had taken place, and everybody had time to take turns smelling.

"It reminds me of something, but not sure what," I whispered to Sara and Areel.

"I might have an idea of what this is." Areel brought a handful of dirt to his nose. "I need to go check something at the artifact tent."

Sara made to follow him, but he stopped her. "Stay here. I'll be back in a few minutes."

I saw him slowly reach the back of the artifact tent, a quarter of a mile north of us, the direction opposite to where we should've been heading back.

"What—?" Sara looked at me, and I shrugged in response.

I heard the nervous barks of German shepherds patrolling the camp. The dogs could smell us, and soon the police would start looking for the intruders.

"We'd better do as he asks." I was getting anxious.

Someone in our group fell with a loud thud, and the dogs went crazy, pulling their handlers with them in their quest to catch us.

Everybody scattered to the four corners. Sara and I ran toward the trail and the high dunes.

The dogs' barking reached a terrifying pitch, and their handlers were pointing flashlights everywhere. Without daring a full turn, I angled my face to take a look behind. Two German shepherds were already on us. I increased my speed until my legs were burning and my eyes watering. To my frantic mind, the dogs chasing us sounded like a stampede of wild buffalos. I swore I felt jaws opening and closing, barely missing the heel of my right sneaker. I almost tripped and fell. At the last moment, when I realized we weren't going to reach the safety of the high grass, I directed Sara toward a tomb that was just between the camp and the beach. The dark mound shone like a beacon under the moonlight. My heart was beating so quickly I couldn't breathe. I froze at the tomb's threshold. Sara yanked me unceremoniously inside, and we both fell on the ground.

"We're inside a tomb." It wasn't right. My butt was already getting wet from sitting on the cold, damp ground.

Sara raised one hand and started enumerating, "Outside, two dogs, the police, and a sure night in jail. Where would you rather be?"

I could hear the dogs coming closer. "Here." I scooted toward the chamber's entry and craned my neck to get a glimpse of what was happening outside. I saw the flashlights illuminating our footprints in the sand. "Definitely here." We were doomed. My eyes got used to the darkness inside, but I wished they hadn't. "I hate this gloomy luminescence." The chamber was faintly illuminated by glowworms.

"It's romantic."

I raised one eyebrow, but I didn't have time to accompany the gesture with words. The dogs were outside the antechamber. I readied myself for the inevitable. My mind was already working on the explanations I would have to invent for my parents, once they arrived at the police station to retrieve me.

A shadow slid through the inner chamber, and I almost cried out loud. One hand covered my mouth before I could, and then I saw Sara looking at me with reassuring eyes. She released my mouth and then touched my arm to direct my attention to the darkest corner. Then, I finally saw him and exhaled in relief. Areel was there with us when a second before, we had been completely alone. He put a finger on his mouth, and I stood still, hoping for a miracle. I could see Areel focusing on the dogs, and I felt a puff of air moving the sand outside the tomb. The dogs sniffed the air and then abruptly changed direction. The policemen followed them while shouting for their colleagues, "There! They're running over there."

We heard the voices and the barking and saw the flashlights moving away from us. Areel made us wait for a full minute and then escorted us outside in complete silence.

My legs wouldn't stop shaking. Somehow, I reached the first dune and dug my way under the tall grass framing the entry of the trail to the beach. I rolled down onto the sand and had to wait a few minutes before my heart would stop racing. Once I reached Sara and Areel down the hill, where they were waiting for me, we moved quietly through the shadows of the dunes. The moonlight now seemed too bright. After several minutes, we reached the spot where we had left the car. Areel parked outside our apartment almost an hour later after driving along uncharted dirt roads for fear of somebody seeing us near the camp and after almost running into a ditch.

Once safely back at our place, I went straight to my room and collapsed on the bed. My legs were still trembling, and my lungs didn't seem to be able to work on their own. My eyes fixed on the lamp hanging from the ceiling, and several thoughts passed through my mind. *What was I thinking? How could I be so stupid? Imagine calling Dad from the police station... I've never, ever, done anything so stupid. Again, what was I thinking?*

Without knocking, Sara entered my room with a cup of chamomile. She looked strangely composed. Right behind her was her shadow, Areel.

As expected from him, he never touched her but never left her side. I idly considered how they managed to keep a constant distance. How could Sara manage that? They looked like two orbiting bodies, never colliding, never escaping each other. It was a morose thought. I knew I wasn't really thinking of them. Elios and

I had been the orbiting planet and its brilliant, handsome star. We were Gaia and Elios, Earth and Sun. How could we be apart?

Sara touched my arm. "Drink some."

I thanked her, gingerly took the cup, and cradled it without drinking from it. Areel remained at the door, uncertain of how to proceed. "You may enter." I finally sipped from the cup. Sara had slipped more than the usual one teaspoon of sugar into the chamomile tea.

She smiled when she saw my expression. "I thought you needed it."

In a déjà vu repetition of the scene that had happened only two nights ago, she sat on my bed and Areel on the chair. I played with the warm ceramic cup, caressing its smooth texture, drawing circles and lines. I had nothing to say; my close encounter with the police had left me speechless. My thoughts went far away. I missed Elios.

"Gaia, Areel has something to say—but you seem upset. We can talk tomorrow." Sara stood, and I realized I had kept my mental monologue going for a while without noticing anything else.

I gestured for her to stay and made an effort to look attentive. "I'm all ears." I turned my head to include Areel, without seeing anything at all.

He waved a hand before my eyes. "I need you to focus. It's important. Please?"

The cold humidity of the tomb was still lingering inside of me, and I shivered.

"Gaia?" Sara's face replaced Areel's hand.

"Okay." *It must be important.* That much I could grasp. I turned to look at Areel.

He waited a moment before talking. "They aren't going to find the thieves."

"Why?"

"Because there was no bonfire."

"What it was, then?" I felt suddenly awake.

"A lightweight shuttle." Areel waited for me to object to his statement.

"It can't be, can it?" I shook my head in disbelief.

He nodded. "It landed there, and then it took off."

"Are you sure?"

"Yes, I'm sure." He gave me a sad smile. "It's a small, stealthy vehicle, normally used when you don't want to be seen. It's fast and silent, it has a mirrored surface, and it leaves almost no residue to be detected. The only smell the engines produce is during landing and taking off, and they can be easily confused with something else—"

"But I did smell something out there."

He raised one hand to request permission to keep talking. "What I think happened is that the hot temperature of the summer night and the high concentration of iron in the soil created that faint burned scent everybody smelled."

"What else?" I wanted him to say it.

"It's not terrestrial technology."

Sara scooted closer to me, and I leaned against her. Then I remembered something. "Are you sure? For all we know, the whole thing could be a classified project. Both Army and Navy have headquarters nearby."

Areel shook his head. "Yes, I'm aware of that—"

"Then we can't just assume—"

Sara softly squeezed my arm. "Let him finish."

"Sorry, go ahead."

Areel tilted his head slightly toward the opened window. "I landed on Earth with one of them."

"Of course." I felt tired.

"Are you okay?" Sara made me turn around to face her.

"I am. Excuse my mood."

Sara smiled and let me go. "It's okay. The three of us went through a lot lately."

I couldn't help but ask him one more time. "Are you sure?"

Areel's eyes went to the window once again and lingered longer, his focus somewhere beyond the nocturnal sky. "I recognize the technology behind it."

"So it's a Solean shuttle."

He turned back to us, opened his mouth, paused, and then shook his head. "Not necessarily. We aren't the only ones with that kind of technology."

"But—" I was nervous because he sounded nervous.

"I already checked with my superiors, in case you are wondering about Solean involvement, and they don't know anything about this. Of course we're in contact with other planets, and we normally exchange information... but we're the only ones interested in the Etruscan artifacts."

"Well, if the Soleans weren't involved, someone else *is* interested." I was wide awake now. "I need some fresh air."

"Let's go to the terrace." Sara pulled me up.

"First, I'm thirsty. Water, soda, coffee, food, anybody?" Two heads bobbed in unison. While they headed out, I went to the kitchen, opened the fridge, ransacked it, and then filled the moka and turned on the stove. When the coffee was ready, I fetched a tray to transport drinks and comfort food and went to join them on the terrace.

Outside, the big umbrella offered shelter from the humidity, and the scent from the citronella candles helped us relax. The night was still warm. I felt strangely rested, and my mind jumpstarted.

"Can you think of anybody who could be interested in Solean ancient history?" I asked Areel after I drank my espresso. I opened a can of orange soda next.

"Other than my people? Nobody." He shrugged and sat on the small bench jutting from the wall. Sara followed him but kept the usual safe distance.

For a while, we remained silent. I was lost in my train of thought regarding Elios. They looked lost in each other.

"I think we're onto something with the inscription on the spear," I finally said. Sara and Areel looked back at me. "Did you talk to your superiors about it?" I asked Areel.

Again, he looked strangely reluctant to talk. "Yes, I did."

"And what do they think?"

"They think so too." Areel exchanged glances with Sara, who smiled back, urging him to continue.

"It's the first time we have enough evidence to form a plausible theory. Thanks to what has been discovered here on Earth, by Elios first and then you, my superiors have nominated a commission to study the Solean artifacts with a different eye."

Maybe it was the caffeine, the sugar from the sodas, or just the high from escaping the police, but several thoughts connected like the pieces of a puzzle. "That's it." Finally the idea that had been nagging at the back of my mind since we had come back to the apartment took proper form. "The stolen boxes contain clues about what happened to your planet. Once the Etruscan exhibit was open to the public, you would've known for sure and consequently reported. I bet the missing link we're looking for is inside one of the boxes."

"It does sound… plausible." Sara walked to the table to see if any coffee was left in the moka.

I had drunk the last cold cup a few minutes ago. "Your kind has lived eons without knowing anything about your lost past. Doesn't it seem strange to you?"

Areel shrugged. "We have good reasons to keep the past in the past."

"Or maybe someone is trying to keep it that way." Sara settled for what I had left of the orange soda.

I felt a strange euphoria possessing me. "Finding the bronze spear must've triggered an alarm and forced them—whoever they are—into the open. It can't be a coincidence that it happened just after I found it." A chill went down my spine. The police catching us seemed almost trivial in comparison. Someone was out there, knowing about us, interested in keeping us in the dark. "Why would anybody want to erase your history? Can you think of any reason?"

Areel's eyes widened as if I had just committed blasphemy. "None. Our history was wiped out by a natural catastrophe."

"But what if there is something else?"

"Like what?" Sara asked.

"Like, I don't know, a reason why Solean people shouldn't know what happened to them." Thoughts were crowding my mind, and coherently expressing them wasn't easy.

"It would make sense only if the Dark on Solo was deliberately caused." Areel made a face indicating how improbable the mere idea was.

I opened another soda can and gulped two long sips of sugar and bubbles. "But what if?"

"If what almost annihilated the Solean culture wasn't a natural catastrophe—" Areel's voice got low, and then he looked first at Sara and then at me. "If someone did this to us, it would be..."

"You are talking about—" Sara couldn't say it either.

"Genocide," I said, and everything clicked into place.

Areel turned around to stare at the clouds illuminated by the first lights of the morning. A freezing breeze extinguished the flames of the candles spread both on the table and on the terrace floor. Only when the empty soda cans started dancing around, hitting the coffee cups and the moka, did Areel seem to hear the eerie noise, and the blizzard subsided.

When he finally turned, I saw his face and felt even colder than before. "I'm sorry," I said to him.

"Areel—" Sara reached out for him, the instinct of giving comfort by touch so ingrained in our human brain. She stopped at the last moment, but he didn't realize what had almost happened. Areel was lost in his thoughts, far away from us.

Suddenly, something made him shiver from head to toe. I felt something too, like electricity in the air, and for a moment, the lights inside the apartment dimmed.

"What is it?" Sara was looking at the kitchen.

Areel covered his mouth with one hand and ran inside. I saw him heading toward the bathroom. Sara ran after him. I followed her to the bathroom. I saw them. I screamed in anguish, and then my thoughts went to Elios. "I love you…"

Everything went black.

18

I woke in a shadowy place, with no idea of where I was or what time it was. I tried to sit on the hard surface I was lying on, but I couldn't move. I realized I was strapped down to a cot and started panicking. My heartbeat became erratic, and my lungs seemed to have problems gathering oxygen. I opened my mouth to scream, but no sound escaped my lips. I felt something moving my right arm. A prick. Nothingness.

Then I woke. Again. And again. And again. A never-ending loop of variations of the same experience. The most terrifying thing was the knowledge it wasn't a nightmare. Once, I felt something, maybe cold fingers, touching my forehead. I tried to keep my eyes open, but I was too tired. I don't know how long I was out. When I regained consciousness, I slowly compelled myself to remember a detail. Anything that could anchor me to the now: the temperature in the room; how dark it was; where the cold fingers had touched my body; anything my mind could manage to retain for the next time I would wake up. I was trying to find a way to determine time and location. I had to keep my mind occupied. I felt hopeless.

Time passed.

Slowly, I noticed my mind was able to remember bits and pieces of the previous time I was awake. Nothing more. Despair still permeated my thoughts.

More time passed.

I'm naked, lying on a hard surface. My first coherent thought. It scared me beyond comprehension. My mind slipped to a safer place. I opened my eyes. It was bright. Something, someone was touching me, on my arms, on my legs, on my chest. When the prickle came, it felt familiar, and I welcomed the soporific effect of the cold liquid spreading through my body.

Next time I opened my eyes, it was night. A silvery light was at my right side, but I knew it wasn't the moon. I still was too tired to think for long periods of time. And I was cold. Nothing, no blanket, no sheet, was covering my shivering skin. A steady stream of cold air hit me, and I tried to curl into a tight ball, but I couldn't. I wished for the bright light to radiate some warmth on me.

I slept.

An incandescent light exploded beyond my closed eyelids and forced me awake. I stared at a white wall in front of me. A humming sound pervaded the room, louder on my right side. I tried to turn my head slightly to the right to see if I could identify what was causing the sound. In the corner of my eye I saw… a white hose. Or maybe it was something else. I couldn't be sure.

Abruptly, one single memory surfaced.

I am Gaia. My name is Gaia.

My name is important.

My name means something else too.

My name is gaiagaiagaia.

Gaia is the name of something else other than me.

It was difficult to think. My head was in terrible pain. The white of the wall was too bright and offended my eyes. I closed them and tried to remember, but the pain was excruciating. It was like trying to jump through fire.

My mind brought forth an image of flames eating at my body. The next thought was about calming waters. The room was first tinted in blue and after that, in green. I felt suddenly better. My head was lighter, and the colors dancing before my eyes reminded me of something I couldn't quite place. Then I saw it. A blue and green globe suspended in the dark blue sky, white surrounding some of it.

Earth?

My name is Gaia. Mother Earth.

To exist I need something. Someone.

Life on Earth can't survive without it.

My life has no meaning without him.

A yellow-orange light caressed only part of my upper body; where it touched me, it felt warm and pleasant and friendly.

Light. Warm. Life. Sun.

Sun…

Elios?

Elios, Elios, Elios. Gaia's sun. My sun.

Suddenly, a flood of memories invaded me, and with them came a question. *Where am I?* My mind exploded with a headache. Thinking of Elios was pleasant though, and I stirred my mind toward memories that included him. At first, I had just the idea of him, an abstract picture of something beautiful, without knowing what made it so. Then details started to fill that picture, some colors here and there and then lips, eyes, freckled skin. My heart dove into the memories, looking for him in every corner of my mangled mind. Images formed.

Elios was in Athens, his lapis lazuli eyes staring at me from a car.

Elios was in a room with me, but I was with someone else.

Elios was part of the view from Queen Anne.

Elios was sitting outside a little coffee shop in Alki beach, the sun kissing his skin, creating black and white shadows.

Elios was sunbathing on golden sand.

Elios was showing me his hair.

Thinking of him was pleasant; it didn't cause me pain. I was tired, my eyelids heavy and swollen, my face wet. The bright light was turned off, and I was in the darkness once more.

Sounds woke me, and I knew I wasn't alone. My heart beat faster in fear. I kept my eyes shut and waited. Someone was busy around my body, touching me, moving things. I could hear the never-ending humming and then steps. The probing continued. There was no comfort in the contact as they were examining me. I needed to be hugged, caressed, comforted, loved, and kissed. Elios… I needed him. Peaceful blackness embraced me.

The next time I was awake, I knew I wasn't in the same place. Everything smelled too clean, sterilized. I couldn't keep my eyes open because the white light was too bright. Even with my eyes closed, the vividness was piercing my skull.

I screamed loudly, and this time my voice was there, hoarse and hysterical. I kept screaming until I passed out. Then I was in the dark, a pitch black, moonless night. I was left in that hopeless darkness for a long while. I thought of Elios. He was my beacon of light.

Time passed.

Nobody came back to check on me. After a while, the sense of being safer than before slowly took root in my heart. I spent all my time trying to remember. More. I needed to put together all the bits and pieces of the scattered images floating through my mind. Finally, I remembered other people. Two in particular. A couple.

A young man, dark-skinned, almond-shaped eyes.

A young woman, fair skin and red-golden hair, beautiful smile.

Friends.

My friends.

Sara and Areel.

They're my friends and were there with me when something happened. But what? It seemed important to remember that. The pain in my head started again; however, it wasn't as painful as before. I stopped trying to remember and relaxed my thoughts.

I waited until the pain was just a shadow, and then I retried. It was important to know what had happened when I was with Sara and Areel. There was something I needed to know. Then an image passed before my eyes. A glimpse of something. *There was somebody else with us.*

I saw the scene in slow motion. It was like opening a window in a windy day in March. My mind was assailed by clear memories. Then, I remembered.

We were in Tarquinia in our apartment, and Areel was with Sara. We had just discovered something important regarding Areel's kind. His ancestors had been victims of a holocaust. He was in great pain. I saw Sara running to comfort him. I went after them to see if I could help. I found them on the bathroom floor embraced in each other's arms, crying and kissing.

I gasped, but Areel and Sara didn't hear me. Everything lasted only a few seconds. They only had a moment together, and then everything exploded. The light was so bright, red and orange like flames eating our bodies, but everything was cold. I heard Sara and Areel scream each other's names when they got separated. My last thought before passing out was my desire to see Elios one more time before dying, and then everything was a blur of shadows and sounds and smells like medicine and antiseptic.

I'm at the hospital. Why isn't my family here to hug me, to tell me everything's going to be okay? Why has nobody talked to me? Why am I naked? I didn't want to be naked. I felt cold, unprotected. I wanted to curl up and cover my body with my arms, but I was still tied to the bed.

Elios. Please help me... hug me... cover my body. I feel so miserable without you. Please hurry. I don't have much time.

For hours, days, weeks, I waited for something to happen in the dark space.

Once my recent memories started coming back, remaining conscious took all my energies. Those memories were painful, and screening my thoughts wasn't easy. I needed to be in control of what I wanted to think. Again, I used my memories of Elios to help me.

His name became my personal mantra. I used it to reach peace of mind, to control my body's reaction to the fearful darkness. When I felt cold, I imagined his body like a warm blanket on mine. When I felt too desperate even to cry, I imagined Elios smiling at me and whispering softly in my ear that everything was going to be fine. When I felt too lonely, Elios was there hugging me tight and kissing my hair and my neck and my lips.

When the memories of Sara and Areel screaming were cutting through my brain like a hot knife through butter, Elios was there repeating to me over and over again how much he loved me and how he would never let anything happen to me.

19

Another hour, week, month, year passed. I didn't know. I couldn't know. Maybe it was only a minute.

I felt better, though. More awake. Nobody had "visited" me for quite a while. I didn't know if it was good news. I got somehow attached to the routine of being poked at regular intervals. It helped me keep track of time, but I was also happy to be left alone. I was afraid of my visitors. Sometimes, their visits were unpleasant. Other times, I wished for unpleasantness.

I tried to understand what was happening. Unfortunately, I didn't know anything about my kidnappers—just that they were so. I'd been taken against my will; otherwise, my family would've been there with me. I welcomed the realization. They would never have left me on my own, especially if I had been wounded or needed medical assistance. I didn't know where I was. I didn't even know how long I'd been there. I was worried about my family. They were probably desperate over my disappearance. Thinking of my parents saddened me.

I knew how protective my mother was and how prone to desperation my father was when it came to their daughters. I remembered when my sister and I were little and went for a walk without telling them. We were on vacation in Villach, a safe and friendly Austrian city, and when, after a few hours, we decided it was time to return to the hotel, we found the whole staff, many of the guests, and three policemen looking for us. The same night, my father drove us back to Rome.

I finally remembered details about my life. About people. About my sister. Clara was surely out of her mind with grief. I hoped there was a way to let them know I was alive.

I wondered about Sara and Areel. The last memory I had of them was dramatic, but if I was still alive, maybe so were they. I wanted to believe that. The more I thought about my current state, the more I was convinced we had run into something with our research. We weren't the only ones looking for the Solean artifacts. Areel had not anticipated such an eventuality. He had been devastated by discovering part of a truth that was much more complicated than any of us had thought. Poor Sara. I felt guilty. If it weren't for me, she would have never met Areel.

Not that I would've done anything differently. I would've traveled along the same path. Even knowing the future, I would've changed nothing. I would've cautioned my friends, though. Yes, that I would've done, and Sara probably would've ended up making exactly the same decisions. Maybe there was nothing I could change. Maybe I was just trying to ease my conscience.

I felt better nonetheless. Thinking there were so many things I couldn't change helped me. It gave me peace, almost as if things were meant to happen that particular way so I could see Elios again. Faith, karma, pure hope—one of them was keeping me sane, although barely. I spent lots of my time theorizing.

Suddenly, my invisible kidnappers reappeared to torment me. I was sleeping a dreamless slumber, never really reaching a deep state of relaxation, when my body was transferred onto another surface, harder and colder than the one I was used to. Busy and impersonal hands touched my body. I could almost feel their distaste. Needles pierced my skin. Not knowing what they wanted from me was terrifying. Not knowing what they were going to do next was worse. The fearful anticipation of physical pain kept me company the whole time. I'd had enough time to get used to being left alone, and now the terror I felt was magnified by the memories of what I had already endured. I knew what was going to happen again.

I was wrong. I wasn't prepared at all for what came next.

They rolled the metallic cot under white lights that were never turned off. The room was kept cold at all times. I shivered until I fainted, over and over again. Some time later, they attached two plastic electrodes to my temples. My head started vibrating while a low buzz resonated around me. My ears rang, and my eyes were blinded by the sharp white halo hovering over me. They kept the level of pain constant. I couldn't think anymore. I was only able to focus on my breathing, in and out, slowly. Once, I found the strength to invoke Elios's name. I was administered an immediate charge of electricity. I saw red dots dancing before my eyes and fainted. When I woke, the pain was tolerable, and I focused on the act of breathing for a while.

Another time, I thought I saw long fingers come into focus. My eyelids were kept wide open, and then a red light invaded my vision. I didn't feel any pain, but I was expecting it and almost couldn't breathe. A mask was put on my mouth and cold, faintly scented air reached my lungs. I lost consciousness right away. When I opened my eyes, the pattern was repeated with a big difference. This time I heard voices. I wasn't used to hearing someone talking that wasn't the voice in my head.

At first, I didn't understand what they were saying. Soon, I realized they weren't speaking a language I knew. I tried to focus on the linguistic pattern the sounds created. Pain invaded my mind, and I stopped thinking. While I was trying to calm myself, I recognized the typical intonations indicating questions repeated at regular intervals. I was waiting for the pain to arrive when I realized they were asking me something.

Someone was speaking in plain English with no recognizable accent. Although from the intonation of their sentences, I knew they were asking me something, and although now they were talking in a language I could comprehend, I couldn't attribute any meaning to the words. It was a terrifying experience. I forgot the words the moment I heard them. I was afraid of how my tormenters would retaliate. Pain didn't make me wait long. It was almost a relief when it arrived. The whole process was repeated countless times. I understood they wanted something from me, but I didn't know what. I was afraid of the consequences of not giving them what they wanted, but at the same time, I had the feeling that once they obtained what they were looking for, I would be disposed of.

I wanted to see Elios again. Deep inside, I was happy I didn't have a clue about what they were after. Remaining alive was easier since I didn't have a choice. I could only be brave. The torture finally reached a familiar pattern, and I found precious few moments when my mind could relax between electrical shocks and blinding lights. My cold body never rested, every muscle ready to jump at the next painful violation. I never understood what they were asking.

After an eternity, I felt in the way they moved and touched me that something was changing. I was left alone more often. Time passed, and the amount of poking, prodding, and inserting of needles became progressively less. The temperature in the room was raised to be just cold. The white light was replaced by a warmer yellow light, but it was never dark. At least I could relax my eyes and find some comfort. The situation had improved. I was still cold but at least not in pain. My thoughts were quite simple; I only had the energy to regulate my breathing. Sometimes, I managed to evoke images of clear blue waters, but it took all my strength to maintain the thought for more than a moment, and after a while I didn't even try anymore. The only desire I had was to see Elios one more time, and that was so powerful and so deeply rooted in my brain, it made me breathe in and out rhythmically. It kept me going even when seeing black shadows and slipping out of consciousness was my entire experience. And it would have been so much easier to just let go of what was left of me. Once, I had the feeling I was finally disappearing, and it was peaceful. As I closed my eyes in acceptance, almost eager to embrace the darkness, a sunny light called to me louder and pulled me out. I found myself cold and trembling, frantically breathing in and out.

I lost track of everything. Time didn't exist any longer. I didn't have recognition of myself. I had become a mechanical motion, pushing and pulling air from my lungs. I remained in this minimal state of being maybe for years, maybe for seconds, when something changed again. The lights went off, and I finally slept.

I regained consciousness and tasted electricity in the air. My room was once more full of activity. The temperature was warmer, almost pleasantly so. When I finally dared to open my eyes, what I saw was hard to believe. I was staring at a scene straight out of a medical show.

Five people were working around my bed, five normal-looking people in a standard hospital room. It was the first time I saw my captors, the first time my eyes and senses weren't incapacitated.

Everything looked so ordinary, not even a single detail that could betray a more exotic explanation. I was dumbfounded by the discovery. Then I realized that if they didn't care to conceal their identities from me anymore, it wasn't good news at all.

They moved my arms and legs, checking something I couldn't understand. The situation was surreal; I was living the last moments of my life, and I felt better than before, both physically and mentally. I would've laughed but decided it wasn't wise to draw any unnecessary attention. I wanted to live my last moments thinking only of Elios. I wanted him to know how much I had loved him, how long I had fought to see him again. I had tried. The memories of his eyes would accompany me to my very end. I was happy I could think of him. It was less humiliating than dying naked and unconscious under unfriendly eyes.

I closed my eyes to embrace his memory and felt him, his presence almost real, palpable. I thought, *Please, now*.

It would've been gracious of my captors to let me go in my happiest moment. Elios's face was always sunny in my memories, and he was smiling at me, exuding warmth.

Then the expression on his face suddenly changed. He was furious. I felt disoriented for a moment and then angry that my bit of happiness was being taken away from me. It wasn't fair. The next image my mind played wasn't what I wanted. I didn't want to die with that image frozen in my eyes.

Elios's face was fierce. The light in his eyes was murderous, his mouth a white line. No cheerfulness was left in the Elios my mind was projecting. I tried to go back to my joyous Elios without any success. Uncaring of the preparation taking place around my body, I kept seeing him, not only his face. He was running through a dark place and looked pale and worried, more than worried, terrified. Elios was worried for me. He was coming to rescue me.

The thought hit me. *He's here*. It wasn't my imagination playing a final trick. I knew Elios was racing down stairs to reach me and save me from these people who were about to kill me. Someone had a scalpel close to my forehead. I felt the cold metal cutting my skin. Without thinking, I jerked my body and reached for the closest person on my right. I bit and scratched someone's skin until I felt blood. It was so fast, nobody had time to realize what I wanted to do. When they did, several hands pushed me back down onto the cot, and someone else dug the blade of the scalpel deep inside me. The pain was immediate. I screamed with all my force and for as long I could manage. I tried to move away from the knife, but the cutting continued until I couldn't see anything anymore.

20

I'm floating. Blood everywhere I look. My legs are dangling. Wind caresses my skin. It's pleasant. A voice I recognize. A soft cloth covers me. Finally warm.

Blackness won the battle with my senses and I effortlessly slipped down a spiraling tunnel of images that didn't make any sense to me. I felt my body shedding pain and unpleasant thoughts at every curve until I felt no more. I slept. I finally slept.

Or maybe I died. I was confused but, for the first time, not afraid. I felt linen shrouding my body and the soft motion of being cradled. I resumed my sleep with the knowledge I could move my arms and my legs if I wanted. All my muscles rejoiced at the good news, and I relaxed, starting with the frown on my forehead and going down to the painful knot residing in my neck. My shoulders followed in a wave of pleasure that engulfed my arms, spreading through my curled fingers and then finally through my thighs and calves to finish the relaxing journey with my ice-cold feet and toes. I moved on the soft and inviting surface until I found the right position, and then I lost contact with the outside world again. In the sweetness of that moment of pure bliss, I felt safe, and I dreamed.

I dreamed that my head was resting on a pillow, soft and freshly scented. Something shaped like a box hovered around me, humming. The room was illuminated gently by warm, dim lights. In my dream, I could smell the scent of freshly cut flowers and could hear music in the distance. While I was enjoying my oneiric life, barely breathing for fear of breaking the enchantment, I felt a presence. I should've been terrified that my peaceful retreat had been invaded, but I was calm, both physically and mentally. Someone sat on the edge of my bed, warmth reaching my skin and stirring my slumber. Quietly, I tasted the quality of the air in my mouth, finding a familiar aftertaste of electricity. The other moved on my bed, deliberately slowly, until the air was charged with a delicate anticipation I could feel on my lips. Time paused, and dizziness smoothed the edges of the overwhelming emotion taking hold of my racing heart.

A sudden realization made my stomach jump. I knew that I wasn't going to die. Finally, I knew the next moment wasn't going to be my last.

I felt hands on either side of my shoulders, and still I wasn't afraid. Waves of pleasant thoughts washed through my mind. The other emanated calm and quiet. My body was covered by warm light. My heartbeat slowed, almost still, when I felt my lips being softly touched by someone else's.

I savored the texture of the lips and the scent emanating from them. I hoped I could live in a never-ending repetition of that moment. There was no past, present, or future. Only now existed, and it was made of soft scents and warm embraces.

Images filled my inner vision, startling my mind and renewing the little shocks of electricity running through my awaking muscles. My skin came alive, registering every little change in temperature and humidity, and with my eyes still closed, I felt Elios.

I felt him. He was kissing me.

Elios was kissing me. And I was alive.

My body and my mind simultaneously caught fire, a beautiful, colorful fire that forced me to acknowledge I was alive. Around me, the world exploded with sounds, colors, and delicate perfumes. Elios was bathing me in pure love.

The momentum of what was happening hit me. My whole essence concentrated on the incredible miracle of his lips on mine. Touching him was the wish I never thought would be granted. His hand brought me closer to him. I inhaled his essence, rain and waterfalls.

Elios slowly caressed my bare back, and even with my eyes closed, I saw a rainbow of colors playing around our shivering bodies. The music resonated more closely, a love ballad, a Celtic melody. I raised my hands to stroke his hair and found it was tied with a silky ribbon. I untied it to let his hair fall freely. I loved the feeling of being able at last to touch him, but I was afraid it was just a dream. I tried not to linger on that thought, but I didn't want to wake up only to discover a different reality.

However, something, a sensation difficult to describe, didn't let me agonize on that doubt. Something reassured me I wasn't dreaming. I brushed his neck with just the tips of my fingers, and he gasped. Elios hugged me closer and kissed me with a different intensity, and then it happened.

I could see Elios… without seeing him. I could hear him talking without using my ears. I saw him in a way that I didn't think was possible. The very essence of Elios was before my eyes and inside my mind. Anything and everything "Elios" was revealed to me: all his thoughts, all his memories, all his knowledge.

I was overwhelmed by the realization that I knew everything he knew. My mind was flooded with the images of what his life had been when he was on Silenzio; how he had escaped the planet by borrowing the alien ship we were currently orbiting Earth in; how he had found me in an alien facility hidden between the inaccessible rocky mountain peaks in the isolated region of the Sarrabus-Gerrei in Sardinia; how he had fought my captors. It was so much to assimilate.

We are on a ship? Were you injured? What are we going to do?

We are together. Nothing else matters.

My thoughts. His thoughts.

"You're right. Nothing else matters." I nudged his nose.

Tears rolled down to wet our conjoined faces.

"Elios." My heart was full of joy.

"I'm here. I won't ever let you go. Never again."

"Elios." I opened my mind to reach his while we were still one. I wasn't sure it was going to work, but I was determined. I found the way immediately. My soul opened like a flower and invited him in. I felt Elios reacting to my gift. I felt his surprise and then joy. My commitment to him was eternal now. I was whole. Only together did we make sense.

I sensed Elios's heart growing bigger at the memories of how I had endured my imprisonment. He was proud of me and sad and horrified at seeing what my captors had done to me. I didn't want him to feel any sadness, not now that we were finally together. I went back to the moment I realized he was at the alien facility. That realization had given me the jolt of adrenaline necessary to rebel and buy a few more minutes of life. I particularly liked that memory. It had been the happiest of my life, until now. Elios relaxed then, and new scents inundated the room, citrus fruit zest and freshly cut mimosa. My closed eyelids showed me a warm red glow, an angelic duet sang for us, and our hair touched our faces, mingled together by the salty breeze. He knew how much I loved the sea. I finally opened my eyes to look at him.

Elios was magnificent. His face had changed in subtle ways that added to his character. New lines around his eyes showed his suffering. His full lips were still chapped by sun exposure, but he had lost his Mona Lisa smile.

He had evolved into a new Elios, one that could scare his enemies to death if that was his intention. I had seen through his eyes the terror on the faces of the people he was getting rid of to save me. Their eyes showed shock at his brutal efficiency, at his fighting skills. When Elios had reached the room where they were going to vivisect me, the only image at the center of his vision was my dying body on a metal stretcher. In his memories, I was white, blood staining my skin, the colors creating a stark and sickening contrast. He didn't see anything else, but his mind took control of his body, and anything and anybody in his way was taken care of.

I saw in his memories the pain and desperation he had to keep at bay while advancing toward the operating room. I looked lifeless, but he couldn't let them desecrate my body anymore. The rage Elios felt when he saw the hand holding the scalpel at my forehead was too intense to bear. I had to fast-forward to the next memory, when he was carrying me out of that prison. Blood covered his hands and the rest of his body, but he cradled me gently against his chest and kept running and fighting. He barely acknowledged the presence of his friends carrying Sara on the stairs. Elios had been tender and soft-spoken before, but now he was something more, love and fury combined in the same person.

"I love you." Elios was looking at me like it was the first time. His eyes stared into mine with a longing and a sweetness that made me gasp.

"This is the happiest moment of my life." I managed to breathe enough to produce a rough whisper.

"Our life."

Elios slowly bent his head to trace the contour of my jaws with his lips. A rush of blood colored my face, and I barely kept my heart from exploding while trying my best to keep breathing. I felt I was burning. Immediately, a refreshing, scented coil bathed our bodies.

"Thanks." My mouth curved in a smile while the rest of my body let me know how much I liked having him so close. I probably needed a cold shower. Elios showed me the image of a cold and misty waterfall in Hana. I liked that. I thought of the melted snow creating a lazy river of crystalline, freezing-cold water on Mount Rainier. I loved that we could communicate instantly. Elios wasn't sure of that, his mind broadcasting his worry.

"It's the most romantic gift I could hope for," I answered with words to his unspoken question. "I hope you'll never tire of my simple thoughts." I smiled at the realization that Elios liked my voice and my accent.

"You are anything but simple. You changed the core of my existence. I'm more worried that one day you'll want to escape from this." Elios pulled our heads closer and bent his forehead onto mine while stroking my arm.

"Never." I laughed back at his silly words and felt a tingle running through my skin. The rainbow around my body changed colors.

"Only you," Elios whispered, already kissing me.

Before being swept away by his lips moving so slowly on mine, I saw we were immersed in a pyrotechnic show. "Forever you." I accompanied the words with images of places I wanted to visit with him: places I had already been and places I hoped we would see together for the first time.

"Soon." Elios kept kissing me while his thoughts were focused on how he could have gladly spent the rest of eternity just looking at me. A microcosm of infinite happiness.

"I like that." I grazed his bottom lip with my teeth. "We are a mini solar system," I said, and at the same time I thought, I am your planet, you are my sun.

"I'm everything you'll ever need." Elios's eyes were kind and bright, little stars of their own.

"I know."

He laid his head on my chest, and I felt our heartbeats synchronizing. I ran my fingers up and down his shoulders and back, absentmindedly designing circles while I kissed his hair.

It was then and only then when I finally realized how different he really looked. My face was so close to his, and I had been so mesmerized by the contact, I hadn't seen the whole picture. I couldn't stop myself from crying. I was still caressing his beautiful, now completely white hair when I found the memory I was looking for. I saw Elios's reflection in the mirror when he discovered his hair had changed color. When my tears wet him, Elios raised his head and met my worried eyes.

"Don't. Don't be sorry for me." Elios tried to calm me, and that made me feel worse.

"Look what I did to you." I had scarred him physically. The whole time I was being kept prisoner, we had shared a mental link. He had listened to my agony, to my shouting, and worst of all, to my silence.

"No, please, it wasn't your fault. I don't mind it at all." Elios made me look at him.

"I really did change you."

When I had disappeared from Tarquinia and had stopped communicating, Elios had projected his mind across the universe looking for me. During my long imprisonment, devoured by senseless pain and constant solitude, without being conscious of doing so, I had looked for him as well. Every time I thought of talking to him, I actually did it. Every time I screamed his name, he heard me. I had been loud and clear inside his mind while his body was trapped in a sleep-induced state as he was coming back to Earth to save me.

The more I scanned his memories, the more I blamed myself for his current state. I could feel his agony at the thought of my death. I could feel him slowly dying inside, from my prolonged silence. For months, he had lain awake, unable to command his body to action. I was terrified by the idea he had contemplated suicide. In the long wake, Elios had rationally designed his death. Had I not spoken in the nick of time, as I did, he would've executed his plan as soon as he had regained the full use of his body. I was horrified at the idea that, without knowing it, I'd had the power of deciding Elios's death. I couldn't even talk about it. It was too much to bear.

Sensing my distress, Elios guided my mind away from the destructive loop in which I was incarcerating my thoughts and showed me how he had embraced the change and why. He was proud of it.

"I actually like it." Elios bent his head again, this time to whisper in my ear, and since he was already there, he took his time to kiss the little spot between my ear lobe and the jaw.

A fresh trail of shivers traveled along my hypersensitive skin. "I see you do."

Elios loudly broadcast how much he liked his new hair color and then said, "It's like a war wound, like a scar. It's my tattoo."

"You are proud of this?" I was amazed at the idea that he considered it a love mark.

"Immensely so." Elios guided my back to rest on the bed and sat precariously on the edge.

Automatically, I pulled his body closer to rest on mine. Suddenly, the room, my body, his body, everything seemed to catch on fire. Every sense was assailed by a different stimulus. My head was light from the lack of oxygen. I could barely think. I craved him. Too embarrassed to have that conversation, I tried to sidetrack my own thoughts. "I want to hear what your tattoo says."

"I'm yours. You made me. You named me. I was born for you." Elios's ragged breathing told me he had problems of his own controlling his mind. Meanwhile, his lips were brushing mine with more urgency than before.

"My whole body is a tattoo that says the same to you." His lips were the center of my focus at the moment; breathing could wait after all.

Elios put his arm around mine. "We are perfect together."

I knew what he meant right away. "I can only be with you." I'd been never able to get physically involved with anybody before. My body had never felt that I belonged to someone else. Even the act of kissing had never really been so enjoyable until now.

"I know." Elios had already seen all my memories of my unfortunate dating life. A sudden and unexpected anger flared up inside Elios's mind. I hadn't anticipated he could react that way to my innocent memories. All my friends had thought I was more suited to join a convent rather than romantically dating someone. I was considered a prude.

One memory in particular was giving Elios almost physical pain. Ironically, the night he was reliving in my memories had been the one I had finally accepted my obsession for him. His knuckles went white. I showed him how the night had ended. "I broke Marco's heart by refusing him."

"You left Rome because of what happened that night."

I nodded. "I was kissing you while I was with him. Your face was the one I saw. Your voice was the one I was calling." I shivered at those memories. "I felt your hands on my body that night, not Marco's." I brushed his lips. "Your presence was so real, so intoxicating."

"I know. I'm sorry." Elios was visibly relieved.

The idea he could be jealous of me took me by surprise. Even with the advantage of mind sharing, he had been blinded by a single, incomplete memory. I was glad I'd never really had a love life. "Doesn't matter." It never really had. "You're my first and my only love." I took his hand mangling the linen sheet and put it on mine. For a moment, the idea that he could be touching someone else came to my mind. I found that I didn't like it. "I'm thankful you never had any human physical experiences," I blurted out, unable to contain the sentiment.

He smiled. "I don't think it could've ever happened. You're one of a kind. Before seeing you for the first time, my life was on a different path. I was on Earth to observe humanity, not to mingle." Again Elios surprised me with another emotion I didn't expect. He was amused by the idea and started laughing. His laugh sounded like moving pebbles on a wet sand beach. I savored every moment it lasted.

"Nevertheless, I can't stand the mere thought of you mingling with anybody else but me." I played with his hair maybe a tad more roughly than I had originally meant. "There was nobody before you." I kissed him lightly.

 "It took me too long to find you." Elios kissed me back and then moved his lips to my eyes and then to my nose, softly brushing my skin without applying pressure.

It had the soothing effect of listening to a lullaby. It relaxed my mind and my body. The colors and the music in the room were getting more subdued as well. The breeze was warmer now because even the temperature of our bodies had cooled down a bit.

Elios kept stroking my arm while our eyes were closed. We kept exchanging memories and thoughts for a while. I mentally showed him the things I would love to share with him. Elios had desires of his own, even vacations on far away planets.

Our bodies lay intertwined on the bed, too narrow for both of us.

Eventually even our minds had to rest.

"I love you, Elios."

"To the end of time, Gaia."

21

I slept continuously for more than two days. For the best part of it, I dreamed of Elios. With him. Our minds kept sharing even in our sleep. I felt whole and healed. In our dream, we had never been apart; we had never left each other's sides after meeting in Athens. That was my idea of a perfect life. That was our dream.

Sometime during those two days, I sensed Elios leaving, but I was too tired to open my eyes, and I let him readjust my body on the bed. His touch was tender, and left me relaxed and in peace with the rest of the world. I went back to my dream. My muscles enjoyed the controlled temperature and the softness of the mattress so much that I envisioned my body reshaping into my former healthy and athletic self. Then I smiled at the idea that I could do that. I would wake from this dream and find that it wasn't a dream at all.

And we were together, and his arms were around my body again. I was sleeping on my side, legs curled, knees close to my chest, and Elios shaped himself around me. Fresh blue veils of misty balsamic vapors hung in the air. My lungs breathed deeply and my body was soaked. Elios kissed my hair and moved it aside to kiss the base of my neck while caressing my arm. The mist disappeared, and a hot sunny light took its place. Now the smell reminded me of freshly washed clothes and lilac flowers. In a matter of minutes, I was clean and dry and happy.

"Sleep well, my love." Elios's voice was as warm as his gentle hands. His lips were at my ear, and I felt a pleasant tingle.

I slept again, feeling refreshed and perfumed. We dreamed, we occasionally kissed, and we moved continuously in the little bed. Then I woke up.

"Hi." The first thing my eyes saw was his smiling face close to mine.

"Hi to you."

Elios came closer to brush my lips.

"What happened while I was sleeping?"

"I talked to Areel and Kam—"

"Kam?" I had seen another guy in his memories earlier, but there was so much information to take in that I had tuned out all the noise and focused only on Elios.

"Kam is a friend of mine."

"Is he Solean?"

Elios nodded. "He left Solo when Areel disappeared off the face of the earth and instead found me. It's only thanks to him that I discovered where you were kept." He paused for a moment. "You'll meet him soon enough." Then, he opened his mind to me, and I went through the memories of the conversation he had had with his two friends.

I already knew all the detail of the sad truth Elios had discovered about his ancestors, but it was too much to bear again. I was thankful when he skipped to the point when he went to see Sara. My friend was sleeping; her mind needed to heal. Luckily for her, the medical technology of the ship was quite sophisticated, especially in the psychology department, and Sara was now undergoing therapy sessions at a subliminal level. I smiled when I saw Pallino's familiar ball of fur curled at Sara's feet. I was sure his presence would help if anything else failed.

Thinking of Sara and her situation made me realize that even after what I went through, I felt quite well. Maybe I was still waiting for the shock to arrive. My body felt too light, and I had a few bruises and some soreness, but other than that I was emotionally fine.

"It's us. Together, we're stronger than we are alone. When we touched the first time and shared our souls, we went through a process that changed us. We healed our emotional wounds with the act of sharing. We're different now. We've changed even at a molecular level. I don't know the extent of our transformation, but I guess we'll know soon enough." He moved a little to make space for me to stretch my legs.

"I do feel calm and in control. The experience I had should've been harder to deal with, but I feel fine. I'm almost worried that it's going to bite me back later. I thought that maybe the happiness of seeing you had temporarily blinded my other feelings, but I don't feel I'm going to crumble any time soon. I think you're right. We did heal our minds."

I stretched my arms, and my stomach started to grumble. Elios and I laughed at something so trivial.

"I went down this path before. I learned the hard way that this body... *I* need to eat." Elios hugged me, being careful not to crush me.

"I'm not easily breakable." I burrowed into his embrace.

"You're stronger than me, in so many ways, but I can't stop fretting about you." He raised my chin with a finger and smiled at me.

"I love being pampered." At my words, possessiveness and rage swept over me and left me without breath. After one look at him, I immediately added, "By you."

Elios closed his eyes, sighed, and then kissed me ruefully. "Sorry, sorry. Human emotions drive me crazy."

"And I also love this new aspect of you." We lingered a few more moments in bed.

Then I noticed something. I wasn't naked anymore. I touched the thin top and the shorts I was wearing and raised an eyebrow, trying to remember when I did that.

"You haven't..." Elios, for some reason, was blushing.

"Thanks." I still couldn't understand his reaction.

"I had to—" He was still looking for words, and we weren't touching, so I didn't have a clue.

"I couldn't sleep in the same bed with you—"

"Oh... oh... oh!" At first I was almost offended by his unfinished statement, but then I understood and finally blushed a nice shade of tomato red.

We had lots of things to talk through, but certain topics couldn't be rushed, and I didn't know where to start.

Thankfully, Elios put an end to our misery. "Would you like some breakfast?"

"I'm starving." I touched his lips with mine just to let him know one last thing, *And not just for food.*

"Not fair, Gaia." Elios mockingly rolled his eyes at me. "Breakfast, please." He kissed me back to let me know his final thought on the argument, *This is not the best moment to start that conversation, but I want to talk about it. A lot.*

"Surprise me with your cooking expertise. I'm really hungry," I said with a big smile. Elios kissed the top of my head, and gently pushed me toward the door.

I walked beside him, feeling my body pulled up toward the ceiling. I adjusted my gait, feeling lighter than I used to. I walked for a few seconds, worrying I would fly up like a balloon. I grabbed his hand like an anchor. Although I wanted to, I fought the urge to jump because I wasn't sure I could trust my instincts at the moment. Nevertheless, my body was reacting surprisingly well after such a long period of forced inactivity.

"The gravity inside the ship is lighter. It makes long trips more comfortable. My guess is that your body was healed in record time by the same power that healed your mind: our sharing," Elios explained while we walked to the kitchen.

Nobody else was there at the moment, and I was glad for that because I needed him by myself. Earlier, I picked from his memories that besides Sara and Areel, and Kam, there was a fourth passenger on the ship, one of the aliens involved in my captivity. I wasn't ready to talk about that. "Give me the grand tour."

He showed me how the automatic kitchen worked, and it was quite self-explanatory, even easier than operating a microwave oven. In just a few minutes, the kitchen provided us a full breakfast. I couldn't name or even understand what we were going to eat, but everything smelled mouthwatering.

"Let me pamper you some more." Elios took a chair from one of the two tables and waited for me to sit.

While he went to arrange our breakfast on a tray, I took the place in. The cafeteria was a cozy spot adjacent to the command center. The ship was small, and every corner was cleverly used. White was the predominant color, with variations of cream and beige. Somehow, it reminded me of my apartment in Tarquinia. Natural white light was shining inside, but there were no windows that I could see. The décor was otherworldly, of course, with scattered linear designs throughout the place, almost reminiscent of the Thai written language. The few pieces of furniture had the same look, elegant thin shapes that curved at unexpected angles.

I knocked on the table. "What kind of material is the furniture made of?"

"Not sure." He was balancing a full tray. "We don't have anything like it on Solo."

I helped him by taking two cups filled to the brim with a red liquid. "We sure don't have anything like that on Earth. This material looks so fragile—"

Elios sat at the table and started serving me from the tray. "It's sturdy enough to have survived a crash."

I had only skimmed through the memories of Elios's confinement on the solitary planet on which he had spent his sentence. "What happened there?"

"You'd call it a miracle. When I thought everything was lost, this ship appeared in the sky of Silenzio to give me new hope."

"Silenzio—Areel told me about it. Was it really silent?"

"Yes, it was. I couldn't communicate with anybody. At first, I thought I would lose my sanity. But then I started seeing you."

The memory of our dates was still fresh to me, and it made my heart race a bit faster. Elios took my hand in his.

"I lived for our dates." He brushed my lips.

"What happened when this ship crashed?"

"I walked across Silenzio to reach the wreckage, hoping the ship was salvageable."

Through our interlaced fingers, my mind connected to his, and I was there with him, the moment he had found a man and a woman inside the ship. Their features alien and beautiful, the couple seemed to sleep reclined in their chairs. I saw Elios reverently reaching for the woman and touching her to see if she was still alive.

"I felt the new life inside her. A small, pulsating light demanding to be."

Through him, I felt it too. Rage invaded me at the thought that someone had tampered with the ship to ensure the couple's death. "Who would want to harm an innocent?"

"According to their society's rules, their union was considered blasphemous."

"I hope they're fine now." I couldn't help but wonder about them and their baby.

"I think they found their haven on Silenzio."

"And you found a way out of it thanks to them." *And for that I will be forever in debt to the alien couple.*

"Me too." He leaned and nudged my nose with his. "Let's eat now."

I nodded and relaxed in my chair, content. I looked around with different eyes, imagining the alien couple going through their daily lives. I could see their love for each other reflected everywhere I turned. The atmosphere was serene, the monochromatic palette calming. I liked it. I didn't feel out of place. Somehow I felt at home.

"Elios to Gaia." He smiled at me. "What would you like to eat?" He indicated the food on the table with a flourish.

"Everything looks good. Surprise me." The feast lying before my eyes was exotic and colorful. The splashes of pink, orange, and green made me think of a new painting. Elios cut little pieces of what looked like a watermelon and fed me a morsel. The act was so intimate it made me think of finding a secluded spot.

"How is it?"

I slowly breathed in and out and then savored the food. "Good as it smells. Salty and meaty, with the consistency of soft tofu." I soon discovered I was hungrier than I thought. I picked up a thin, elongated fork and ate from the plate he had prepared for me, commenting on each exhilarating flavor. Elios reached for the two cups I had laid on the table and offered me one. We toasted with our raised vessels while kissing each other, and then we carefully sipped the drinks. The swirling liquid had the most surprising flavor I had ever tasted. It was warm but not scorching—even if it seemed to be boiling on the surface—and the flavor was nothing like the color; it was refreshing like lemon but red like blood. It was sweet and spicy. I put the drink down and I couldn't help but smile.

"What is it?"

"This is my first meal after—" I searched my memories for the answer and shook my head. "I don't know when I ate last."

Elios's expression became pained. "Six months."

"I was kept prisoner for six months?"

He took my hand in his, and I saw the time flying by while he was paralyzed but awake, counting the seconds to reach Earth.

"Thanks... for everything." I brought his hand to my lips and brushed it.

"Anything for you." Elios leaned to kiss my lips and then added in a lower voice, "I'd do anything for you."

Images of the carnage he had committed to save me flooded my mind. He was impassive to the graphic recounting, a dark halo surrounding his actions. "I'm sorry. I didn't mean for you to see that."

"I know." When I was around, he confined his darkest thoughts in a hidden corner of his mind, but they were always there, lingering. I squeezed his hand and then pressed it on my heart, smiling reassuringly at him. "Nothing is going to happen to me."

Elios pulled me onto his lap. "I know... because I won't let it."

We finished our first breakfast together talking about little things. It didn't matter that we already knew everything about each other. We just loved talking.

He gently helped me to my feet but left one hand on my waist. "I want to show you our room."

"Okay." I took one step toward the hallway.

He didn't follow. "Is it okay with you if we sleep together? In the same bed?" He bit his lower lip.

I didn't understand his question. "I think we just did."

"That was done under more dramatic circumstances." He released the hold on my waist and lowered his eyes to the floor. "I'm not sure you want me around day and night."

I reached out my hand and splayed my fingers on his chest. "It is exactly what I want. Forever." I stepped closer to him, left one hand on his heart, and raised the other to caress his neck slowly. A smug smile formed on my mouth. *And sleeping with you is the least of my concerns at the moment.*

Elios's eyes shone with a brighter light and, for a moment, I felt his heartbeat accelerate, and warmth spread from his body to mine. Then, he removed both my hands gently, but firmly, and efficiently cut me out of his mind without giving me time to listen to his thoughts.

Playing the same game, eh? "Sooner or later, I'll discover what you were thinking." I smiled brightly. "You'll see; I'm a fast learner."

Elios smiled back with a cheerful sparkle in his eyes. "Believe me, you'll know it soon enough if you don't stop teasing me so."

We walked down the narrow hallway and stopped in front of a transparent glass door, which I viewed with suspicion and a raised eyebrow that Elios read correctly.

"It becomes opaque at a vocal command."

I blushed, which immediately ruined all my preceding attempts to play the temptress. My lack of experience was not helping. The door opened and silently slid inside the wall.

Elios looked at me and whispered, "I love you, Gaia." Then he bent to kiss me and scooped me up in his arms, and I found myself carried into the room like a newlywed.

My eyes filled with tears, and I hid my head against his chest, wanting to say something, anything, and not finding the words. I opened my mind to Elios to let him know how I felt. Then I saw it and couldn't repress my tears anymore. Over "our" bed, Elios had hung one of my paintings. On the creamy wall, there was now a splash of red, pink, and light blue.

"I couldn't leave it behind. When I saw it in your apartment in Tarquinia, it spoke to me," he said, and gently lowered me to my feet.

I had painted my red geraniums and pink hydrangeas under a cloudy sky, hoping I would be able to show it to him one day, and here it was, now, in "our" room. The possessive pronoun before the words "room" and "bed" made my heart race against my ribcage.

"While you were sleeping, I arranged the room. I hope you like it."

"You edited your memories." I hadn't realized he could do that.

"Yes, I did." He lowered his eyes. "I wanted to surprise you."

"Thanks." I walked around the room. The bed was larger than the medical cot, and the furniture was elegant and simple, almost Japanese in style. The bed frame was dark, maybe made of wood, and linear. The two chairs by the side of the bed were decorated with the same pattern I had seen in the kitchen, in the same material as the bed. There was a small desk, which looked like an antique, with a delicate-looking chair. At first glance, I saw a window opening on a blue sky. *It can't be, can it?*

"It's a screen that can project any image you want." Elios voiced a few commands, and a green forest appeared outside the window.

It was unsettlingly realistic. I could even hear the distant sounds from the woods. I looked at it for a few seconds trying to understand why it looked so familiar and then smiled when I recognized the place. "Oh, this is the trail I showed you on Mount Rainier." I thanked him with a kiss.

Elios muttered another command, and now the window showed the same spot where I took a picture last time I had been there hiking with Sara. Before my eyes, there was the little waterfall I had immortalized, framed by the green of the foliage and the white of the mist, with the pleasant addition of the sound of crashing pebbles and birds singing in a tree. The only difference from my memories was the presence of some white snow in small patches scattered here and there.

"It is now," Elios said.

I realized my hand was still holding his, so Elios was involuntarily listening to my thoughts, but I was too overwhelmed to say anything.

"The image you're looking at is being taken right now. It's a live broadcasting of the location I chose." He went to sit on the bed beside me without releasing my hand. "I still can't believe we are here, now." His voice gently meshed with the natural sound coming from the window.

"I can't wrap my head around all of this." I smiled and went to sit on the bed by him. "I'm worried you're going to disappear." I kissed the back of his hand and put it on my heart, which was still beating too fast after the impromptu threshold ceremony. At the memory, my face became red.

It means exactly what you think. Elios's statement was loud in my mind and had the effect of putting my heart in an even more agitated mode instead of calming it.

"We already exchanged our vows. We did it the first time we saw each other. I will wed you in any form you think is most proper, but our union transcends any human or Solean form of companionship." Elios kissed the top of my nose while passing his hand through my hair.

You are my wife, my companion, my soul mate.

I was speechless and repressed a sob.

"Oh, it wasn't my intention—" Elios said.

"No, no. You didn't say anything wrong. The opposite. You're perfect. This moment is perfect." Tears swelled in my eyes. "I'm just terrified it's going to end."

Elios silently lay on the bed and pulled me down with him, washing away the tears with kisses.

"I'm being silly. I know." I chuckled between tears.

When he had kissed every inch of my face twice, Elios raised his head to look at me again.

"I don't know what just happened to me." I was still shaken. "Just don't let me go."

"Never again." He brushed my cheek, and I leaned against his touch.

"I love you."

"My love." He projected wave after wave of images of wedding ceremonies, some from around Earth and some from other planets as well.

I played along with him, imagining our wedding celebrated in some bizarre fashion. Our minds relaxed, and we focused on our bodies lying intertwined. The light from the window was now dim, the afternoon becoming night out there in a forest so far away from us. The animals had grown quieter. The only sounds came from the waterfall. The moon was rising, casting a silver luminescence on our bed. Elios's white hair glowed in the pale light. His eyes were lit by a different fire, the blue and green resembling swirling water.

Elios moved lightly on the bed and covered my body like a warm blanket. I found myself breathing underwater, bathed in fluorescent light. He was as light as a feather on my body, but my lungs stopped pumping air altogether.

All the molecules in my body rejoiced at the contact. I felt renewed at cellular level. When his fingers skimmed over my face and my throat, my heart exploded. In a haze, I saw the rest of the room was also exploding with colors, music, and new exotic scents.

"Do you realize the effect you have on me?" My head was so light everything was moving around in the aquarium that once was our room. I was on the verge of swooning.

"You have the same effect on me. I'm defenseless in your hands." Elios was trembling; his voice and breathing matched mine.

"I love you. I love you. I love you." With my last bit of rational thinking, I repeated the words like a lullaby, oblivious to the world outside our bodies.

Elios kissed the hollow of my throat while lowering the strap of my top. The trail his gentle fingers left on my skin was accompanied by my constant shivering. Acting instinctively, I raised the hem of his white shirt to bare his burning skin. My hands ran over his chest, circling the shapes of his muscles with my fingers, feeling the shivers that rocked his body. Our minds had reached such a level of sharing that we had lost consciousness of our single selves. I couldn't say where Elios's thoughts started and mine ended. I sensed in his mind how my skin felt under his touch at the same time he experienced my joy at caressing his face. I wanted with all my heart to lose myself in that magic and never come back to reality.

The air was saturated with the exotic spices and the scent of our bodies when a coherent thought finally emerged in the chaos of my mind. When I realized its nature, I was already regretting it, but Elios was faster than me to decipher my garbled ideas. Slowly, he moved to my side, visibly making an effort to regulate his breathing while facing the ceiling with his eyes shut. The atmosphere in the room changed abruptly. The colors dimmed until they vanished and only the silvery light coming from the forest remained. Cold fingers squeezed my heart, unable to retrieve the beautiful emotions we had shared until a moment ago. I reached for his hand, missing the physical contact already.

I hated myself.

Why did I have to think of that? What does it change if we have our first time here or somewhere else?

"Because the first time is a memory that lasts forever. And I agree with you." His voice was low, between every word a pause. His hand reached mine, our shoulders already touching, his eyes now looking at me. "I love you. I want that perfect memory."

"I need you. In every possible way. We've been through a lot to waste time now." My mind and my body were fighting an internal conflict.

"The fact you had *that* thought *then* means a lot." Elios's smile reached his eyes.

After one look at him, I regretted having had any thought at all. "It doesn't mean I'm not ready." I had been ready for Elios for years now. I wanted to scream in frustration at my stupidity.

"I know you are, as you well know that I am." Elios was now reclining on his elbow, holding his head with the hand that should've been tracing the pattern of my face. "But I want to give you the gift of an unforgettable memory. My wedding present to you." His voice was now steadier than a moment ago. His eyes suddenly became serious, and he brought us both back to a sitting position. "Would you accept me? Would you do me the honor of accepting my gift?"

"Thank you." I choked on the rest of what I wanted to say and hugged him instead. *You just did it. You just made it perfect. I'm the luckiest girl alive.*

"I'm the lucky one, my love. You would've found happiness" —Elios smiled at my outraged expression at his words— "even without me."

"I'd never—"

He put a finger on my mouth to stop me. "But I would never have understood what it is to be alive without you." Elios kissed my eyes and then my nose and then reached my jaw. "I wasn't meant for love. My destiny was to spend my life alone. You changed me."

I gently pushed him away from me. "Without you, I would never have found happiness." *With time, I might have started a family with someone, but I never would have found real love.* It was so sad to think so, but it was the truth. The thought made him sad too. "My heart can't belong to anybody else." I started kissing him. Slowly at first. My hands roamed over his body. He shivered, and I shivered. I pulled him onto me.

Gaia?

But there wasn't any need for an answer. There weren't any doubts in my mind; I was exactly where I wanted to be. There wasn't anything, anybody. Only Elios and I.

My clothes disappeared. His clothes disappeared. We were skin to skin. I had never experienced in my life such bliss. We kissed, a deep, breathtaking kiss that left me dizzy. He circled my shoulders with light fingers. Then my collarbone. Up to my jaws, down to the side of my breast. Light exploded behind my closed eyes. When he reached my hipbones, I arched my back, gasping for air inside his mouth.

He stopped, and I looked at him. I nodded. He lowered his body on me and I welcomed him, ready to finally be one. Maybe I fainted. When I had thought I reached bliss before, I was wrong. Nothing could compare to the joy of our union. I was so happy, so overwhelmed by it that I cried. We moved together, and it seemed the most natural thing in the world. It was right. We were right. We reached the stars together and stayed there. Our mouths locked, our hands frantically exploring our trembling bodies. We didn't come back to reality until much later.

Then we remained silent, letting our thoughts talk until we remembered how to properly breathe, and the colors in the room changed to soothing pastel shades matching our moods.

Outside the window, the night was black, and the moon was surrounded by millions of bright lights shining like diamonds in the dark.

22

We slept embraced and stayed in bed until the sun shone again outside in the forest. We forgot to have dinner and other necessities, like drinking water to keep hydrated. When we woke up, we realized our error.

The following day, we tried our best to keep track of things, mostly because we weren't alone in the ship. Wrapped in Elios's warmth, it was easy to forget Areel and Sara weren't the only ones sharing living arrangements with us.

Kam, Areel and Elios's friend, had come all the way from Solo to help Elios when he had needed him the most. Without Kam, Elios wouldn't have found and rescued me. He kept to himself since Areel spent most of his time checking on the sleeping Sara, and Elios and I weren't the best company. The arrangement had worked fine, and I had yet to meet him officially.

The other guest was the alien spy Kam and Elios had found in Santa Severa, a small city north of Rome. Elios and Kam had followed a trail that had eventually ended at the medieval castle of Santa Severa. There, they had been ambushed by the alien and barely escaped with their lives. The alien had confessed where I was kept in Sardinia and was now in their custody. While I was sleeping, Areel, Kam, and Elios had talked about how to handle the prisoner, and they had opted to put the alien in deep sleep, to avoid having to deal with him on a daily basis and to ensure he would have the best possible treatment under the circumstances. They didn't want to succumb to their feelings toward the prisoner and treat him in a way they would regret later in life.

The plan was to travel to Solo, where the three of them were going to request a formal hearing with the college of Superior Observers and explain what had happened and what they had discovered. The idea made me nervous. Elios was a fugitive, and I didn't see how telling the whole truth was going to free him from his charges. Sensing my distress, he shielded his thoughts to give me the edited version of what was going on in his mind.

Before leaving our room, I asked for a special treat. "I'd love to see the place where I lived in Rome."

He looked at me with a perplexed expression.

"Just the outside of my parents' building."

"I don't think it's a great idea."

"Please, just a moment." But I was lying. A moment wasn't enough, and we both knew it.

"You don't know what you're asking for."

"Please..."

Finally, Elios indulged me. Overwhelmed by a river of emotions, I kept staring at the familiar sight on the screen, and he let me until I saw my family going in and out, running errands. My mother's and father's faces looked tired. My sister's was impossible to see, her eyes covered by long bangs that hadn't been there last time I'd seen her.

Elios leaned to press a kiss on my shoulder. "They think you are back in Seattle."

I had seen in his memories the phone call he had exchanged with my mother where she had told him I had left Italy. The Pures had planted fake memories in my parents' and sister's minds to cover my abduction. "I know, but I need to talk to them, to hear their voices." I couldn't remove my eyes from the screen. I was waiting for my family to appear again, if only for a moment.

"It's too dangerous right now. The same power behind your abduction could get hold of your family if you contacted them. They would do anything to stop us from reaching Solo."

The thought that anybody would subject my sister to a fraction of what I had endured made me feel sick.

"What can I do, then?" I looked at him.

Elios shrugged and reached for me. "We have to wait. We can't leave any crumb for our enemies to follow."

I knew it, but it still stung.

"I'm working on something." He took me in his arms and cradled me.

"What—"

He gently shushed me. "You must trust me for now." He left a trail of kisses on my face.

I sighed but let him comfort me, and when I was feeling calmer, I reached for his hand and pulled him out of the bed. I couldn't stand another moment before that screen. "Let's go visit Sara."

We hurriedly dressed, then silently walked to the other end of the ship where my friend was sleeping her worries away. After a single knock on the door, Areel said to come in.

"How is she?" I looked at them, Areel sitting by the bed and Sara lying on it.

He gave us a half smile, his hand gently stroking hers. "She looks more alert today."

Sara had her eyes closed in a serene expression, her head connected to the pillow by two probes. From Elios's memories, I knew the pillow was a medical device for psychological treatment. Pallino was curled at Sara's feet, but as I approached the bed, he stirred and offered me his head to pet.

"Are you still trying to reach for her mind?" Elios walked around the bed and stopped at the headrest.

Areel nodded. "I feel she can hear me now."

I laid one hand on his shoulder and softly squeezed. "It worked for us. I'm sure it will work for you as well." I leaned over Sara to give her a peck on the head. She smelled nice. "What is it?"

"I wash her skin twice a day with an infusion I make."

"What's in it?"

"Herbs and minerals to help with her skin regeneration."

I thought I recognized one of the scents. "Jasmine?"

He openly smiled now. "And a hint of freesias."

"She'll be fine."

"I know she will." He looked at me for a moment, and then his eyes went back to her, and we knew we were two too many.

Elios gestured for me to exit the room, but at the door he turned. "Dinner is going to be ready in a few minutes."

Without taking his eyes off of her, Areel murmured he was coming later.

We headed to the kitchen, and Elios started cooking the old-fashioned way, by chopping and sautéing vegetables fresh from the hydroponic pod. I helped him, but it was clear he needed the activity to shake off Areel's sadness. Kam joined us when the cooking was almost done and I was sitting at the table, nursing a hot tea.

"Hi there." I didn't know what to say to him. It was awkward. I knew him the same way Elios knew him, but I had never physically met Kam until now.

The feeling must've been mutual. "Hi." After looking at the crowded kitchen counter where Elios was cleaning up after himself, Kam sat at the table at my right. "Pleasure to finally meet you."

"Likewise." I stared at the contents of my mug. Finally, I raised my face to look at him and whispered, "Thank you."

His eyes widened at my words.

"I owe you my life and Elios's."

"I would've done anything for him."

"I know."

His eyes widened more and turned toward Elios.

"We're one," Elios said, and my heart did a backflip.

Kam seemed to think about what Elios had just implied and then shrugged. "Better this way. I know nothing of Earthly pleasantries." He smiled at me. "We don't have to waste time explaining things. I like it."

I liked it too.

Later, Areel joined us for dinner, but only his body was there. He kept looking at the hallway while hurriedly eating what Elios had prepared. The colorful morsels that tasted like meat but resembled nothing like it left the plate to reach Areel's mouth, but he didn't seem to be aware of that. He ate the last piece, drank the contents of his cup in one single gulp, and stood up, only to be stopped by Kam's words.

"So, has she given any sign she knows you're there?" Kam looked at Areel and, when he had his attention, added, "Anything at all?"

For a moment, I thought Areel hadn't heard Kam's question. Then, he touched Kam's hand. Without asking permission. Elios and I gasped at the same time. Kam instinctively tried to free himself from Areel's hold, but the transfer was already taking place. I witnessed the moment Kam's expression changed and he lowered his eyes, ashamed of his indelicacy.

"Areel, please stop." Elios was behind him.

Areel raised the hand he was holding Kam with, and Kam stormed out of the room. One tear falling down his jaw, Areel looked at us as if expecting us to rebuke him.

Elios went to sit and pulled out a chair for Areel. "Kam didn't mean to be cruel. He doesn't know—"

"Now he does." Areel didn't wait for Elios's comeback; he turned and left.

I leaned on Elios and rubbed his arm. "Everything will be okay. Don't worry."

Later that night, Areel came back to the kitchen, where Elios and I were talking to Kam, who had tiptoed in for some water and stayed.

Areel didn't look surprised to see his friend there. He stepped closer to the table and paused before Kam. "I'm sorry for touching you without permission."

"You have a lot on your mind." Kam waved his hand in the air.

Areel shook his head and lowered his eyes. "It's inexcusable."

"No, you were right to force me to see through your eyes. I wouldn't know what you're going through otherwise. I'm sorry."

Areel seemed to crumble at Kam's admission. He sat on a chair and took his head between his hands. "What if she wakes and doesn't recognize me? What if—"

"Don't think about that." I couldn't help but think his doubts were reasonable, but he couldn't focus on that. The technology on which the ship's medical machinery operated was based on alien physiology, and we were all concerned about possible side effects on Sara's mind. Her condition when she was brought aboard was such that Areel had taken upon himself the responsibility to treat Sara on the ship. Not treating her was not an option, and neither was leaving her somewhere in Italy for her family to find her. Areel had taken the risk to cure her and couldn't wait for the end of the treatment to see if he had decided correctly.

Days passed. The weight on his shoulders was crushing him, but Areel stoically waited and never complained. Day after day and night after night, he stood by her side. Several times, we found him asleep on the floor, his hand on hers, their fingers intertwined. The rest of us tried our best to comfort him. We managed to make him eat at regular intervals.

The atmosphere inside the ship varied; it ranged from despair to hope, from happiness to depression, and anything in between. Being confined in small quarters didn't help Areel's and Kam's moods. Elios and I had each other and felt guilty that we couldn't help being happy.

Then, Sara woke up. It had taken slightly longer than programmed, but after twenty days of sleeping therapy, my friend opened her eyes.

Elios and I were heading toward the kitchen—after another blissful night—when we heard a commotion coming from Areel's room. We ran, bracing for the worst. We found Sara sitting on the bed eating breakfast, Areel at her side, fussing over every single movement she made, and Pallino fighting for attention.

"Sara!" I ran to her and hugged her tight. "I missed you so much—"

"I'm back."

I felt her smiling against me and released my hold to look at her. "You look... good."

Sara turned toward Areel and then back to me. "He was with me the whole time."

"I know." I saw Areel lower his eyes to hide a tear.

She acknowledged the silent presence behind me with a tilt of her head. "Elios."

I went to stand by Elios.

"It's nice to see you again." He took my hand.

She nodded. "It is. Thank you for coming back for us."

It was Elios's turn to lower his eyes.

Sara looked behind our backs. "And you must be Kam. Nice to meet you, and thanks to you too."

I hadn't heard Kam enter the room.

"Nice meeting you too." Kam didn't step closer to the bed. "You'll probably want to get used to…" He looked around, encompassing the whole space. "To all of this."

"Yes, I think she needs to rest now. You can come back later." Areel accompanied us to the hallway before we could protest.

Sara smiled from the bed and winked her eye at me.

"As soon as your mastiff goes to sleep, I'm back."

She laughed at my words and threw me a kiss. "Later."

"Later." I waved my hand one more time before Areel closed the door on us.

Kam looked at the opaque surface and then raised one eyebrow at us. "You're all like that?"

"Pretty much." Elios dropped a kiss on my head and right on cue Kam turned around and left.

"Was that necessary?" I kissed him properly.

"Yes."

We went back to our room, breakfast forgotten.

A few hours later, Sara went for a tentative walk, accompanied by Pallino, and found me in the small kitchen preparing something to drink while waiting for Elios, who had been called by Kam. Now that Sara had joined me, I was glad for Kam's intervention. I needed some time alone with my friend.

"I was so worried for you." I shouldn't have said it, but it was out. I hugged her for an eternity, and then we hugged again, until we couldn't stand it anymore. "Areel?" I was surprised he hadn't appeared yet.

"He was exhausted and finally fell asleep." She looked around, her stance uncertain.

"Here." I showed her the only couch in the room. She thanked me and sat, her eyes darting here and there, probably trying to identify objects and make sense of what she was seeing. Pallino jumped on her lap and promptly curled into a purring ball.

"Everything is so…"

"Incredible," I finished and sat on the couch with her. Pallino raised his head, and I reached out to pet him.

"Areel prepared me," Sara gestured, pointing at the ship, "but seeing it is something completely different."

"How do you feel?" I took her hand in mine.

"I feel weird but fine." She gave me a tentative smile; her face was illuminated by an excited expression, almost childish. "I'm rested, and I feel lucky, mostly. Other than that, I'm trying to come to terms with what I already know."

I went to prepare the red drink Elios had fixed for me. I walked back to the couch with two glasses full to the brim. "Have some."

She looked at the glass I was offering.

"Good for the nerves. I promise." She accepted the drink. "This is real. Completely real. Isn't it?" She smiled at me and scooted on the couch until she found a cozy spot. She adjusted her body with her legs to the side and started sipping the aromatic beverage slowly.

"You aren't dreaming."

"Areel explained what happened when we disappeared several months ago. It's hard for me to believe I was unconscious for so long. I mean, it's as if I were dead. It felt strange when I opened my eyes." Sara took another tentative sip.

"How does the therapy work? We were all concerned." I bit my lower lip. "I mean, it's okay if you don't want to talk about it."

"No, it's okay." Sara finished her drink before adding, "The therapy itself is pleasant. I was kept in a light sleep stage and fed input from the outside to integrate my memory and facilitate my reintroduction to reality. At the beginning, it felt like a strange dream populated by familiar people in an unfamiliar setting." She paused. "Like…" She worried the hem of her sweater for a moment. "I don't know how to explain it." Pallino rubbed his head against her arm.

I touched her knee. "Like what?"

"The scents, for example. They were different from anything else I've ever smelled." Her nostrils flared as if she was trying to catch those odors once again.

"Did it scare you?"

She shrugged. "No, it didn't scare me. But it disoriented me." Her eyes wandered for a moment and then focused on something beyond my head. "Even the colors were different."

"But you never opened your eyes." If she had, we would've known through Areel.

She thought about it for a moment. "I saw colors in my dreams. And they were… strange."

"What else?"

"Areel's voice." She finally looked back at me and smiled.

"He never left your side."

She nodded, her smile brightening. "There were times when I was aware of his body beside my bed."

"He talked to you. Constantly." I laughed.

"I think he brought me back, little by little."

"He was so worried you could've forgotten about him."

"I know. Most of the time, I was aware of the feelings around me, and it pained me not being able to reassure him."

"He never lost hope."

"No, but right before regaining consciousness, I felt his anguish getting stronger, and that probably triggered my awakening."

"I'm so happy to have you back." I hugged her once more. "A snack?" She nodded, and I took the empty cup and moved to the kitchen, where I put hers and mine in the sink.

She laid Pallino on the couch and followed me. "So, Areel told me briefly what happened and how we were rescued by Elios and Kam, but he was vague about the reasons we got abducted."

"We got in the middle of something way bigger than us—" I dreaded having this conversation. "And I feel responsible for dragging you into it." I couldn't shrug the guilt from my conscience. "Please forgive me. It wasn't my intention. Had I known…" I lowered my eyes to the kitchen counter.

Sara reached for my chin and gently compelled me to look at her. "By the time we were kidnapped, I would've followed Areel to the end of the world. Nothing you could've said or done would've changed my mind."

"Thank you." I felt a huge weight being removed from my shoulders.

She walked around the counter and laid her arm on my shoulder. "So, you were saying?"

I leaned against her. "It's a long story."

"I've got time to spare, and I'm wide awake." She looked at the empty cups waiting to be washed. "What did you put in those drinks?"

Her exaggerated expression made me laugh. "Nothing, don't worry."

"So, what happened exactly?"

I turned on the washing function and the sink took care of the cups before Sara's incredulous eyes. "Handy, eh?" In a matter of seconds, the cups were cleaned, dry, and ready to be used again. I took some bread from the cupboard over my head and then reached for the ingredients to make what would look like a sandwich but taste like something completely different. "It turned out we never knew the entire truth. But what we found was enough to put us in danger. Our discovery raised alarm among the Pures." I filled a plate with the snack I had just assembled and slid it toward her.

She accepted it. "The Pures? Who are the Pures?"

"This is where the story gets long and complicated." I went to brew a hot beverage that resembled a strong Earl Grey tea.

"Again, got nothing but time at the moment."

I checked that the temperature of the tea wasn't scalding and poured some for her. "The Pures are the aliens who caused the destruction of the Solean civilization. Ironically, had they left us alone, their secret would've been safe. Elios would never have come to my rescue, and everything would be just like before. Even what Areel found wasn't enough to understand a third culture was implicated. Nobody on Solo would've connected the dots because several pieces of the puzzle were still missing."

The alien race of the Pures had committed the error of overestimating what we knew. I had seen the whole story in Elios's mind and the knowledge was haunting. No wonder Areel had been uncooperative.

Both the sandwich and the mug lay untouched before Sara. "What reasons did the Pures have to destroy the Solean culture?"

I wasn't hungry either and kept moving my cup from one hand to the other. Some of the liquid spilled out. I dipped my finger in it and drew lines and circles on the counter. "The Pures feed from others races' emotions. They aren't able to feel anything by themselves."

Sara shivered. "Did they feed from the Soleans? Is this how everything started?"

"Yes."

"They drained the Soleans until they were left without the will to go on living."

I shook my head. "It wasn't their intention. Not at first. Soleans' emotions were so untainted, so undiluted, the Pures got addicted over time. Eventually, Solo wasn't enough. Now, they can't function without constant administration of their drug." Here it was in a nutshell.

She took in my words, let them percolate in her mind for a moment, and then asked, "What were they doing on Earth? Were they looking for their next fix?"

I nodded. "They've been scouting Earth for a while, almost two thousand years, but the presence of Elios as an Observer slowed them down."

"I still don't understand the presence of the Solean artifacts."

"The Pures brought the Solean artifacts with them, for sentimental reasons."

Sara gave me a puzzled look.

"Solo was the first planet they reached, and they loved the Soleans, in their own way."

"I thought you said the Pures caused the Solean holocaust."

"Yes, but I also said it wasn't the Pures' intention to emotionally drain the Soleans until they went crazy."

"Still—"

"When the Pures realized what they had done on Solo, they mourned the end of the Solean civilization. A more-sensitive fringe of Pures wanted to fully acknowledge their sole responsibility in the massacre of an entire planet. They started bringing Solean artifacts with them wherever they went. They didn't want to forget what they had been capable of. The mementos were a constant reminder of how their initial love for Solo had degenerated into annihilation, how their vice, their addiction, had drained innocent souls of their feelings and desires."

"We were the next ones?" Sara's eyes got bigger.

I nodded again. "Among other planets before us. Yes, that was the plan, but we turned out to be difficult subjects. Our feelings are too raw, too strong for them, like undiluted heroin. They were experimenting on me to find a way to extract and change the intensity of our emotions, but it didn't work. Elios stopped them before they could try one final theory on me." It was still difficult to talk about my ordeal.

"I'm alive only because of him," I said, barely keeping my voice from breaking. My hand went to the silver scar on my forehead. Although completely healed thanks to the alien technology, I could feel the ridge where the scalpel had cut through my skin. "I was conscious the whole time of our imprisonment. My desire to see Elios was my only strength. I didn't have anything else—just the hope of being with him." I sniffed softly, trying to stop before anybody else entered the kitchen and saw me crying. I didn't want Elios to see me that way.

"Oh, Gaia, I'm so sorry. At least I wasn't conscious. I can't even imagine what you went through." Sara softly hugged me.

I burrowed into the familiarity of her embrace. "Everything is in the past now. We're together, and that is all that matters." I disentangled myself, gave her a reassuring smile, and then went on cooking a meal for the rest of the crew.

"Do you know what's going to happen? To us, I mean." Sara gently laid her hand on mine to stop me from cutting a finger with the knife I was slashing a salad with.

I blinked once and saw how close I'd come to losing my index finger. When I looked up, she was biting her lower lip, and her eyes were focused far away, somewhere outside the ship. "We can decide. We're free to stay and follow them to Solo."

"And leave our families." Sara's voice was sad.

"Probably forever, yes." My voice didn't falter, but my heart was aching. "Or we can go back to Earth," I said, and the pain in my heart grew even sharper.

"And leave Areel and Elios to their fate," Sara finished for me.

"Yes, and this time it would be forever."

I thought about that a lot—at night when Elios tried his best to hide his worries and during the day when Elios looked at me when he thought I wasn't looking at him. I had to divide my heart into two pieces, and there was no mending that. He knew it. "You should carefully consider the consequences." It was the only solid advice I could give her.

"How can I choose between Areel and my family?" Sara was holding her head with a shaking hand. "We can't have both, can we?"

"No, we can't." I put the knife down. "And it's so painful just saying it out loud." I looked at the large amount of vegetables I had cut, not knowing what to do with them. "And the worst part is that Elios doesn't want to talk about it."

"Why?"

"Because he feels responsible."

"For what?"

"For me having to choose between him and my family. Elios has committed serious crimes against his kind, and I don't think he's going to be pardoned and sent back to Earth."

"But you've decided already."

"Yes, I have." I had tried, but I couldn't imagine a life where I couldn't touch him, caress him, or sleep embraced in his arms. "I can survive anything but regret." I shrugged and then reached for her hand and squeezed it. "You must follow your heart."

Sara's plate lay untouched on the table. She was playing with the fork, her eyes unfocused once again. I'd had a few days to sort my feelings. She had just received the crash course. For the first time, I could understand Elios's reticence in talking with me. He thought that any single thing he might say could influence my final choice. He was wrong. Still, I didn't want to have that kind of power over Sara. She was a strong and independent young woman but quite frail at the moment, and she had to find the strength to decide, as painful as it was.

"You'll decide what's right for you."

"I know." Sara managed to smile a little.

"Is there anything else you want to talk about?" I hoped she was ready to move to another subject. "The guys will appear around the corner any moment now."

Sara looked at me with renewed interest. I waited for her to speak, slightly confused by the expression on her face.

"Speaking of guys, is it true that you and Elios are sharing a room?"

I didn't expect that question. I nodded.

"Have you…?"

"Yes." I blushed.

"Finally. " She gave me a satisfied look. "So?"

"So, what?"

"Was it worth waiting all this time for him?"

"Yes."

"How was it?"

"It was beautiful and unexpected and romantic. Perfect. It was simply perfect." A sudden gush of emotion made me tear up.

Sara's eyes became liquid as well. "Look at me." She dabbed her tears with her sleeve and then repressed a sob with a laugh. "I can understand what you just said, you know?" She paused, her eyes distant.

I wait for her to finish her thought.

"I want to have that moment with Areel. I want to feel the sparkle of magic between us."

"If that's what you want, you'll have it."

She finally smiled. "And you know what?"

"What?"

"I would've waited for him."

"You love him."

"I do. More than I thought I'd love anybody."

"Glad to hear it," Areel said, standing behind Sara. He bent to kiss the top of her head.

We'd been so taken by our conversation we didn't notice him entering the room.

"How much did you hear?" Sara tried her best to hide her embarrassment.

Areel enveloped her in his arms. "Enough to be incredibly happy." While he was the image of satisfaction, Sara was rapidly changing shades of red.

To my great relief, Elios came and interrupted the two lovebirds. For once, I understood why Kam found it difficult to stomach our effusiveness. It was truly nauseating.

23

"How do you feel, Sara?" Elios asked her, standing beside me. We had moved to the sitting area. Areel and Sara had curled up on the couch, Pallino between them. Elios moved two chairs from the kitchen for us.

"I feel well, like in a dream," Sara answered.

"Sometimes, I feel I'm dreaming too." Elios took my hand.

The sheer contact sent shivers through my spine.

Elios caressed my wrist. *Good.*

We're not alone. I gave the other couple a glance and was relieved they weren't paying any attention to us.

Elios traced a pattern with his fingers, brushing the sensitive skin at the base of my hand. *We could be.*

I stood up in a sudden hurry to reach our room when Kam arrived.

Without preamble, he stated, "We'll approach the critical point of no return in less than two days."

I fell back on my chair. "But I thought we had more time."

"Can't we wait for Sara to get used to things?" Areel's voice was a croaked whisper. His dark eyes locked onto Sara's pale face.

"The conditions for the jump are ideal only for the next forty-two hours. Past that limit, we'll have to wait another full Earth revolution." Kam dragged a third chair over and sat with us.

"We can't wait another year in orbit. It's too dangerous." Elios took my hand again. *Are you okay?*

I wasn't.

"We're lucky Sara woke up just now," Kam added, his eyes on Areel. "We should've left already… with Lex turning out to be a Pure—"

Elios gave him a look I couldn't decipher.

"What is he talking about?" I stared at him. I remembered Elios talking about Lex and I knew who the man was. He was Elios's father figure and one of the Wise Ancestors who had sent Elios to Silenzio. Lex's parting words for him were among the saddest memories Elios guarded in his mind. But I hadn't found anything else regarding him being a Pure.

Elios looked down and then up again, pain etched on his face. "He's the one who betrayed all of us. He isn't Solean—"

"He's one of the Pures in charge of keeping the truth about what happened before the Dark hidden," Areel finished for Elios.

I touched Elios.

I can't accept what Lex did. Had to keep those memories buried. It's still too painful. Later…

I squeezed his arm. *Don't worry. We don't have to talk about it.*

Kam coughed, and we turned to face him. "I hate to interrupt, but we should get back to the problem at hand. We must leave and we must leave now. You"—he looked first at Sara and then at me—"have to decide what you want to do."

The finality of Kam's statement hit me. Until that moment, my mind had been otherwise engaged, my reunion with Elios taking central stage. But now, the decision I had already taken weighed me down in its stark reality. Elios said something. My head was spinning. I had to leave that room. I didn't want to hear anything. I didn't want to talk. I didn't want to declare my decision out loud. Because if I did, then it was real. Then, I would be leaving my family behind. Without a goodbye.

You don't have to.

I don't have a choice.

But you do.

No, I really don't. I regretted not having gone to our room sooner.

"Yes, you and Sara have to decide now whether you want to follow us to Solo or go back to Earth," Elios said out loud for everybody else's benefit. He did his best to hide from me the fear behind his words. It was just a second. He shielded his mind right away, but in that brief moment, I saw his soul and all the air in my lungs was forced out, as if a fist had squarely hit my chest.

"You can't go back to Solo," I pleaded while my mind was screaming.

"We are not talking about my decision." Elios words were final and full of sadness. "I won't force you into a life of constant running and hiding. I want to have a chance for us." He shut his mind to me.

"We can go somewhere else."

He shook his head. "You have to decide. Please."

I knew it was taking him lots of strength to control his voice, but he still gave me a mental nudge to reinforce his words.

"I think we should discuss pros and cons since neither Gaia nor Sara seems to grasp all the consequences of taking this journey." Kam's words were distant, almost as if under water.

Or maybe I was the one under water, falling down without breathing. When the meaning of his words finally reached my brain, I wanted to scream that we knew. We understood the consequences more than he did.

"Kam's right. Let's talk about it." Elios sounded practical. "You can travel with us and ask for asylum on Solo, independently from our fate."

I heard his voice as if under layers of cotton. I already knew all the things he was going to say. I hated that we had to rehearse a script I knew all too well, but it wouldn't have been fair not to give Sara another opportunity to think things through and decide.

"Or we can take you back to Earth," he finished.

When I had talked to Sara, saying pretty much the same things, it hadn't sounded so awful. My mind hadn't melted in a pool of bleak despair.

Sara asked something, but my brain wasn't reacting to voices that weren't Elios's. Areel answered her question, and then Elios spoke again.

"If you decide to go back to Earth, you'll be safe, and you'll be able to rejoin your families."

I sat on the edge of the chair but kept my hand on his leg. "But what about endangering our families?"

He closed his mind to me. "You and your families will be safe."

Sara tilted her head and for a moment escaped Areel's hold. "How can you be sure?"

Areel answered, "The Pures are after us. Once we leave Earth, they'll immediately follow—"

I raised one finger to stop him. "Then, you'll be endangering yourselves by taking us back to our families. The Pures must be waiting for you to make that exact move. They don't know where you are yet."

Elios locked eyes with me. "It's a risk we are willing to take."

I sent him my frustration. "It's a risk I won't take."

"But it's the only way for me to know you'd be left alone." He kept his mind closed.

Bits and pieces of a conversation that took place so long ago came back to me. "Why would you be so sure?"

I'm working on something. I played that memory for him.

He closed his mouth in a thin line.

"How?" I asked Areel, who lowered his eyes to the floor.

Sara squeezed Areel's hand. "What are you planning to do?"

A long moment of silence followed.

"We'll manipulate your memories," Kam finally said.

"What do you mean?" I turned to face only Elios.

"It's the only way." His voice faltered at the very end.

"Why?"

"Because the Pures won't have any use for you once you don't remember anything about us." He stroked my hand. "And Solo would never accept sending another replacement to finish the mission on Earth with you knowing about us all along."

"It was part of my mission, if you remember," Areel added.

I nodded and then shook my head, too shocked to say anything. Everybody talked at the same time.

"You are asking us to make an impossible decision." Sara's words. My thoughts, coherently expressed.

I took Elios's hands in mine and opened my heart to him. "Is that what you really want?"

He didn't answer.

Anger and frustration bubbled inside of me. "I can't believe you're asking me to forget you. And I can't believe you hid this from me."

I was fully aware of the shock Elios felt at the pain accompanying my words. He didn't spare me his this time; it was too much for him to hide. I moved away from him and cut our mental connection, unable to withstand the despair of our combined emotions.

Then Kam spoke again. "I'm sorry for all of you. I'll wait for your decision in my room."

After a while, I realized Elios and I were alone in the kitchen.

I had eyes and ears only for him. I had to say things, unpleasant things, and I didn't know where to start. My heart was beating faster and I was stabbing my fingernails into the palms of my hands.

"I have my family—" Thinking of them without crying was a struggle.

"I know. I understand," Elios said.

"No, you don't." I caressed his face. "The mere idea of not remembering you breaks my heart."

"It could all be for nothing." He leaned into my hand.

"How can you say that?"

"You are leaving everything behind for me, because of me, and I don't know what's going to happen once we reach Solo. We could be separated."

"Then we'll have now." I kissed him. "Now it's worth it."

He moved away from me and lowered his head. "I want you to be truly, completely happy."

I tilted his chin up with a finger. "I choose you."

"I want you to choose *you.*"

Elios felt too guilty to let it go, but I couldn't bear to talk about it any longer. I had decided, and I wasn't going back. "I did."

Elios moved me carefully, as if I was going to break in his hands, and I found myself on his lap, hugging him. Moments like these were the reason behind my decision.

"Would you reconsider? Please?"

And like that I had enough. "Stop it. Now." I had never talked that way to Elios. It wasn't just that I had almost shouted at him, which in truth I'd already done, it was the sharpness in my tone that made the two of us shiver. "I'm selfish. I'd give up anything just to have a moment with you. Don't you understand?" I was staring down at him; my body had moved without being asked. I was angry. I felt ashamed of being capable of reacting that way. I felt bad I had lost my temper. I felt I was betraying my family. I felt so many different sentiments I thought I would explode. My mind was melting under the stress. The only thing I knew was that I wanted to touch him and be reassured, and we were arguing instead.

I wanted to say I loved him. So I fled the kitchen instead. I sat on the floor of our room, determined not to fall apart. I saw the window screen, and warm tears rolled down my cheeks. And I fell apart. A few moments later, I was staring at a blank screen. Where it had been the view of a street in Rome, now there was simply nothing. Nothing at all.

My vision was blurred, my thoughts were incoherent, and somewhere far away someone knocked on a door. I just sat and thought of nothing. After a century, or maybe just a second later, that someone knocked again. Behind curtains of warm water, a familiar shape entered the room and carefully and silently sat down on the floor beside me.

"Sorry," he said, and then when he saw I didn't reject him, "I'll do everything in my power to make you happy."

"Just tell me everything will be fine." I needed to hear that. I needed him.

"We'll be fine." Elios was looking at me like he meant it, and that was enough for me.

Later, we slept embraced, Elios's hands caressing my face slowly and soothing my restless mind. My heart was still aching, but Elios's body beside mine was a source of infinite joy.

The night passed quickly, and Kam knocked on our door very early in the morning. We found Sara and Areel already in the kitchen. They had probably spent the night awake; their eyes were tired and their movements slow, but they seemed serene. Areel had cooked breakfast for us. We sat down, waiting to hear what they had to say.

Sara spoke with a calm voice, and I involuntarily held my breath.

"I'll go with Areel." That was all she said.

Only then did I realize how much I had wanted to hear that. I was almost embarrassed to admit it, but I wanted to have my friend by my side now that our lives were being uprooted. I turned to hide a solitary tear. I felt grateful for all the different kinds of love I was experiencing, and one forgotten memory found its way out to remind me how lucky I was.

Once, while traveling by train through the Italian countryside, I had met two young mothers who were going to meet their husbands at the naval station in Livorno. Between one train station and the other, they told me their story. They traveled for hours just to have a glimpse of their beloveds whenever their ship reached an Italian port, which happened once or twice every eighteen months. One of the fathers hadn't seen his newborn child yet, and the other had seen his daughters just once in the last two years. I had wondered then how love could survive through absence and uncertainty, and I had admired those young couples so adamant in their sentiments.

Now I could understand.

24

The rest of the day passed quickly.

Unfortunately for us, so did the rest of the trip. Although it took us eight months and five wormholes to reach the outskirts of our destination, to me, time ceased to be a quantifiable experience after I decided to stay with Elios. We just shared every breath we took and every thought we dared to think. We ate, and we slept, and we had the most beautiful dreams together. We treasured every single minute spent holding hands, and we never grew tired of looking at each other.

Our interaction with the rest of the fellow travelers was minimal, due to the fact that Kam had decided to go into deep-sleep and Sara and Areel kept to their room most of the time. The four of us shared occasional meals, and we had pleasant little chats, avoiding discussing what we really wanted to talk about. We all tried our best to hide our worries from each other, and we failed miserably.

The love I felt for Elios was so strong that anything was bearable, even knowing we were quickly approaching Solo. I lived every moment with the same intensity as if it were the last because I knew it might be.

Sooner than I wanted, our vacation ended, and not in the way I had imagined.

* * *

"I knew it was too simple." Elios's words drowned in the noise.

We were attacked a ship-day before we were scheduled to approach the Solean atmosphere. Our vessel could evade danger but wasn't equipped to defend itself or even fire back.

"We can't retreat. One of the engines has just been hit." Areel read the message showing on the control panel. Sara was by his side, shaking badly.

"I knew it was *way* too simple." Elios was looking at the commands in front of him. "The Pures' facility was deserted, and we managed to get in and out with three people and encountered almost no resistance." He was talking about the night Kam and he had raided the facility where Areel, Sara, and I had been held captive.

"That's not completely true. You did mow down a lot of enemies." I was standing next to him, trying to soothe his nerves. Lex, Elios's Ancestor Guide, the man he considered his father, a Pure, had sent him a message before the first blast had rocked our ship. He wanted all of us dead. "*I deeply regret it has come to this, my son,*" Lex had said before ending the communication. I could still remember how Elios had defended him, one night on Earth. So long ago.

"I should've thought he'd know my plans." Elios shook his head in despair. "Of course he'd be here waiting for me to come back home."

"It was the only decision we could make," Kam said. He was operating the flight console manually.

"I should have seen this coming." Elios looked at me and then lowered his head. "I should've done better by you."

I didn't have time to reassure him. Another blast rumbled the hull. When I realized it, I was already on the floor.

Elios was thrown against a wall but recovered immediately and came to help me.

"We're together. It's going to be okay," I said in his arms.

"I'm sorry. It's all my fault. I was so naïve."

Another blast sent us in opposite directions. He hurried to my side once again as soon as the quake ceased. "We have to find a way out of here," he said while reaching for the radio panel. "I'll send another distress call."

Areel had already explained we couldn't jump. The closest wormhole was one day away.

Elios's words were almost unintelligible. "Lex is counting on a fast kill."

But I heard him. Everybody did.

He continued, louder, "We can't let that happen. If we stall the other ship long enough, sooner or later a Solean vessel will notice us. This is a busy stretch of space. " After sending the distress signal, he vented to the ether, "Lex, have the courage to show your face."

I knew he needed answers. Lex had betrayed him, and it hurt him. And it hurt me. "Elios?"

The ship was rocked by another blast. This time, the hit was more serious.

"Lex is probably not even on that ship," Kam said.

Beside me, Elios stirred. He had been in a trance-like state for a few minutes. His eyes shone with resolution when he said, "I'll use his own teachings against him again." He kissed me and let me know his plan.

"Yes." I hugged him tight and gave him a peck on his lips. "It will work."

We walked to Kam, and he understood before Elios could explain what we wanted to do. "Are you sure?" he asked Elios. "Are you sure?" he turned and asked me.

Before closing my eyes, I looked around and found Sara. I smiled at her and then took Elios's hand firmly in mine. "Everything's going to be okay." Kam moved out of the way, and Elios and I took control of the ship.

At the beginning, only darkness surrounded us. Elios linked our minds together and looked for the right path toward the light, where there was a tiny speck of white beckoning far away. It was the light I had followed when I was losing my sanity during the long months of captivity. From that moment on, we were one.

Our mind connected to the ship. We moved slowly at first and then faster, and we left the light behind us. Myriads of bright little points dotted the pitch black, and we moved again until the stars zoomed toward us at dizzying speed. Finally, we saw the ship attacking us and the dark aura surrounding it. We pitied them and their joyless lack of hope. The ship moved increasingly more slowly. It almost stopped, and we could see the blasts coming toward our vessel frozen in space. We moved us from one point to another, avoiding hits as we went. We were our ship, and we enjoyed our new freedom. The other ship, malevolent and dark, grew impatient and attacked with its entire arsenal. We simply moved, lazily enjoying the dance, escaping their hatred with fluid and joyous jumps.

Irritated by our perseverance in escaping them, the Pure's ship threw an energy net to block our progress toward freedom. We let the net close to our hull, and at the last second we skirted away. Our maneuver prevented them from attacking one more time. They had felt victory close and had underestimated our resilience. Soon they were angry and couldn't maintain an analytical point of view. They opened fire one more time without realizing we weren't alone anymore.

A stern voice resonated in the control room, breaking the link between our minds. "Cease fire immediately, and surrender."

I felt Kam moving around us to take back the console.

"Identify yourselves."

Colors exploded and blinded me temporarily.

"They are flying away," Areel cried.

"It doesn't matter anymore. Their attack is proof enough. Our memories will incriminate Lex," Kam said.

I felt the urge to laugh and cry at the same time. "We are free!"

Elios gently squeezed my arm. "I still have to face a Court judgment…"

"I will not be betrayed by one of my own. Never." The message from Lex resonated loud and clear inside the ship.

"I was never one of yours. You never deserved my affection and my loyalty," Elios answered, but the other ship was already disappearing, pursued by the Solean vessel.

He smiled at me.

* * *

I found myself contemplating Elios's birth planet with a mix of awe and trepidation. The window screen in our room showed us a constant stream of images originating from various locations on Solo.

"It's so peaceful," I said to him.

Elios showed me all the places he wanted to go with me.

When we finally reached the Solean atmosphere, I simply stared at the beauty of the purple sunset bathing the green planet, feeling thankful that such a gift had been given to us.

Our ship was finally escorted down to the landing strip by an official vessel, but everything happened in a blur while I was clinging to Elios's arms.

The portal of the cargo bay opened.

I kissed Elios.

No regrets.

25

A dignified man, apparently in his fifties, entered the hull, flanked by two younger men. "Elios, the College of Superior Observers requests your presence. Follow us."

Elios and I stepped forward, but the man raised one hand to stop us.

"Both humans will remain onboard."

"I won't leave her behind." Elios hugged me closer.

"It isn't for you to decide." The man looked from Elios to me and then back to Elios again. "You well know we have the means to ensure your cooperation. Don't force me to use them." The man looked at both of us this time, almost with concern. "Please, Elios. Be reasonable."

Elios struggled with the request. I heard his thoughts, but they were chaotic and too fast to follow. Finally, the man stepped closer and gestured for Elios to give him his hand.

The man closed the gap between us. "Trust me."

After a moment of hesitation, Elios let go of me and took the proffered hand in his. His face lit up, and then he severed the contact with the other man and turned to face me. "I must go with him."

I wanted to object, but he took me in his arms. *Everything is going to be fine.*

He was already gone by the time I realized what was happening. Areel and Kam had followed him soon after while their prisoner had been disembarked, still in his cryogenic bed. Sara and I were left on a lonely ship docked on an alien planet.

Hours passed. We moved from one room to another, too nervous to rest, too worried to do anything else but worry about our fate. Our conversations were a monotonous repetition of the same questions and answers.

"What's happening?"

"I don't know."

"Why aren't they already here?"

"How long has it been since they left?"

"Are they coming back?"

"What if they were found guilty?"

"Elios and Areel did break their oaths…"

"What if I'm not going to see him again?"

"They would never have left if they knew we were in any danger."

"They would never have left us."

"Why has nobody come back yet?"

"I don't know."

Outside, the night was illuminated by stars so bright they shone like diamonds in the sky. At the sight of the alien constellations, I felt a sense of profound sadness. Instinctively, I had looked for the familiar astral bodies crowding the sky I knew and found none. *Where are you?* After that, I turned my back to the cockpit and strolled to the kitchen where I went to fix something to eat. I wasn't hungry, but there wasn't anything else I could do to keep me sane. Accessing the video screen in our bedroom wasn't an option. I could only think of places on Earth to look for, and I knew better.

Sara followed me but remained silent, the only soft noises coming from Pallino, nestled in her arms. We had tired of talking some time earlier. Now there was only waiting. And we waited. And waited. Light streamed inside the ship, and the Solean sun found us still waiting. When I thought I couldn't take it anymore and decided to take action—since nobody would let us know what was happening—I went to open the cargo bay door only to find Elios and Areel coming back.

I was in Elios's arms before he could enter the ship proper. I didn't let him talk. My mouth pressed to his, my body seeking his warm embrace. Then we were in our bedroom, and I didn't know how we had gotten there. He cradled me softly, and I cried. Relief and joy drove my senses crazy. Between sobs, I finally managed to ask him what had happened.

"Areel and I were found guilty of breaking our oaths."

My heart sank, and I wished I had made love to him before asking anything.

"We're not allowed to come back to Solo." He stroked my hair. "It's one life sentence on Silenzio."

His fingers massaged my scalp, and positive thoughts radiated from him. Then I realized he had been projecting his memories the whole time. I was in such a state of distress I had involuntarily blocked the communication. I gasped. "Is it true?" I couldn't dare believe what he was saying.

I felt his smile when he kissed my head. "The College of Superior Observers unanimously decided you and Sara must follow us. You know of our existence."

I didn't care about the reason why we weren't to be separated. For a long time, we forgot about anything else. Later, I remembered something he had said. "What did you mean by *one* life sentence?"

"Once on Silenzio, I won't have access to another body. I'll grow old in this one." He traced the contour of my face. *With you.*

I couldn't help but feel guilty at rejoicing at the news. His lifespan would be a fraction of what it was supposed to be. "I'm sorry…"

He took my chin in his hands and gently raised my face. "Look at me."

I did, but tears were already wetting my cheeks.

He wiped them with a few kisses. "It's the most beautiful gift my superiors could give me."

"But—"

"I asked for it."

"You asked for it?" I saw him smiling, and some of his happiness leaked to me.

"Areel, Kam, and I are considered heroes. Our memories proved our role in unmasking the truth about Lex."

"But you said you were found guilty." I caressed his jaw. I couldn't stay this close and not crave his contact.

"We are guilty of breaking our oaths of chastity, but we came back knowing our fate once we reached Solo."

"The College of Superior Observers realized your sacrifice?" From what I had heard of those people, I couldn't believe that could be the case.

He smiled at my line of thought. "They asked us to decide our own sentence."

"They did what?"

Between laughs, Elios said, "Heroes must be rewarded." He brushed the tip of my nose. "And Earth is safe."

"Earth is safe." My heart swelled at the thought. "Your superiors decided to send someone else to finish your mission?"

"Yes."

"Is it going to be Kam?"

"No, Kam wouldn't be objective. The Council has decided on a veteran. And he has been ordered to alter your families' memories. At least your parents won't suffer from your absence."

I wanted to laugh and cry at the same time. I was overjoyed by the fact my parents wouldn't worry about me, but I felt hollow at the thought they wouldn't remember I had ever existed. Sadness prevailed, and tears escaped my eyes.

He hugged me tightly and wiped my face. "You do know if there had been even the slightest chance for us to go back to Earth, I would have fought for it."

Before he could replay for me the memories of the hearing in which he had discussed his plea to save my planet, I gently pulled away from him. "I know." Then I touched his lips with my fingers. "I know," I whispered.

* * *

We arrived on Solo at sundown, and we left at sundown. Once the ship was replenished with anything needed for its last trip, Kam came to say goodbye to his friends, and it was bitter-sweet. I thanked him for everything he had done for us.

"Take care of him," he said, pointing at Elios, who was checking the cargo.

"He's my whole life."

Elios heard me and smiled.

Kam exchanged a few words with Sara as well and then left. Elios and Areel followed him from the cockpit window and didn't look away until their friend disappeared from sight. A few minutes later, we were given permission to take off.

* * *

The cargo bay door opened. Silenzio's fresh air rushed in from the outside. The salty breeze from the sea tickled my nostrils. I shivered. Elios draped a blanket over my shoulders.

"Ready?"

I nodded and he kissed me on my lips. I looked ahead. A new life awaited us.

He took me in his arms and stepped toward the bright light outside. "Welcome home."

My heart exploded. I'd never been happier in my life.

No regrets.

Dear Reader, if you liked this book, please consider writing a review. As an indie author, I rely solely on word of mouth to promote my stories. Just a few words from you will ensure my work is discovered by other readers.

Monica

To keep up to date with Monica's new releases and promotions scan the QR code with your smartphone or mobile device.

Backstory and Acknowledgments

I have been writing Elios's and Gaia's stories for so long, it doesn't seem possible I am finally at the stage of thanking everybody who was involved in the project. But here we are, four years later and several books already published.

Thanks, Mom. You would have loved both *Elios* and *Gaia*. Thanks, Dad, for reading my books in English and not having asked, not even once, I translate them in Italian.

Thanks, Maria Luisa. You were the very first one to read the rough draft of both stories. I can't forget how you took the time out of your schedule to send me mails full of notes.

Thanks, Claudia. You too were there at the beginning of my journey, and your enthusiasm about my writing endeavors was contagious then, and it is contagious now.

Thanks, Gaia and Giuseppe. As usual, just because.

Thanks, Roberto. Without you, none of this would be possible at all.

PERSONS OF INTEREST

I wrote this book

Red Adept Publishing edited and proofread it

Roberto Ruggeri patiently formatted it

You, dear reader, hopefully enjoyed reading it as much as I did writing it

BIO

Monica La Porta landed in Seattle several years ago, where she lives with her family. Despite popular feelings about the Northwest weather, she finds the mist and the rain the perfect conditions to concoct new universes. When Monica isn't writing or reading, she can be found painting on her digital tablet or sculpting. Whenever the sun shines, she comes out of her cave and treats her beloved beagle, Nero, to long walks into the Washington wild.

You can find Monica La Porta here:
Blog: http://www.monicalaporta.com
Facebook: https://www.facebook.com/monicalaportaauthor/
Goodreads: https://www.goodreads.com/MonicaLaPorta
Twitter: https://twitter.com/momilp
BookBub: https://www.bookbub.com/authors/monica-la-porta
wattpad: https://www.wattpad.com/user/momilp

OTHER BOOKS BY MONICA LA PORTA

To keep up to date with Monica's new releases and promotions scan the QR code with your smartphone or mobile device.

The Priest – Book One of the Ginecean Chronicles

Mauricio is a slave. Like any man born on Ginecea, he is but a number to the pure breed women who rule over him with cruel hands. Imprisoned inside the Temple since birth, Mauricio has never been outside, never felt the warmth of the sun on his skin. He lives a life devoid of hopes and desires. Then one day, he hears Rosie sing. He risks everything for one look at her and his life is changed forever. An impossible friendship blossoms into affection deemed sinful and perverted in a society where the only rightful union is between women. Love is born where only hate has roots and leads Mauricio to uncover a truth that could destroy Ginecea.

Pax in the Land of Women – Book Two of the Ginecean Chronicles

Love doesn't obey preordained rules. Sometimes, social status and gender mean nothing. The purest of affections can be born between two people living in different worlds. In a society where women rule over an enslaved race of men and love between a woman and man is considered a perversion, Pax's and Prince's union is destined for a tragic end. Coming from an existence of privilege, Pax has never endured harshness. She has never had any reason to doubt the rules Ginecea was built on. Everything changes when she is sent to spend her summer on a desolate farm and is exposed to the ongoing brutalities against defenseless men. A wrong turn leads her to witness Prince's thrashing at the hands of the guards. One look from him and Pax's perfect life is shattered, the memory of his dark eyes haunting her night and day. As a pure breed, born to one of the most prestigious family in Ginecea, she would have never thought it possible to fall in love with a man. Marked as a sinner, Pax abjures her ancestry to save Prince's life. She hopes they can disappear into the desert, but social prejudice and political schemes give them no respite. The Priestess, the ruler of all Ginecea, has other plans for Pax Layan and her family. Second in The Ginecean Chronicles, Pax in the Land of Women is a dystopian tale set on the planet Ginecea.

Prince at War – Book Three of the Ginecean Chronicles

The City of Men has been destroyed. The pure breeds want him dead. Prince is still running for his life. This time, he's not alone. Pax and the rest of the survivors count on him to keep them alive in the unforgiving desert. Pursued by the heartless Priestess and the President of Ginecea, Prince and Pax fight to find a haven for their unborn child. He knows the two women won't stop at anything to achieve their goal. But he can't fathom the true reasons behind their motives. Ginecea wants the heads of anyone who helped the fugitive men and nobody is safe. Not even the fathered women, slaughtered by a Priestess crazed by hate. The world is in an uproar and Pax and Prince stand in the eye of the storm. Prince at War is the third book in The Ginecean Chronicles, a series set in the dystopian world of Ginecea where women rule over enslaved men, and heterosexual love is the ultimate sin.

Elios – Elios and Gaia Series

He had no name until she gave him one. Elios has existed for eons, yet he has never lived. As a Solean Observer, his latest assignment is to study human nature. When Earth reaches its final days, he will be the one judging whether humanity's memory deserves to be preserved. This is not his first mission, and he is confident that he will make Lex, his Ancestor Guide, proud once again. Then, in Athens, Elios locks eyes with Gaia, and for the first time in his long life, he develops feelings he doesn't have a name for. An impulse stronger than any he has ever felt will drive him to follow Gaia first to Rome, where she lives, and then across the ocean to the United States when she goes to study abroad. In Seattle, unable to fight his sentiments any longer, Elios finally approaches Gaia. What starts as an innocent desire to talk to her just once, soon becomes a fire Elios can't quench. And yet, bound by his oath as an Observer, he can't have any physical contact with her. Struggling between his duties to Solo, the planet that gave him birth, and Gaia, who has become the only reason for his existence, Elios must decide. But fate, in the form of an archeological finding discovered inside an Etruscan tomb, decides for him and Gaia, separating them. Although Elios is a companion novel to Gaia, they can be read in either order. They are both stand-alone stories from different points of view. You met Gaia and Elios in her book; now hear his story.

Gaia – Elios and Gaia Series

While vacationing in Greece, Gaia locks eyes with a stranger, twice. Two years later, back in Rome, she should be enjoying college life; instead, the memories of his lapis lazuli eyes and Mona Lisa smile still haunt her. Gaia longs to meet him again and unwittingly sabotages her romantic life by refusing to move on. Only her anthropological studies about the mysterious Etruscans make her feel alive. A chance to breathe new air is presented to her when she wins a full scholarship to study abroad at the University of Washington. In rainy Seattle, Gaia finally meets the man of her dreams, but he proves to be... otherworldly. Meanwhile, in her field of studies, what starts as an interesting archeological finding about a six-fingered human image, soon evolves into the discovery of the millennium, but not where Earth is concerned. Although Gaia is a companion novel of Elios, you can read these in either order. They are both stand-alone stories from different points of view. You met Gaia and Elios in his book; now hear her story.

The Prince's Day Out

Once upon a time, in a faraway land, there was a young prince who lived confined to his bedroom. Accompanied by his sister, he traveled to the most incredible places thanks to his imagination. Follow the Prince and the Princess's fantastic journey through a magic kingdom where seagulls transport cities and ships sail on pearl necklaces instead of waves. Twelve whimsical drawings illustrate the story.

Linda of the Night

Linda was born with hair the color of the mature grain and eyes of the lightest shade of blue. Tall and willowy, she's the ugliest girl alive. Kept inside her house by her parents for fear of being ridiculed for her hideous appearance, Linda dreams of being like the dark-haired, curvaceous girls who live just outside her walls. One night, she dares the inconceivable and leaves the safety of her home. For the first time alone, Linda walks for hours until she is lost—only to find her destiny in the arms of a mysterious stranger.

www.ingramcontent.com/pod-product-compliance
Lightning Source LLC
Chambersburg PA
CBHW070859250626
47159CB00003B/1117